"No," James said quietly, his stomach leaping into his throat. Jumping up from his desk, he rushed back into the lab and turned on the lights. He approached a silver box about the size of a computer printer. Next to it was a disposable pen that he pressed to his index finger. When he pushed the button on one end, a small needle jumped out, pricking his finger. Blood instantly blossomed from the puncture. Next he held up a tiny plastic square, transferring a dot of blood onto it. He set the bloody square onto a tray that slid out from the machine.

Adrenaline surged through him as the tray slid back into the machine and a timer appeared on the display reading thirty minutes. Now he just had to wait.

VIRUS THIRTEEN

Joshua Alan Parry

A TOM DOHERTY ASSOCIATES BOOK • NEW YORK

This is a work of fiction. All of the characters, organizations, and events portrayed in this novel are either products of the author's imagination or are used fictitiously.

VIRUS THIRTEEN

Copyright © 2013 by Joshua Alan Parry

All rights reserved.

A Tor Book
Published by Tom Doherty Associates, LLC
175 Fifth Avenue
New York, NY 10010

www.tor-forge.com

Tor® is a registered trademark of Tom Doherty Associates, LLC.

ISBN 978-0-7653-6954-3

Tor books may be purchased for educational, business, or promotional use. For information on bulk purchases, please contact Macmillan Corporate and Premium Sales Department at 1-800-221-7945 extension 5442 or write specialmarkets@macmillan.com.

First Edition: April 2013

Printed in the United States of America

0 9 8 7 6 5 4 3 2 1

For my father

ACKNOWLEDGMENTS

I would like to extend my thanks to all the friends and family who patiently supported me during the near half-decade process of making this book. It was an arduous road, but they believed in me the entire way.

A special thanks to my longtime friend Sam Mortazavi, who was kind enough to take up the monstrous task of reading and editing countless early drafts of this novel before it was sent to the publisher. I'm incredibly thankful that he took it upon himself to come on this long journey with me. I am also grateful for Stephanie Flanders, my editor at Tor Books. Due to her hard work this novel has become a reality. I cannot thank her enough. Last but not least, I'd like to thank my father, who has been a constant source of inspiration in all facets of my life. I couldn't ask for a better dad. He has provided me with all the tools for success, and I thank him for it.

VIRUS
THIRTEEN

1

For Dr. James Logan, it was not just another painfully dull lecture on his latest research. Today he was announcing a breakthrough that would change the world. After nearly a decade of work, James and his wife, Linda, had finally done it. The couple stood in the shadows just left of the stage. They both stared absently at the podium, the glare of lights shining down onto it like an alien tractor beam. The audience was buzzing; hundreds of reporters, students, and scientists had packed themselves into the auditorium.

Without warning, a small man appeared at their side. The man had a professorial bush of a mustache that waved in an absent wind as he talked.

"Are you two ready?"

James nodded and squeezed his wife's hand.

The man nodded and brushed by him, trotting out into the blinding sea of light. The mass of humanity hushed as he began to speak.

"Ladies and gentlemen. First of all, just let me say that we are honored that GeneFirm chose the University of Texas to come and present their new medical breakthrough. We hope in the future that this university can continue to work with GeneFirm in the research and development of new cures and therapies. Now it is my pleasure to present Dr. James Logan and Dr. Linda Nguyen, the husband and wife team who head the gene therapy department at GeneFirm Incorporated, the largest and most esteemed biotech company in the world. Interestingly, James and Linda were both children of GeneFirm scientists, both engineered and raised on GeneFirm's massive research facility west of the city. They went on to earn their doctorates from the University of Texas before moving back to GeneFirm to start their careers. The two of them have authored dozens of papers on gene therapy and are among the brightest rising stars in our scientific community. So without further ado, I present to you Dr. Logan and Dr. Nguyen."

James gave one last squeeze to his wife's hand as they stepped into the haze of the auditorium lights. James stood six feet tall with a slim, yet muscular build. Linda was almost the same height in her high heels, her skin tone a wonderful brown next to the stark whiteness of her husband.

James stopped in front of the microphone. He looked out over the crowd with pleasure, barely able to contain the excitement coursing through him.

"Good morning and welcome. Thank you all for being here. We are very excited to share our research with you today; however, before that I would like to start off this morning with a little history lesson for the students in the audience.

"In terms of preventable deaths, the cure for cancer has been one of the single greatest medical discoveries in human history, perhaps only surpassed by the creation of the vaccine by Edward Jenner. While the development of the smallpox vaccine can be accredited to our bovine friends and the cowpox virus that afflicted them, the cure for cancer originated in a remarkable parasitic trematode isolated from the Ganges River. The Ganges was quite possibly the most polluted river on the planet at that time. It is ironic that the toxic environment mankind created, which increased the incidence of cancer in the first place, eventually became so carcinogenic that it led to a cure, a mutation-resistant flatworm called *Schistoma immortalitas*. From this parasite, Dr. Weisman, the founder of GeneFirm, managed to isolate a group of genes that had paradoxically mutated the ability to resist further mutation. By inserting the flatworm's mutation-resistant genes into humans, he was able to create a strain impervious to carcinogens and random mutations. In other words, he created a human genotype that was effectively cancer proof."

James was speaking of the original Dr. Weisman, somewhat of a godhead among the people of GeneFirm. Dr. Weisman had been dead for quite some time now. Dr. Weisman II was currently the CEO of GeneFirm. But no one ever mentioned "II" to his face. This would not be very politically correct. To call a clone "the second" or "number two" was a slur of sorts, since most of them didn't gravitate toward the idea of not being unique individuals. Apparently it was very much a part of human nature to want to be an original. It was no wonder that most of the clones, created back when it was still legal, were inevitably prescribed a mood stabilizer, antidepressant, or some other cheery combination of psychiatric medications.

James swept his hand out. "Of course there is controversy shrouding all of this. This great leap in disease prevention has resulted in a crippling overpopulation of our planet. Many complain that eliminating cancer has made humanity unsustainable. But I ask you this: how could it be ethical to do anything else? As a doctor, if you have a treatment that is effective, how can you not use it? The Hippocratic oath says that above all else we must do no harm. So to answer the critics, I argue that it would be absolutely amoral to consciously let a child be born today with the potential to develop cancer, or any disease for that matter. Our goal for the future should be to limit the birthrate and develop more sustainable ways of living, not to limit medical treatment. You cannot stop the progress of man."

James paused. Out of the blue, he was beginning to feel light-headed. He had been having episodes like this for the last couple months; he had always been in perfect health, so he didn't quite know what to make of it. Looking down, he was puzzled to see that his hands were flushed bright red. James wobbled for a moment at the podium; an awkward silence was fast falling over the room.

Linda quickly pushed by her husband, replacing him at the microphone. She flashed a brief look of concern in his direction. Not wanting the moment to be ruined, she cleared her throat and continued.

"Unfortunately these cancer-proof genes, in each and every one of us, are not inheritable, meaning that the genes must be inserted into the embryo and then the embryo implanted back into the mother. This has not only proven to be very costly for our health care system, but it also leaves room for people to fall through the cracks. For instance, those individuals who freely conceive—illegally—without cancer-proof engineering, or those who do not have access to conception engineering in third world countries. For decades, GeneFirm has been trying to develop a way to make the cancer-proof genes easily deliverable and inheritable."

James was having trouble hearing the words coming out of Linda's mouth. Her voice soon disappeared completely, leaving only a buzzing in his ears. The room was also getting extraordinarily hot. With one hand he loosened his tie, which at the moment seemed to be constricting around his neck like a python. He gulped painfully, his mouth dry. Breathing was becoming a chore.

At the podium, Linda continued talking, unaware of what was unfolding behind her. She never saw her husband begin to sway back and forth.

"Well, that is all about to change. I am excited to tell you that our research has led to an incredible breakthrough: the creation of a viral vector that can deliver the cancer-proof genes to an individual and make them a permanent fixture. I'm talking about a set of inheritable cancer-proof genes that can be delivered through a simple injection. This will revolutionize the world. From the largest cities to the most remote and poverty-stricken areas, we now have a permanent cure for cancer—a cure for everyone."

Linda's chest puffed up in pride. She addressed the audience confidently, "Now we'll take questions."

There were hundreds of questions, but none of them were answered. James toppled to the floor behind Linda and began to shake, his head slapping the ground again and again like a freshly landed fish gasping for air.

As the airplane banked sharply to the left, the captain's voice came on over the intercom announcing their imminent landing. A man in a window seat looked out over the American landscape beneath him with a scowl. Where once there was a grand expanse of green, there were now only concrete plains. Throngs of cars choked the roadways—boxy machines crawling everywhere like an army of mindless ants. Flying over cities during the day always depressed him. At night it was a different story, when the sun disappeared leaving only the sterile glow of city lights, transforming the ground below into a mirror image of the space above. But during the day there was little beauty about the city. Just filth. Like a termite mound made of bug spit and wood shavings, standing ugly against the horizon. It was the final flight of his long trip. In the last couple weeks the man had circumnavigated the globe like a space-age Magellan. But it was the same story everywhere he went: overpopulation, crime, infrastructure decay, and smog so thick it stained your teeth.

Unfortunately this last flight had been disturbed by a small child in the seat next to him. Three? Four? Not old enough to show any common decency. The child had been busy playing some obnoxiously loud video game on his father's phone for the last couple hours. The game involved a cartoon polar bear on some kind of gluttonous seal binge, mauling gun-toting humans along the way. The irritating growls, pings, and chimes of the game grated against the businessman's nerves, like an ice pick to his forehead. The child's father, sitting in the aisle seat, was busy snoring loudly.

He thought now was as good a time as ever. Out of his suit jacket he produced a tiny plastic spray bottle. There was only a tiny bit of fluid left inside; enough for one more dose, he hoped. He stared down at the child slapping the buttons on his asinine game. The child eventually tilted his head upward and the two locked eyes.

Without warning, the man sprayed the kid in the face. The child's head recoiled, his features contorting as the mist met skin. To the man's disbelief, the kid seemed completely unfazed by the event, returning without comment to his video game, the sounds returning once again to shred what was left of the man's waning patience.

"Stupid fucking kid," he whispered, "turn that off."

The bottle remerged from the man's coat. This time he did his best to spray the mist directly into the boy's eyes.

This time the boy started crying and rubbing his eyes furiously. That's better, thought the man. He lay his head back and closed his eyes.

To his relief, the stewardess' voice crackled again from the intercom: "Please make sure your tray tables and seats are in the upright position and that your seat belts are fastened as we prepare to land. The weather on the ground is sunny and sweltering with a high of 110 degrees. Welcome to Austin, Texas."

2

An intimidating black car with two equally intimidating men cruised down a busy street in Austin, Texas. Passersby could tell this was a government
car by the crest on the door panels—the distinct insignia of the Department of Homeland Health Care,
by far one of the most loathed and feared branches
of the bloated bureaucracy that was their federal
government.

"So who are we paying a visit to?"

"The guy's name is Pat Henderson. Another
porker. On his last checkup the doctor signed him
up for a health retreat but he never showed. So now
we got a warrant to assist him in making the next
one." Agent Macdonald gave a big toothy grin. "I
know he would just hate to miss it."

Agent Marnoy attempted to acknowledge Mac's

humor, but all that showed was a thin sneer in the corner of his mouth.

"Oh, come on, Marnoy, don't try to smile so hard, you might hurt yourself."

Marnoy was a brutish-looking man with the kind of crookedly angled nose that can only be formed via repeated blows to the face. Throughout life he had taken plenty of these, both literal and metaphorical. Marnoy's mother had been a giant black Amazon of a woman, while his father was a stocky Jewish bodybuilder. It had been a difficult childhood, to say the least. With life being so unkind to him, at the age of thirty Marnoy was the human equivalent of a prized pit bull, kicked and bit his entire existence. He had grown into a man eager to lunge at the throat and hold on until life had paid him its due.

Agent Macdonald, on the other hand, was a light-hearted man and about as fat as you could legally get under Homeland regulations. Underneath his nose lounged a lazy caterpillar of a mustache. He looked more like an Italian chef than an agent of the government. Phenotypically at least, he had missed his calling. The man should have been working around checkered tablecloths and spitting out little clichés like, "you like my tasty meatballs?"

Marnoy scowled, "This is what it has come down to, Mac. I have a lifetime of chasing down the obese ahead of me."

"Hey! This is my job, too, man. Don't go bashing it. It's not so bad."

"Yes it is."

"Whatever. Listen buddy, you'll eventually get that promotion. You were born to move up the ranks, I promise you. You're working your ass off and it's going to pay off. Plus, it's not like this is the job that I thought I would be doing either, but you don't see me complaining. I never thought for an instant that I would end up blowing out my rotator cuff and not going pro." After a pause he added, "I guess I had some clue. I was never that good at baseball!" Mac chuckled to himself. "But look at me now. My wife and I bought a house and filled it with dogs, cats, and kids. All that happily ever after kinda shit. It will happen to you one day, buddy, if you're not careful."

The fact that Mac found humor in every aspect of life annoyed Marnoy to the point that he felt like swerving the car into oncoming traffic. Humor had a tendency of hitting him like water on summer asphalt, instantly turning to steam.

"But that's just life, my friend. Our job isn't that bad; hell it's even fun sometimes. We just have to have the strength to accept the things we can't change."

"Isn't that the motto for Alcoholics Anonymous?"

"So I used to drink too much—sue me." Mac laughed again. "It's still a good motto."

Conversations with Mac were always useless, thought Marnoy; the man was filled with an endless barrage of positivity and bad jokes.

Something caught the corner of Marnoy's eye.

"Oh, hell no!" Marnoy screamed and slammed on the brakes, turning the wheel hard while making a complete U-turn, tires squealing.

Completely unprepared for the force of the sharp turn, Mac was thrown against his door. "What's the deal, man?"

Marnoy ignored him and accelerated, taking a

sharp turn into an alleyway before coming to a screeching halt in front of four terrified teenagers. A lanky boy in the middle stared wide-eyed at the car, frozen solid with a cigarette dangling limply between his thin lips. The front fender of the car was inches away from his shins.

"Smokers."

"Dude. Come on. You almost gave me a heart attack. Thought you saw a terrorist or something."

"Game time!" Marnoy shouted as he jumped out of the car. It was moments like these that provided a rare spark of enjoyment in the dark moldy mass of his heart.

Mac smiled, the initial shock wearing off. He barked out, "Game time indeed!" By the time he was out of the car, Marnoy was already shouting at the teens and waving his gun.

"Get on the ground!"

All four of the stunned kids instantly hit the pavement. Marnoy fed off the fear in their faces.

"Where the hell did you get it?"

"Get wha—what?" cried one of the kids.

"Don't play with me. Where did you get the cigarette?"

"I found it on the ground, man. I've never seen one before. Please, it's not ours!"

Mac whistled as he leaned up against the hood of the car. "Wrong answer. He won't like that."

Marnoy was now kneeling next to the kid, screaming in his ear, "Where did you get this? Cigarettes are illegal! You want to go to jail? You wanna go to a health retreat?"

The lanky kid who had been smoking was crying

buckets, his tears creating two dark spots where his eyes were pressed against the cement.

"Told you he wasn't going to like that," said Mac. "Listen kids, I would just tell the guy—he's a very angry man, and frankly a little unstable. He didn't get enough hugs as a kid. But I think you figured that one out already."

The cigarette the kid had been smoking was smoldering nearby. Marnoy bent over and picked it up. He held it up to the face of the crying boy.

"You know what this does to you? This will fucking kill you! I'm talking about chronic obstructive pulmonary disease! Lung cancer! Systemic vascular compromise! I think you need a lesson."

Slowly he brought the cigarette close to the boy's face until it was almost touching the skin. The kid could do nothing but whimper, "I swear we just found it, I swear. I swear! I've never even seen one before."

Then the waterworks really turned on. The kid cried so hard he was losing his breath.

Mac, a father himself, could only take Marnoy's antics in small doses and stepped in. "That's enough, let's sign them up for Tobacco Rehab."

"Please, it's not ours! Don't sign us up."

"Stand up and put your wrists out now!" said Mac.

The teens slowly stood up. Four right arms extended out. Marnoy pulled out a little black rectangle from his pocket and touched each kid's wrist. Four names popped up on the device's display.

"All right. Jeff Husk, Zuy Luu, Gregory and Donald Power. You will all report next week for rehab.

You will be contacted shortly with more information." After saying this, Marnoy couldn't help but add, "You're lucky this time. You four better hope I never see you again, because next time I'll be sending you to a health retreat."

With that he snapped his teeth down hard, making the crying kid jump. The agents climbed back into the car and pulled back onto the street.

Marnoy was in a much better mood; he was actually smiling, if you could call it that—he hadn't had much practice with that particular facial expression. He turned to Mac and said, "Now where were we? Oh, yes, Mr. Pat Henderson. This little piggy went 'wee, wee, wee' all the way home."

3

"**W**hat do you mean I can't see him? I'm his wife!"

The nurse looked up and shook her head. "Listen lady, I've already had four different 'Linda Nguyens' come up here. I'm not falling for it. You can go over there and hang with your news reporter cronies. You're not getting any information out of me."

It was obvious that the news of her husband's collapse had spread rapidly. Linda rode with James in the ambulance but had been forced to wait in the hospital's lobby for hours. They told her they needed to take James for an emergent surgery due to a hemorrhage in his brain. She was a nervous wreck and wanted answers. The whole thing had been such a mess. James had seized right up to the point where the paramedics had to administer a benzodiazepine suppository right there on stage. How embarrassing. This day had not gone at all like she planned.

Linda grabbed the nurse's scanner and waved it over her own wrist. Her information instantly popped up on the screen. The nurse carefully read it over and then looked up and gave Linda a sympathetic look.

"I apologize. We've just been trying to keep these news people out of here. They've been chomping at the bit to get more information. Come on back. You better come quick, though. I think those reporters heard you."

It was too late. A microphone was shoved in front of Linda.

"Dr. Nguyen, is it true that your husband just had brain surgery?"

Her only response was a very poignant extended middle finger directed at the crowd as she disappeared through the double doors. The gaggle of reporters stood there, staring sadly at the swinging doors where Linda had just been, like dogs waiting for their owner to come home.

The nurse led a worried Linda back through a series of chaotic hallways until they came to a room. The nurse stopped and looked at her.

"Your husband just got out of surgery and I'm sure you would like to keep him company. I'll make sure the surgeon comes to see you shortly."

A lump had formed in Linda's throat; she managed to squeak out a soft "thank you." The nurse went back down the turbulent hallway, leaving Linda all alone. She hesitated, then slowly reached out and pushed open the door. A loved one in the hospital was such an unreal experience. There he was, his head wrapped in a turban of white bandages, lying in a tiny robotic world of beeps, bips, and blinking lights. With each heartbeat the monitor next to him chirped slowly and methodically. She walked over to the edge of the bed, held his hand, and began to cry softly, her organic sounds balancing out the room's machinery. She studied James' face and realized she hadn't really looked at it in a long time. He was a beautiful man, the same man she had fallen in love with. At forty years of age, he still had a baby face. Not one wrinkle had carved its way into his skin; not even a single gray hair sprouting on his head. He still looked more like a college student than a middle-aged researcher, filling her with an unreasonable sense of jealousy. This youthful look had vexed him for most of his life, especially back when the two of them used to try convincing bartenders they were of a legal drinking age. Of course, this would often fail, and it would be her cleavage to the rescue. Men seldom argued with that.

There was a mirror on the wall across from her. She hoped it was the dark lighting, or all the crying, but she was depressed to see that she looked older. Unlike James, her face showed the small insults of passing time. Age, the stealthy attacker.

Suddenly the door opened behind her. The air in the room stirred with the pressure change, making a shiny bag of IV fluids sway from its perch. Linda turned to see a dark man enter the room looking rather sheepish in his oversized white coat.

He held out a soft hand to Linda. "Hello, I'm Doctor Solomon."

Linda nodded.

His name was embroidered on his white coat and below it, Department of Neurosurgery. He shared James' baby face, but there was no way he could have been practicing more than a couple years. This made Linda nervous. She noticed the young doctor's inability to look her in the eyes while he took a seat on a little black stool, which squeaked as he sat down. It squeaked again as the doctor nervously pivoted back and forth. After Dr. Solomon realized where the sound was coming from, he immediately stopped moving and sat up straight.

"The surgery went well. The hemorrhage in his brain was evacuated."

"Why did he hemorrhage?"

"Well, this is where we are at a loss. He had a mass in his brain."

"A mass?"

"Yes. We are currently waiting on the pathology results, but it seems to be a tumor."

"A tumor? Impossible." Linda put a hand on the wall to brace herself. It was her turn to feel lightheaded.

"Which is why I want to clarify a few things." Doctor Solomon pulled out an electronic tablet and tapped it with his pen a few times. "Was your husband a free conception?"

Linda laughed weakly. "You and I both know that you have access to all of James' electronic medical records. You know exactly where he was born. You even know who his conception engineer is."

"I understand how ridiculous the question sounds."

"So it's really cancer?"

"It looks very much like your husband had a meningioma that was responsible for the hemorrhage and subsequent seizure. Once again, we won't be sure until we hear from pathology."

"Will he be alright?"

"Luckily the cancer did not seem to be aggressive. We found it in a very early stage and were able to resect all of it. He has a good prognosis; however, we are at a loss for how this happened. His DNA sequencing on record shows that his cancer-proof genes are intact. I've never seen cancer in someone with cancer-resistant genes. "

Dr. Solomon's look became more serious. "I have ordered another sequencing of James' DNA in hopes that we can find some clues to what caused this. In theory, there could have been an error in his original sequencing, and by some inexplicable chance James' embryo managed to make it through. If this is true, then he may be at risk again. Are you alright?" Dr. Solomon's brow wrinkled in concern.

Linda had grown silent. It looked like her mind had wandered somewhere far away. She was looking a little pale. Dr. Solomon could understand why; this situation was unthinkable.

"I have also been contacted by Homeland Health Care; as you could imagine, they are very interested why someone with the cancer-proof genes has developed cancer. I just wanted you to be aware you may hear from them soon."

The sleek black government car sped down the off-ramp.

"So what do we know about our boy Mr. Henderson?"

"I'm going to take a complete shot in the dark here and say that this guy eats entirely too much. The report says he is five foot eight and two hundred and twenty pounds."

MacDonald whistled as he did the math in his head. "A BMI over thirty! You don't see many of those these days. How the hell did he manage to make it this far without getting sent to a retreat?"

"Oh, you know, same old story. Guy works from home, turns twenty-five and his metabolism drops, he becomes depressed, eats more, next thing you know you got a snowball of cellulite."

"That image will haunt my dreams forever."

Marnoy turned the car into a ratty-looking apartment complex and parked. "Home sweet home."

The two men got out of the car into the scorching sun, sweat beading on their foreheads.

"It's hot man. Damn this global warming shit," Mac said as he wiped his brow. "I feel like I'm one of those melting glaciers right now."

"This is Texas. If you don't like the weather, just wait. And by the way, this guy lives on the third floor, so I hope you've been doing your workouts."

The two men climbed the three flights of stairs. At the top Mac was bent over and gasping for air. Marnoy noted that his partner's waist line had been progressively swelling. If Mac wasn't careful, he would end up at a retreat himself.

"Here we go, Apartment ninety-two." Marnoy rapped hard on the door.

Little pig, little pig, let me in.

After a minute or two, the door creaked open. A chubby moon of a face peered out through the crack. "Aw, shit! What do you guys want?"

Marnoy flashed a wolf smile.

"Mr. Henderson, we are with the Department of Homeland Health Care. Your doctor referred you to us. Can we come in and talk to you for a minute?"

Or I'll huff and puff and blow your house down.

The boy looked at his feet, swearing underneath his breath.

"Okay come on in. But if it's about my weight, I've been working out every day. I've lost ten pounds!"

"I'm sure you have," Marnoy said as he glanced down at the kid's bloated gut.

When the door opened they walked into the pigsty that Pat called his home. The small kitchen to the left of the entryway was lined with a maze of dirty dishes. In the corner the trash can was teetering at maximum capacity like a game of trash Jenga.

"Have a seat, Mr. Henderson," Macdonald said.

The young man sat down on his couch and Agent Macdonald pulled out a computer pad and started his well-practiced spiel. Marnoy hated listening to this part, so he wandered off into the kitchen.

"Hey, where's he going?" said Pat as he craned his neck to see Marnoy.

"Don't worry about it, dude," said Mac. "Let's see, according to your parole doctor, your body mass index is thirty-three, waistline is thirty-nine inches, and your blood pressure is one-fifty over ninety. Mr.

Henderson, you are clinically obese and hyperten-
sive. These facts, combined with your family history
of heart attacks, mean that you have three major
risk factors for cardiovascular disease; therefore you
are eligible for a six-week health retreat program."

And by eligible, Mac really meant mandatory.
And by "health retreat," he really meant nightmarish
boot camp.

"I can't! I have to work."

Mac looked up. "Mr. Henderson, consider this a
paid vacation."

Without warning Marnoy burst back into the
room holding a half-eaten tray of brownies.

"Chocolate brownies! You bet I'm writing this
up. You're not even trying, are you Pat?"

"Dude, get out of my fridge."

Marnoy just cackled like a witch and disappeared
back into the kitchen.

Pat looked helplessly at Macdonald. "What about
my job? I'll get fired!"

Before Mac could respond there came another
interruption from the kitchen. "Cookies! Chips!
Coke! You are so screwed!" This was followed by
more of Marnoy's sinister laughing.

Mac rolled his eyes. "Marnoy, shut up will ya!
I'm doing my thing in here."

The only reply was, "Fudge? Fudge, really? Who
has fudge lying around?"

"Pat, it's illegal for your employer to fire you for
going to a health retreat. Cardiovascular disease
used to be the number-one killer in the United States
of both men and women. This also means that it is
one of the most expensive diseases for the govern-

ment. Prevention is key to keeping health care costs down. Do you understand?"

The fat kid had the self-defeated look of a hog caught in a trap. He knew he was stuck and there was no way out. He nodded his head slowly in acceptance and stared down at the stained carpet.

"This is unbelievable. The government doesn't give two shits about me. They are just trying to save money," said Pat.

Marnoy ran back into the room holding up a box.

"Funfetti cake mix! Funfetti!" he said, almost choking on the words. "Are you a thirteen-year-old girl? What kind of man has Funfetti cake mix? Oh man, you're killing me."

Marnoy popped back into the kitchen. Pat and Mac could hear him digging through the pantry.

"A van will be here tomorrow morning to pick you up. Take the rest of the day to get your things in order. They should be here at six a.m. One piece of advice, don't be late. They hate that. Can I see your wrist?"

Pat held out his left wrist.

"Your other wrist Pat."

With much resentment he stuck out his right arm. Mac waved his scanner over it.

"We're all done here. Let's go Marnoy—get out of the guy's cupboard."

The two agents left the apartment, leaving the boy with the buffalo hump to ruminate on how his next six weeks would be spent—undoubtedly very sore and very hungry. He knew what the so-called health retreats were. It was Homeland Health Care's brain-child: a place where unhealthy habits are skewered and slow roasted over the coals of a rigorous exercise schedule, health propaganda, and six very meager meals every day. Pat knew people who had gone. They all came back thinner, with lower cholesterol, broken dependencies, and—most important—an incredibly strong desire never to return.

Outside, Marnoy followed Mac back into the parking lot. "That apartment was disgusting."

Macdonald wiped more sweat off his brow. "I think you made your feelings perfectly clear in there. Why do you have to harass the guy like that? Slate and his scantily clad goons are going to eat that kid alive."

"They most certainly will," Marnoy said as he started the car.

4

The girl with cat eyes was painting. Her slitlike vertical pupils watched each brushstroke carefully as she applied thick globs of color to the canvas. A swift knock on the door made her jump slightly. No one ever knocked on her door; therefore, the only explanation was that her probation doctor was back. With no intention of talking to that asshole, she continued to paint. This time she stroked the canvas with a bloody mixture of oil pastels, leaving a thick red laceration. The knocking on the door became more rapid and her brushstrokes became faster and faster, as if to match the rhythm of the knocking. She could hear the probation doctor's muffled shouting.

"Modest? I know you're home. Your car is outside. I need to talk to you, please."

Modest, she thought. Her parents must have really

hated her. She really could never fathom what was going on in her parents' heads when they did what they did to her. Mushrooms? LSD? Marijuana? They must have been rolling all of that shit up and smoking it together. The end result was Modest, a girl with cat eyes and pink hair. The hair wasn't dyed. Her eyes weren't fake contacts. It was all the real deal. Her rich prick of a rock-and-roll-icon grandfather had paid some unethical conception engineer to turn his daughter into a complete freak, the kind of freak he had always wanted to be.

Modest continued painting with short jerky movements. A sleek four-legged outline was emerging like a shadow on the canvas, rust red and metallic gray against the canvas's white emptiness.

The knocking became more frantic. Modest started to breathe heavily, and her forearm burned from her viselike grip on the brush. The knocking turned into pounding. Finally the banging worked a screw loose somewhere inside her. She screamed in frustration and began to stab the canvas like Caesar's incarnate. The easel collapsed during the attack and the canvas dropped backward to the floor. In the dim light, the hunched form of a feline stared back at her from the ground. Her hands were balled up so tightly that her knuckles went white as she stamped over to the door. She threw it open.

Her probation doctor's eyes widened in surprise.

"Stop pounding on my damn door!"

"I was just knocking," he said, looking confused, wondering what drugs she was on at the moment. "We need to talk, Modest."

"About what?"

"Well, first of all, you haven't been showing up to your A. A. meetings or your exercise classes—both of which, I remind you, are mandatory."

She cocked her head and feigned a cough. "I've been sick."

The small gray-haired man looked at the skinny pale girl with her wild pink hair and sinister-looking eyes. He thought she did look pretty sick, but more of the mentally ill variety.

"Well, maybe it's time for you to return to a health retreat so we can get you feeling better. How do you feel about that?"

"Fuck you! I'm not going back!"

"I'm sorry, Modest, but you worry me. I'm afraid you don't have a choice. You're relapsing. I've arranged for the van to pick you up at six fifteen a.m. tomorrow morning. Can I see your wrist?"

Modest glared at the scanner he held in his hand. "This is fucking bullshit!"

"Modest, can I please see your wrist?"

With her cat eyes burning, she lifted a limp hand, barely, just enough so that he could quickly swing his scanner past her arm.

Trying to avoid eye contact, he peered past her shoulder and saw empty bottles of vodka cluttered on the coffee table in between layers of dirty dishes and half-eaten meals. She was definitely drinking again, but the smell of her had already given that one away. She smelled like the sticky floor of a bar on Sunday morning.

"Thank you, Modest. Don't forget, the van will be

here to pick you up tomorrow. I don't want there to be any complications." He waved good-bye to the brooding figure in the doorway.

Modest slammed the door as hard as she could and collapsed against it. She sat there hugging her knees, slowly rocking back and forth. The tears came next; she cried so violently she began to hiccup, unable to catch her next breath. She cried until she couldn't anymore; sapped of energy, she lay there sniffling on the ground. Not another one of those damn retreats. This would be her fourth. She knew this wasn't about her health anymore. Nobody got more than three trips to a retreat. It was that bastard, who was behind this, she was almost sure of it.

Modest crawled over and snaked her hand under the couch, emerging with a small bottle of whiskey. With trembling fingers, she unscrewed the cap and took a terribly long chug. When she lowered the bottle her face twisted with bitterness. Disgusted with herself, she smashed the half-full bottle against the wall. Whiskey and glass rained down on the carpet, forming a dark patch—just another blemish in a room full of stains.

5

Linda was disappointed to find herself in the dream again. The air was sticky and stagnant with summer. Moonlight reflected off the glassy dark water of the lake. Her college roommate, Mary, was there, too. Both of them were clad in black, with panty hose stretched over their heads making their faces look squashed and disfigured. In the shadows they looked like hideous monsters. She realized there was something in her hand, and to her horror she saw it was a gas can.

Linda knew what came next, but she couldn't stop it. She wanted to shout, "Don't do it," but she couldn't move her mouth.

The two girls advanced quickly over the grass until they came to a chain-link fence. With wire cutters, Mary quickly clipped a hole in the fence that they could slip through. They stealthily passed through corridors of construction equipment—bulldozers, cranes, dump trucks, stacks of wood and steel. Finally they stopped at the base of a shell of a building. It loomed above them like the petrified skeleton of an ominous giant. Now Linda had changed her mind. Burn it! Burn all of it.

This building was just another affront to the lake, an ugly eyesore of a greedy and consumerist culture. She hated this building and everything it represented. The smell of gas was strong. Gas was everywhere. That's because she was dousing everything around her with it, and Mary was doing the same. A match appeared and was struck. The tiny flame gave birth to a fiendish offspring that enveloped everything around them.

It was a spectacular sight. Orange and yellow danced around her and became hot against the dark night's sky. The fire shot its way upward until it was a burning pillar reflected in the still waters of the lake.

But now she was trapped. The fire was all around her with no way out. The paralyzing fear of death overcame her.

She was on fire and there was no way to put it out. She screamed as the flames crept up her body. Soon she was a burning pillar as well. Again, she cried out for help, but no sound came. Instead flames crept down her throat, roasting her from the inside. She could feel her esophagus liquefy and start to boil out of her mouth.

With a jolt Linda was awake. No more fire. Her

skin was clammy and her heart was racing. For a split second she had no idea where she was, some dark unfamiliar room. Then the beep, beep, beep of the heart monitor brought the situation crashing back down on her.

It was a dream she had been living with for quite some time, but she had been living with the guilt even longer.

That night had happened so long ago that it had become difficult to distinguish the dream from the actual memory—the two so often bled together in the heat of her recollection. She wondered that if she didn't remember something happening and there was no proof, no pictures, no witnesses, did it really happen? Would that past eventually fade from memory, erasing the truth? She hoped so, otherwise she would carry this secret to the grave.

Thinking back on it, that night wasn't about the cleared forest, the lake, or the pollution: it was her own personal witch burning. However, in the end, it was her reckless youth and ideals that burned that night. Out of the ashes, a more cautious woman arose and her activism slipped into a deep hibernation.

It wasn't until the next day that they discovered two firefighters and a security guard had been killed in their self-righteous inferno. Over the guilt of what they had done, Linda and Mary disbanded. They didn't count on having any real casualties in their battle for the lake. Being young and foolish were her only excuses.

◎

"Linda, you look like you just saw a ghost."

"Jesus Christ!" Linda cried as she swung around in her chair. A mountain of a man stood in the doorway. "You scared the living shit out of me. Damn it, Ari! I almost had a heart attack."

"You kiss your kids with that mouth?"

"Shut up, Ari. What are you doing here?"

He had to duck his head to fit through the doorway. The man's features were now visible in the dim light of the room, including the sharp angles of his chin and cheekbones. His hair was so blond he almost appeared albino. Linda had always wondered if he was suffering from a clinical case of gigantism as well. He wore a dark blue suit with no tie, his shirt unbuttoned one too low for her taste—perfectly tailored and incredibly expensive, as one would expect from the son of Dr. Weisman, the heir to the GeneFirm empire.

"My father sent me to bring you two back to GeneFirm. He wants James to be cared for by our doctors."

"Thank goodness for that, Ari. I don't trust this place."

"Nor should you; GeneFirm has the finest doctors in the world." Ari leaned back into the hallway and said, "Alright, let's get him out of here."

A horde of people burst into the room, and in a flurry of movement James was unplugged, unhooked, and transferred over to a stretcher and then wheeled out of the room. Ari and Linda followed behind.

"We're going to get harassed by the media when we try to leave."

"Unlikely."

"What are you talking about? They've got this place surrounded. They almost tackled me on the way in here."

Ari just stared back with a blank expression. He pointed with his giant index finger toward the sky.

"Dr. Weisman sent a helicopter?"

"Only the best for our top scientists. And by the way, I saw your little stunt on the news last night. The middle finger, eh? Whatever happened to 'no comment'? You were always the classy girl growing up, weren't you?"

"No, they didn't . . . ," Linda said dropping her head. "They put that on TV? I hope my kids didn't see it."

"Somehow I doubt your kids watch the nightly channel nine news."

Linda and Ari piled into a large elevator along with James' stretcher and rode it all the way to the top floor of the hospital. The group pushed through a set of doors and onto the helipad. Waiting for them was a black helicopter with the GeneFirm logo—a husk of corn, half peeled, with a phalanx of DNA protruding out in place of a yellow corncob.

It was daybreak. Dawn's violent streaks of color were already thrashing over the edge of the horizon. James was carefully loaded into the helicopter. Linda took a seat next to him. Ari got in last and shut the door. With a deafening whirl of steel the high-powered metal stress test lifted off the ground and began to thump its way west. She watched the hospital and the multitude of news vans get smaller and smaller until they were out of sight. She enjoyed the thought of those reporters shaking their fists at the sky as they watched their story fly off into the dawn.

As the sun rose higher, the signs of the city began to disappear, slowly replaced by rolling hill country. The green treetops stretched on for miles beneath them. They passed over the expansive Lake Travis, sparkling blue below. Soon she could make out the tips of the great white spinning blades of GeneFirm's wind turbines. As they approached, more oversized propellers jutted upward into the air. The towering fans were everywhere. The helicopter turned slightly, and Linda held her breath as the peculiar sight came into view. She had never seen GeneFirm from the sky before. Rising up from the forest was a glass pyramid shimmering in the orange light. This was GeneFirm's main campus. Surrounding the pyramid were dozens of boxy glass buildings where most of the company's research took place. In front of the pyramid was a neighborhood of cookie cutter houses. Linda could pick out her house because of the white fence she had strong-armed James into putting up last year. She could see the red brick building where her children attended school, then the grocery store, the recreation center, the hydrogen station, and the neighborhood pool. The GeneFirm neighborhood was like a flashback to the 1950s, a standing replica of the once-lost American dream.

"We're home," shouted Ari over the drone of the helicopter.

6

Pat was startled awake by an angry shrill that filled his room. It took him a couple of confused seconds to figure out that the foreign sound was actually his alarm clock. He hadn't used it in a long time. Big red numbers flashed 6:00 A.M. harshly in the dark. He couldn't remember the last time he woke up this early and didn't care to. It was downright painful.

Just a little more sleep, he thought. He rolled over, drifting back into his dreams.

Ten minutes passed quietly by. The tranquility of his room abruptly ended when his bedroom door shot open and slammed into the wall with a loud crash.

"What the hell?" yelled Pat as he jumped out of bed.

Two large men strolled through the now open doorway. They both wore cowboy hats, boots, and jeans—the whole Western getup.

"Good morning sunshine! I'm Driver Dan and this is my ugly brute of an associate," said one of the burly gorillas with a deep Southern drawl.

"Get out of my room! Who the hell are you? You can't just burst in here like that."

Pat's rant ended when one of the cowboys grabbed his hand, bending his wrist to such an obscene angle that his legs went limp with pain.

"Ow!" he cried. "Ow! Stop that!"

In seconds Pat, clad only in his boxers and a white t-shirt, was herded down the stairs of his apartment building. The men dragged him across the parking lot to a white van with the Homeland insignia on the doors. When they reached the van, Pat was crying, snot spilling down his face.

"Now are you gonna be a good little heifer or are you gonna give us more trouble?"

"Let go of me!"

Driver Dan shook his head and looked at the other cowboy. "Some bovines just don't get it, do they?"

"Nope."

He applied more pressure to Pat's wrist, making him drop to his knees on the pavement.

"Please stop it, please! It hurts."

"You gonna stop fighting us?"

Pat nodded.

"That's a good pig. Now get in the van."

The side door of the vehicle slid open and Pat was greeted by the wide-eyed faces of the other captives inside. He squeezed his way into the back row of the van, where he threw himself down on the seat, trying his best to stop crying. The van door shut and the two cowboys climbed into the front seats.

The engine started up and the driver asked, "Ya'll like country?"

Nobody said a word but the stereo came on anyway. The van filled with deafening country music, a smorgasbord of crashing slide guitars and harmonica.

"Yeehaw!" shouted Driver Dan as he stomped on the gas, sending the van rocketing forward.

The guy sitting next to Pat stuck out his hand. "Hi. My name is Tony."

Pat looked over solemnly and croaked, "Hey."

"Looks like those two hillbillies manhandled you pretty good. If they would've tried that with me I would've bludgeoned them to death."

Tony was a whale of a man. His midsection protruded like a beach ball beneath his blue jumpsuit. The guy was huge, at least 400 pounds. Pat wondered how Tony had managed to achieve all that weight under the government's watchful eyes. His forehead was spotted with sweat. Around his neck the jumpsuit was already dark with saturation.

"Man, is it hot in here or what?"

"Kinda," said Pat as he inched away from the sweaty beast next to him.

The van took a sharp turn and the passengers groaned as they squished into each other. Tony rolled into Pat, soaking him with his perspiration and nearly crushing him to death.

"Oops. My bad buddy. Looks like I got you a bit wet. Damn this heat."

Pat tried not to look too horrified as he furiously wiped off Tony's bodily fluids.

"So I used to play in the NFL. I was an offensive lineman. Can you tell? Anyway, one game, a linebacker came in low and *pow* . . . blew out my knee. He screwed it up real good. Just like that, my career is over, and now I'm here. The government doesn't seem to care about how fat and unhealthy we professional football players are until we stop playing. Ain't that convenient? Probably because they get to tax the hell out of our salaries."

"I'm sorry to hear that," Pat said, but he wasn't really. He wondered why the big Italian was hellbent on having a conversation despite the loud music and psychotic driving.

Tony drummed his fingers on the seat in front of him. "But hey, a six week vacation from work ain't too bad."

Up in the front, Driver Dan yelled loudly, "We have one more camper to pick up. After that we will be on our way to the Lake Travis Health Retreat, so just sit back and relax."

As if to directly contradict his last statement, Driver Dan proceeded to run a red light and take another sharp turn, allowing anything but relaxation.

"Did he say 'camper'?" Pat whispered to himself in disbelief. "Christ, we really are headed to fat camp."

The van drove on for another ten minutes, and then swerved onto a side street, pulling up to a rundown apartment complex. A pale girl, looking utterly miserable, sat on the curb with her arms wrapped around her legs. Her ghostly skin tone contrasted starkly with her bright pink hair, which was just long enough to cover her ears. She had the whole cute-and-helpless look going for sure, like one of those white lab mice awaiting the guillotine of research. She wore a pair of ridiculously large pink sunglasses, neon purple lipstick, and what looked like a hemp poncho striped with a rainbow of all-natural dyes, undoubtedly extracted from local indigenous berries and plants; it looked more like a kite that had been broken over her head and wrapped around her. The girl's face was devoid of emotion. The sun was still below the horizon, so she had to be half blind sitting there in those stupid sunglasses.

Driver Dan once again hopped out, but this time he showed a gentleness that was completely absent in Pat's recent experience. The cowboy even offered a hand to help the girl into the van. However, she just scoffed and ignored him, climbing in by herself. Pat wondered if the courtesy Driver Dan showed the girl was because she wasn't overweight. In fact, she wasn't even close; she looked severely malnourished. Pat knew the world seemed to think he and other large people were second-class citizens. The mere fact that the government shipped them off to retreats like they were some kind of diseased lepers was enough evidence to prove the stigma of fat.

Dan got back in the driver's seat and introduced the new arrival. "Everyone, meet Modest. This will be her fourth time back to the health retreat, so give her a round of applause. If you want pointers on what not to do, she would be the person to ask."

Modest promptly told him to fuck off, which gave him a good hard laugh. "That a girl."

"Why is she so modest?" Tony yelled from the back.

Pat slapped his forehead and said, "Tony, her name is Modest."

The girl's face remained emotionless, hidden behind her glasses, offering no confirmation.

"Ah," Tony hummed, scratching his head.

Driver Dan shouted, "Okey dokey. Let's get this party started. Next stop, Lake Travis Spa and Resort!"

His passengers didn't find this amusing.

"Just ya'll wait. Six weeks from now, you will all look and feel like a million bucks."

Pat highly doubted this. More like six weeks from now he was going to be sore, overworked, and starving—just the thought of the pain that was quickly approaching made him feel sick.

Dan cranked the music up again, louder this time, ignoring the protests that arose behind him. This time a new country song played, the theme of which seemed to center around "titties and beer."

Trying to ignore the music, Pat eyed Modest from the back of the van. The girl's hair was just a few inches longer on the right than the left side. The asymmetry of her hair cried a tale of frustration, clumsy scissors, and a drunken homemade haircut. Her skinny arms hung at her sides like limp ropes. She didn't look too unhealthy, though, maybe just depressed. Her skin was pasty; she looked like she hadn't slept for days.

Pat found himself strangely attracted to her. She reeked of counterculture, depravity, and alcohol. The van now smelled like sour whiskey. He had to wonder if her clothes had been soaking in the stuff overnight. Thanks to this aromatic clue, the reason why the frail girl was packed in a van with a bunch of her chubby brethren was apparent. These health retreats weren't just for the overweight. They were designed by the government to avoid more expensive medical bills down the road. Pat had been given the same old speech about "preventative medicine" by his doctor a million times. The fixation of the government on these major costly diseases left a bad taste in Pat's mouth. This meant that the more obscure, incurable, but less costly your health problem was, the more you were going to be screwed. Homeland Health Care was all about budgeting its humanitarianism. For example, he was at risk for heart disease, and therefore the eyes and ears of Homeland Health Care followed him relentlessly, because a person that suffers multiple heart attacks in his lifetime racks up hundreds of thousands of dollars of hospital and doctor fees. But what about the diseases that aren't cured so easily, like depression or schizophrenia? What incentive does the government have then?

Pat knew this all too well. His older sister personified this rhetorical problem. They didn't send her to a retreat. No white van came to pick up her poor demented soul. She was deeply disturbed, and the doctors just prescribed pills, pills, and more pills. Where was this ruthless brand of "preventive medicine" for her?

7

"Ugh, my head. Who whacked me with a shovel?"

"James! You're awake!"

Linda got up quickly from the chair she had been napping in. She moved to the side of the hospital bed, picking up his hand.

"How are you feeling?"

"My head hurts so bad. Where am I? What happened?"

Linda was delighted that James was finally coherent. He had been in and out of consciousness all day.

"We're in GeneFirm's hospital now, but you had surgery back in Austin."

He raised a hand slowly to his scalp and felt the thick mound of bandages. "Surgery? Why?" he asked with a furrowed brow.

"Why don't you get some more rest? We can talk about this later."

"Just tell me."

Linda hesitated, not sure if he was ready for the news.

"Honey, please . . ."

"You had a seizure due to a brain hemorrhage."

"Really?" James asked with interest, still not looking terribly worried. "Do they know why?"

"Yes, brain cancer," she blurted out.

James laughed. "Nice try."

Linda's expression looked like it had turned to stone.

"That is impossible."

"They were able to remove all of it. The cancer hadn't spread yet."

James could only shake his head in disbelief. "You're kidding me, right?"

"Damnit, James! I was so worried. I thought I was going to lose you."

James saw tears well up in the corners of his wife's eyes. "Alright, alright. Don't get too worked up. So maybe they think it was cancer, but it can't be. It was probably just some vascular malformation or something. You can't trust doctors to diagnose cancer these days, they just don't see it anymore."

James could see how worried Linda was, but she needed to know that it couldn't possibly be true.

Suddenly there was banging on the door that startled them both. James straightened up as the door opened, flooding the room with light.

A figure in the doorway barked, "It's dark in

here. What kind of hanky-panky are ya'll up to? I'm turning on the lights."

The voice belonged to the hunched figure of Dr. Paradee, chief of the GeneFirm hospital. James didn't know exactly how old he was, but he estimated over 100. Using an ancient gnarled wooden cane, the doctor waddled over to the bed. With each step he had to lift up his hip and swing his leg forward in a wide arc. His neck was bent at an unnatural ninety-degree angle, causing his chin to almost touch his chest. Time had been unkind to the good doctor's spine. His head was bald as an egg and covered with liver spots, while his face was a crooked web of wrinkles.

"When did he wake up?"

"Just now."

" 'Bout damn time. Now I hear those quacks back in Austin said they found 'cancer' in your brain. That's a bold statement considering it's not even possible. I want a piece of that biopsy for myself. You can't trust those fools working for the government," said Dr. Paradee, staring intently at the couple before continuing. "Now I've been caring for both of you since you were shitting in diapers, so you can trust me."

They both nodded.

The old man continued in his blunt manner: "No one, and I mean no one, engineered with the cancer-resistance genes has ever developed cancer. Plus, we have one of the greatest conception engineering programs in the world, so I can say with complete confidence that the both of you are genetic perfection. It was probably just a cyst or a benign mass that those idiots misdiagnosed. You're as healthy as an ox. Now I'm going to give you the rest of the day to recover, but then I want you out of here. Get home to your kids, because you're taking up too much of my damn space. Any questions?"

"Thanks, Bill. I don't believe it either," James said.

"As you shouldn't. Ya'll have a great day now." With that, Dr. Paradee wheeled around and limped his way out of the room, dragging his bad leg behind him.

James looked at his wife and said with a smirk, "He has such a way with words, doesn't he, dear?"

Linda didn't smile.

It was high tide at Austin Bergstrom International Airport. Waves of people crashed against the serpentine security lines, only to trickle slowly through the gauntlet one by one. It was a zoolike atmosphere, as usual, and Marnoy felt a little claustrophobic.

"Man, this is such a bad idea."

"Aw, quit your bitchin'," Mac said as the two men squeezed through the throngs of people headed toward their respective terminals.

"We just have to check for compliance with emergency quarantine procedures and then we're out of here. Shouldn't take long at all."

Both agents were wearing blue face masks. The sight of the masks sparked fear in the already anxiety-laden passengers who passed by.

Marnoy shook his head, "This thing is the real deal. A biological weapon. They haven't gone public with it yet, but why else would the director send us out here? I bet half these people have already been exposed."

A woman overheard this and stared at them with a look of shock.

"What the hell are you looking at?"

The lady gave Marnoy a nasty look and disappeared into the river of bodies headed downstream.

"So several hundred cases of a new strain of flu appeared simultaneously in cities all around the world. So what? It doesn't mean bioterrorism," Mac said sarcastically. He sighed and rubbed his belly. "I'm starving, by the way. I really don't want to do this, but I'm going to grab something quick from the food court."

A string of fast-food restaurants was coming up on their right.

"Are you crazy? Why don't you just let everyone behind the counter sneeze on you?"

Mac contorted his face. "Oh, relax, dude. This thing isn't that bad yet. Although I'm not really in the mood for health food."

"Wow. Mac wants fast food? You must really be hungry if you're willing to eat something good for you. Where's your fatty, grease-laden lunch from home?"

"For your information, my wife was freaking out about the flu epidemic this morning and forgot to make me lunch. You know I would never eat out if I could avoid it."

Mac entered the food court and his partner begrudgingly followed. In Marnoy's opinion, with every minute wasted there they were putting their lives at risk.

Mac told the bored teen cashier his order: "A soy-cheese bison burger with a calorie-free coke."

"Nice masks, dudes," said the cashier while rolling his eyes.

"Nice job, dude," Marnoy shot back without missing a beat.

"Damnit Marnoy!" Mac said. "Could you please save your insults until after I get my food safely? Now they really *are* going to sneeze on it."

By the time Mac paid, his food was slapped down on the counter in front of him, fresh off the heat lamps. According to the menu, the burger contained five grams of fat, thirty grams of protein, forty grams of carbs—a well-balanced meal meeting the regulatory requirements of the Department of Homeland Health Care.

Mac's bison burger was alright, a little dry.

Marnoy just sat there with his arms crossed, watching him eat. "You shouldn't have taken your mask off in here."

"Too hungry."

"Well, I hope it's worth it."

8

◎

Pat awoke as the van came to a crunching halt on a gravel road. It took him a second to compute his surroundings—the innards of a white van, its large passengers, the heavily wooded area around them. Only a mess of pink hair sticking up from the seat in front of him jogged his memory. The unwanted reality of the situation came crashing down around him. His confusion was quickly replaced with dread.

At some point during the winding drive through the foothills he had fallen asleep. Next to him, Tony was snoring. It wasn't your ordinary run-of-the-mill snoring, however. To Pat it sounded like the invisible hand of death was doing its best to choke Tony in his sleep.

Driver Dan put the van in park and turned off the

engine. In the uneasy silence that followed, Tony's snoring was the only sound.

The passengers of the van shuffled awkwardly into the blinding morning sunlight. They shifted nervously in their shoes, feeling like cows freshly arrived at the slaughterhouse. Tony was still asleep in the van; Pat had tried to wake him, to no avail. Dan climbed inside and slammed a fist into Tony's swollen gut. Tony awoke with a holler, recoiling so hard that the van rocked back on its tires.

"Good morning, sunshine! Get your ass out of my van," said Dan, with a big smile.

Tony's rubbed his bruised stomach. He didn't move; he just locked eyes with Dan. The two sat there for a second, caught up in a hate-filled staring contest. Then, with surprising speed, the Homeland Health Care gorilla pounced on Tony the hippo. The other cowboy eagerly leapt into the backseat to join in on the ruckus. Pat could tell that the two captors had done this well-orchestrated dance dozens of times. In a flash the two had dragged Tony out of the van and pinned him against the hot gravel like a calf at the rodeo.

After a minute or two, Tony stopped struggling and lay there defeated, huffing for air. Looking around, Pat could tell everyone was mortified. The tone had been set for the rest of the health retreat. After watching the ex-offensive lineman get his ass whooped, there would be very few issues of compliance among the group. Pat turned away from the pitiful scene. His back was sore and his butt ached from sitting so long on the van's uncomfortable seats. He already missed the comfort of his soft leather

couch. The gravel road shifted beneath his shoes as
he took a few steps and looked around. This place
was beautiful, nestled right in the green foothills
surrounding the lake, which sparkled swimming-pool
blue off in the distance over the tree line. Far down
below, he could see a lone boat gliding across the
water, the foamy white V of its wake stretching out
behind it.

The van was parked in front of a bizarre-looking
series of buildings that Pat could only assume was
the health retreat. He had never seen anything quite
like it. No doubt their tax dollars at work. The
building consisted of five white domes connected by
cylindrical passageways. The dome in the middle was
the largest, while the domes issuing from it on either
side got smaller and smaller. The buildings looked
like they belonged to a colonial outpost on Mars,
certainly out of place here in the middle of the hill
country. From above, a casual observer might mistake the buildings for a clutch of goliath-sized eggs
protruding from the nest of the forest.

An electronic drone filled the woods around them.
After a few seconds, he realized it was actually music, some kind of new age bullshit with violins, harps,
and a host of other instruments designed to soothe
the mind. The music sounded like someone had let
Kenny G get too close to a synthesizer. It was irritating. Pat always had the paradoxical urge for violence
whenever he was subjected to that "eastern philoso-
phy, meditative, peace of mind" crap.

From the forest around them, a soothing male
voice spoke up over the music. "Welcome, my guests.
I'm very excited that you've come to share this

amazing experience with us. Today is the first day of your new healthier, happier, and more peaceful existence. Please open your mind and heart and then enter."

When the voice finished, two glass doors at the front of the main dome slid open, beckoning them to enter. The owner of the omnipresent voice sounded more pleasant than Driver Dan, but maybe it was a trick to lure them into the building where they would be ambushed by more thugs in the name of fitness. For now there was no turning back. He would have to take his chances inside, but he feared what awaited him inside those white walls.

9

The GeneFirm neighborhood was only a couple hundred yards away from the hospital. James was feeling much better, so he wanted to walk home, much to Linda's discomfort.

"You should've let them drive us home."

"I'm fine, Linda. I'm feeling like a million bucks."

"You make me nervous."

For the moment, they had escaped the hot sunlight, thanks to the shadow of the glass pyramid behind them. James looked up at the hulking triangle; the sight of the pyramid brought back a flood of memories. It was hard to believe that he had spent almost his entire life living under the shadow of this thing.

"Do you remember how big the pyramid used to look when we were kids?"

"Aw, is your near-death experience making you a bit nostalgic?" She laughed, but caught herself. "I'm sorry. Probably too soon to joke about it, huh?"

James nodded, with a smile. "Too soon."

"Sorry, hon. But I know what you mean, it seemed like it went up for miles when we were younger."

James wrapped an arm around Linda.

"I remember in high school when we swore we would never come back to this place. Seventeen years was enough. Now look at us."

"Well, we really couldn't turn down Dr. Weisman's offer, could we? Paying off our student loans, cheap housing, and jobs at GeneFirm? Away from all the pollution and violence of the cities? I'd say we're blessed."

"My fresh craniotomy aside, I'd say yes, we are. There is no escaping this place, huh? Three generations of Logans have worked here. Same with your family."

Linda smiled. "This place is a lifeboat of civilization. The best and brightest living in peace here in the forest. Why would we ever want to leave?"

James kissed her cheek. "I agree, but that's a bit dramatic, don't you think? The world isn't that bad out there."

"Debatable."

Once they were across the field, they turned onto the first street they came to. It was normal-looking enough, and that was purely by design; it gave its residents the perception of suburban normality. But even the street signs had names that would make a molecular biologist blush, names like RNA Circle, Polymerase Run, and Gap Junction.

James and Linda grew up several streets down from where they currently lived. Sometimes James felt like he had just crash-landed in the past, always hesitant that he would turn a corner and come face-to-face with his childhood self.

They turned onto Helicase Lane, and their house came into view. Their two children, Augustus and Olivia, were on the front lawn playing Frisbee with an older woman dressed in flower-patterned pants, a tie-dye shirt, and a wide-brimmed floppy gardening hat.

James chuckled at the sight of her, "Wow. Look at Aunt Rose."

"Give her a break, she's just eccentric."

"Eccentric is a very nice word for someone who should be on medication."

Linda tried not to laugh.

The kids looked like two little clones of their mother. Augustus was nine years old, and Olivia was seven. Both had straight black hair and olive skin. It seemed their mother's Asian genes had completely crushed whatever genetic contribution James had to offer them. Wherever his genes were in his kids, they sure as hell weren't showing themselves on the surface.

If he really did have cancer, which he still refused to believe, would his children inherit his vulnerability? He knew that was impossible. His kids had the cancer-resistance genes, just like he did. He tried to push the irrational fear out of his mind, but he couldn't help but feel anxious.

The kids saw their parents coming down the sidewalk. Their forgotten Frisbee crashed harmlessly into the grass as the kids ran over, screaming in excitement.

"August and Olive, I missed you two so much," said James as he scooped up Olivia in his arms.

"James, be careful, don't overexert yourself!" Linda cried.

Both kids were now staring at James' bandages.

"What's wrong with your head, Daddy?" asked a concerned Olivia.

"My head is fine, Olive, I just got a very, very, bad haircut."

Linda wrinkled her nose. "Have you two been intentionally rolling around in the grass?" she said, changing the subject.

James stuck his nose in Olivia's hair and made a face. "Whew! You stink. I think it's time to run upstairs and get cleaned up."

Olivia giggled. "I don't stink. You stink."

James set her down, and the two kids took off sprinting toward the front door, jockeying for who would get the first shower.

Linda shook her head in amazement as her kids ran frantically into the house. Little Olivia screeched a high-pitch squeal the whole way.

Linda turned to the older woman. "Thank you so much for watching the kids, Aunt Rose."

Aunt Rose was James' aunt, also a researcher at GeneFirm.

"No problem, you two." Rose looked at James fearfully. "Is it true? They say it was cancer."

"News travels fast around here," said James.

Rose stepped forward and swept James up in a big hug, glancing nervously at Linda. The hug was becoming awkwardly long. Before she let go she leaned in close to James, whispering into his ear, "I knew this day would come. I hoped it wouldn't, but it did." Without James noticing, she slipped something small into his shirt pocket.

"Listen, Aunt Rose. It's not cancer, Dr. Paradee says . . ."

"Oh, Dr. Paradee!" she yelled. "Of course he knows everything!"

Linda stepped in to rescue James from Rose's madness.

"Anyways Rose, thank you for watching the kids on such short notice. We owe you. We appreciate it, we really do."

"It was my pleasure! I love your children. Sweetest kids on the block. Not the sweetest ones in the neighborhood, but on this block for sure. They have very good inner light, very pure," she said, lifting the brim of her hat and staring intently at Linda.

James couldn't help but roll his eyes.

"Well, thanks again, Rose. Have a great night." James tried to wrap up the conversation and lead his relative off the front lawn.

Rose wouldn't be sent away that easily. She turned back to Linda. "So I assume you've heard about the viral outbreak?"

"What outbreak?" James was now interested in hearing what the woman had to say.

"Another biological terror attack, they say. Homeland Health Care is already restricting flights and setting up quarantines. Hundreds of people are infected. I would suggest that you don't let your kids go to school anymore. It's no longer safe."

"Aunt Rose, please, I'm sure it's not that bad."

Rose leaned toward James and whispered, "Trust no one." Then she stepped back and said loudly, "Good day to you both. And let's hope the great magnet has mercy on our souls!"

With that, Rose slowly backed up, turned, and speed-walked down the street, suspiciously looking behind her with every other step.

Linda had a puzzled look on her face. "I'm a bit worried for her. That might be the last time we ask her to watch the kids, I think."

"Listen, babe, she's harmless. I think watching our kids is good for her, gets her out of her house. I mean, the woman lost her husband and her daughter, plus her son ran off. She must be insufferably lonely. That would make anyone go crazy."

Linda sighed as she watched Aunt Rose walk away.

10

Out of all the horrors Pat expected to find behind those glass doors, he was still grossly unprepared for what awaited him.

Inside the dome everything was white: the walls, the floors, the furniture, everything. Standing in the middle of the room was a man with shoulder-length blond hair. He wore spandex biking shorts and nothing else. Pat just looked on with disgust at the man's washboard abs and toned physique. As soon as the man spoke, Pat knew that it was the same frustratingly peaceful voice that had goaded them inside.

"Hello! I am Dr. Slate, the director of this health retreat. You just caught me in the middle of my workout."

You've got to be kidding me, thought Pat.

He wanted to see this man's medical license. This

wasn't a doctor; he was a walking and talking advertisement for men's cologne.

"You are all about to go through a wonderful metamorphosis."

As Slate said this, his eyes fixed on Modest. For a second or two, he seemed to temporarily forget what he was saying. Modest seemed incapable of turning her eyes away from the doctor. For a brief second, Pat felt a surge of jealousy roll through him at the sight of the pink-haired girl eating up Slates' ripped abs and sunbaked skin. He wondered if this was part of the treatment program: putting a girl in each group to gloat over the hot doctor in order to motivate the rest of the fatties to get fit. If it wasn't, it should be. He wanted Modest to look at him like that.

Slate continued, "I want you to remember this moment, this exact moment, when you all came to me as people who disrespected their wonderful gift. The gift I speak of is life, of course, and my goal, if nothing else, is to help you discover love and respect for that which you have taken for granted. When you leave here, food will taste richer, you will be filled with an unprecedented energy, and most of all, you will embrace your life, living every day to the fullest."

The only thought in Pat's head was, kill me now.

"Now I would like you all to give a warm welcome to the two wonderful people who are here to help you on your great journey. Mandy and Thomas, come on in!"

Pat had assumed wrongly that Dr. Slate was the most cruel and unusual thing he had ever been subjected to. When Mandy and Thomas appeared through a side door, he realized his mistake. He hoped it was just a night terror and that he would wake up in a cold sweat screaming, but he had no such luck.

"Hey ya'll! My name is Mandy and this is Thomas!"

Mandy was a petite blond girl, while Thomas was an equally blond but much less petite dude.

Thomas waved at them all with a smile plastered above his protuberant butt of a chin.

When Pat laid eyes on Mandy, he ground his teeth together in instant sexual frustration. She wore a pair of tiny white shorts that hung just an inch too high to successfully cover the smooth curves of her ass. Her blond locks and glowing blue eyes immediately diced Pat's heart up into a million little pieces. The miniscule white blouse she wore was about one button shy of decency, her cleavage threatening to make a jump for freedom at any moment. All in all, her uniform looked more like a slutty nurse costume than any kind of legitimate professional outfit.

Pat was overwhelmed with the cruelty of it all. He had already accepted the fact that a fat, pasty white guy like him would never be in the same league as this girl—scratch that, not even on the same continent. He would never get a shot at taking the world championship title that was Mandy. She was like the Super Bowl and he might as well have been the Chicago Bears in the midst of another losing season.

On the other hand, Pat could do with a little less of Thomas. A whole lot less, in fact. The guy was obviously a bodybuilder. His all-white outfit was somehow more revealing than his female counterpart's. The guy had on embarrassingly tight shorts that accentuated his man-package while simultaneously exposing most of his hairless thighs as well.

Pat unconsciously stole a glance over at Modest. She had stopped eyeing Slate and now she stared in Mandy's direction with a look of jaded disgust.

"I'm so glad to have you all here. We are going to have so much fun," Mandy said as she clapped her hands together.

She then lifted those perfectly manicured hands and pointed to a doorway behind her. "If the ladies would follow me, I will take you to the women's sleeping hall. All you guys can follow Thomas. Alright, let's go!"

Modest and the other female campers slowly followed Mandy. Pat stared intently at Mandy and Modest as they walked away through another set of sliding glass doors on the right. He wanted both women, even though they couldn't possibly be more different from each other. When they were gone from view, depression unexpectedly crept up and slapped him, or maybe it was just Thomas slamming an iron pan of a hand down onto Pat's back.

Thomas stepped up next to him. "Okay guys, you heard the lady. Let's go."

The group followed Thomas through the doors to their left, which opened up to a half-cylindrical white corridor.

"I guess I can start off by telling you all a little about our retreat," Thomas told the group brightly as he walked backward in front of them. "The original health retreat that was built here eighty years ago was completely destroyed by a particularly nasty warming storm. You may have noticed this building's interesting architecture. The dome structure is designed to withstand the severe warming storms that Texas has been suffering from, so nobody worry. If there are any storms, which there will undoubtedly be during your stay, you will be perfectly safe."

They entered another smaller dome; this one was filled with a host of workout equipment.

"This is one of our gyms. You will be spending a lot of time here, so I won't bore you with any details. But a quick overview: we have more than fifty machines in this room. As far as free weights go, we've got plenty, don't worry."

Pat looked around at all the torture devices and muttered, "I'm not worried about that, I promise you."

"What did you say?" Thomas shot back.

"Nothing."

The bodybuilder smiled at him. "That's what I thought. Anyway, we will have plenty of fun in this room."

Silence fell over the group as they walked on. The sight of the gym hit home with them; the ugly reality of the next six weeks now had a face.

From the back, Tony spoke up for the first time since his beating out in the parking lot.

"When are we going to eat? I didn't get breakfast this morning. I'm starving."

Thomas nodded his head in sympathy. "I understand that feeling. Breakfast is the most important meal of the day. Sadly, you missed breakfast, which is served at five a.m. So you all will have to wait for smoothie time at eight a.m."

"Smoothie time?"

"Yes, smoothie time. It happens to be my favorite meal of the day."

"You got to be kidding me." Tony choked on the words as he repeated, "Smoothie time?"

"We have a little motto here at the retreat. Here we work for what we eat. So we've got plenty to do before that next meal. You're going to have to do your best to cope with that hunger. Can you do that for me?"

Tony didn't reply. He was still trying to come to terms with "smoothie time."

At the end of the next corridor, they came to a clothes rack full of bleached white cotton. Pat's stomach turned when he realized what he was looking at. To confirm his suspicions, Thomas reached over and pulled a hanger off the rack.

"Each of you has been provided with a uniform that you will be required to wear for the remainder of your stay. They are all just like the one I'm wearing."

Shit, thought Pat. Hopefully not "just" like the one you're wearing.

"You will be responsible for keeping your clothes clean and orderly. You have two pairs. Just make sure to put your dirty pair in the hamper next to the rack so we can clean it for you."

Pat lowered his head, preparing himself for the embarrassment. He could already feel his cheeks getting red.

On cue, Thomas read the name tag on the first uniform: "Pat Henderson?"

The pile of white was thrust into his arms.

"Here ya go!"

"Gee, thanks . . ."

"Now, after you get your uniform, go through these doors and find the bed with your name on it. Get dressed and meet me back out here in a couple of minutes."

The sleeping hall had a misleading title. It was anything but a hall. The doorway opened up into another circular dome. White cots circled around the outer edge of the room. In the center of the room octagon-shaped beams of light lit up the floor in a spiraling pattern. The light source came from octagonal windows scooped out of the arching dome above.

Pat slowly walked around looking for his name on one of the plastic placards that sat on each cot. They were ordered alphabetically. He saw Tony's bed and began to pray that he wasn't sleeping next to the man whose snoring could wake the dead. But to his dismay his cot was just a few feet away from Tony's.

First Pat stripped off his jeans and squirmed his way into the white shorts that were indeed embarrassingly short, exposing his white lumpy legs. He let out a sigh; the image of how Thomas looked in his uniform shamed him. He took off his own shirt and did his best to squeeze into the tube sock of a muscle shirt he had been given.

Well, they had won, he thought, feeling incredibly self-conscious. His belly stretched out the shirt like it was maternity-wear. Meanwhile, the shirt was surprisingly loose on his arms and chest—the over-all look was not at all flattering. Luckily there was no mirror, but he imagined he looked like an up-right albino slug.

After everyone had put on their clothes, they all stomped out of the room looking like they had just licked a shit sandwich.

Thomas was waiting there to greet them. "So, here at the retreat we believe in the power of the saying, 'Out of sight, out of mind.' These uniforms are designed to uncover your insecurities and re-mind you daily of why you are here. I know the clothes feel much too small and tight right now, but I promise by the end of this retreat they will fit per-fectly. Now if you would all please follow me, I will take you to orientation."

The group followed Thomas back down the se-ries of white corridors. Pat felt like a stupid fool, but couldn't help but smile at how ridiculous they must have looked. One guy with the body of a Greek god leading several overweight men in white tights—like the nurse section of a gay pride parade, minus the rainbow flags and glitter.

Pat marched on, his smile fading as he wondered what humiliation awaited him next.

11

James and Linda had only been absent for a couple days, but their two children had taken the opportunity to mount a large scale offensive against the sensibilities of the house. The remnants of mud, grass, dog hair, fruit juice, and other mysterious stains snaked their way around the floor of the living room.

Linda's eyes went wide. "What happened here?"

"How did the kids manage to do all this?" James asked as he waved his hand at the disaster zone that used to be their living room. Shocked by the state of the floors, he yelled out, "Where the hell is the vacuum?"

Linda got behind James and rubbed his shoulders.

"Relax, James. But Aunt Rose is officially never watching the kids again. You have to wonder if she actually helped them make this mess. And who knows what kind of garbage and conspiracy theories she filled their heads with."

"Next time we'll find the kids smoking pot and wearing tinfoil hats to protect them from alien mind control. Honestly, we should have known better. This isn't half as bad as her house, though. She is one of those pathological hoarders. Dr. Weisman told me that after she dies he's having her house condemned."

"I don't doubt that," Linda added. She bent down and picked up one of Olivia's dolls. "I heard there's decades of junk in that house."

"My mom used to tell me that Aunt Rose rigged her house with booby traps after claiming people were breaking in and searching through her things. That's some clinical paranoia, alright. Who would want to steal any of that junk anyhow? Old bicycles, ancient papers, soaps, notes—all absolutely worthless. I won't be surprised when she ends up crushed beneath six hundred pounds of lab journals."

"James! That's absolutely terrible," cried Linda, after stifling a laugh. "I found the vacuum. Looks like Clementine got ahold of it."

The vacuum was a small cylindrical robot that whirled around the house seemingly motivated by its own free will. It swept, mopped, removed stains, you name it. At the end of a long day's work, the little robot would go and charge itself at its docking station. To James, it was the most useful member of the household, and he loved it like a child.

Linda found the robot flat on its back, its shiny

covering scratched and gnawed at every angle by a pair of sharp teeth. If it weren't for the presence of their dog, James would guess that someone had thrown his beloved robot through a wood chipper.

"Damn that Clementine!"

The jingle of a collar rang out down the hall, followed by the emergence of a neon orange Labrador. It ran right past James and straight into the loving embrace of Linda.

"Oh, that's a good girl. Did you miss mommy?" Linda hugged the dog and scratched behind its ears.

"Good to see you, too, Clementine." James glared. "Don't pet the stupid dog! She should be punished for what she did to my vacuum."

He went to the corner of the room and flipped the little robot over. It gave a little chirp, as if to thank him, and whizzed off toward a clump of muddy grass on the carpet. A ratty strip of plastic coating dragged behind it like a sad tail. The little vacuum had a large task in front of it. Clementine barked and sprinted after the roving cylinder.

"No, Clementine! Leave it alone!"

"Stop crying over the stupid robot."

"Whatever, I think this dog got the pain-in-the-ass gene inserted into her, too. I want a refund from GloPets; they really messed this creature up when they put those sea coral genes into her. I swear, I don't care if she glows in the dark, she's not right in the head."

Linda chuckled. "James, you're just sore because she likes to poop on your side of the bed."

"Yeah, no kidding! That's real messed up, by the way. Next time we get a GloCat!" James exclaimed, pointing a threatening finger at Clementine. "All this stress can't be good for someone who just had brain surgery. I'm going to go take a shower before dinner and, so help me, if that damned dog pooped on my side of the bed again, I'm going to make myself a glow-in-the-dark fur coat."

Linda was still laughing in the kitchen as he strode away. When he got to the bedroom, he breathed a sigh of relief that the bed was unsoiled. Of course, this only meant that somewhere else in the house Clementine's excrement awaited him. He would go on that particularly shitty scavenger hunt later.

In the bathroom, he finally got a good look at himself. He was a wreck. Between the dark rings under his eyes and the black stubble of his unshaven face, he looked like he had spent much longer than a couple days in the hospital. He found the end of the bandage on his head and slowly unwound it. The entire left side of his head had been shaved. Right down the middle was the dark scabbed-over line of the incision. With the bandage he looked bad, without the bandage he looked like an escaped psych patient. He stripped down and climbed into the shower.

One of the greatest things about this smart house was the fact that the shower temperature was always perfect. He didn't know exactly how it worked, nor did he care. Maybe the house monitored the body temperature of each individual via a sensor that would then regulate the water temperature. James' shower temperature was not Linda's, this much he knew. If he wanted the shower colder or hotter all he had to do was just say so and the shower would do his bidding. It was great. Most of the house worked on voice recognition—from the lights, to the toilets, and even the oven. You had to be careful with the oven, though, in the event the house misinterpreted the statement, "Linda, you look smoking hot," because then you just ended up with a blackened dinner.

"James . . ."

He wiped the water from his eyes and looked up. Linda was standing on the other side of the glass shower door, completely naked. She had always been a very sneaky nude, ambushing him more times than he could count, not that he ever complained.

She opened up the shower door and stepped in.

"Should you be taking a shower right after surgery like this? Isn't that bad for the incision?"

"I'm not getting it wet."

"I can see that it's getting wet, James. Here, use my shower cap."

"I really don't want to."

"Use it," she said sternly.

James reached out and grabbed the plastic cap. "As you wish, my lovely despot." He stretched it carefully over his head, doing his best not to touch the incision.

It had been a long stressful day for the both of them. Now that they were back in the comfort of their own home, his worries began to fade. Standing inches away from the near-perfect female form of his wife, with the warm water trickling down around him, life's volume suddenly turned down while his libido awoke from its opioid-induced slumber. Linda undid her ponytail and shook her shiny black mane down around her, the hair just long enough to cover her nipples. Her dark eyes blazed from behind the dark strands of her hair. He pulled her in close to him. Hot streams of water beaded down between them and pooled in the crevice formed by their touching chests.

"I love you so much," James whispered between kisses to her slender neck.

He lifted her by the thighs and pressed her against the cold shower wall.

"James, take it easy!"

"I am. But you're just so hot, I can't help my . . ."

"Ow! Too hot!"

On his command the shower had turned the heat up, scalding both of them, sending James hopping sideways and taking Linda with him to avoid the uncomfortably hot water.

"Damn it shower, not you! Colder! Colder! Too cold! Just right."

Linda couldn't stop laughing. "When are you ever going to learn?"

"I hate technology. Now where were we?"

He pressed against her again. For the moment, their combined warmth was the extent of their world. Cancer, work, the kids, terrorists, all those stressors that clung to them like mud on a carpet were washed away under the whisper of the showerhead.

12

Pat stared up at a stage with a large projection screen above it. Around him there were rows upon rows of stationary bikes arranged in a half circle. Most of the bikes were already in use; cellulite jiggled and sweat was aplenty as people Pat had never seen before pedaled away. There were probably over fifty people on the bikes. His group must have been the last batch of new arrivals.

Thomas led them to a row of unused bikes.

"You all can get started spinning. The orientation will start shortly."

Pat exchanged looks with Tony. His facial expression summed up what both men were thinking.

"Are you shitting me?" Pat said as he climbed onto the nearest bike.

Tony shrugged. "Don't worry, bud. It's just a little exercise. It will be good for us."

"Easy for the pro athlete to say."

Pat started to pedal slowly, just enough to look like he was doing something. A minute later Thomas appeared on stage next to a couple of stationary bikes that faced out toward the crowd. He attached a little microphone to his collar and hopped on the bike.

"Hi, everybody. As some of you have probably noticed, there is a watch in the right cup holder of each bike. Please take this out and put it on your right wrist."

Sure enough, Pat found the watch, but the screen didn't say anything about time. Instead it read 0 CAL.

Thomas continued, "Now the watch you just put on is actually a calorie counter. It has a computer chip in it, much like the identity chip in your wrist, that will help us monitor how many calories you're burning during your workouts. How we work things here is simple. You have a meal with four hundred calories coming up, but in order to receive that meal you must burn at least six hundred calories. If, by the end of this session, you haven't reached that goal, you will have to wait for the next meal. Does everyone understand? Okay, now everybody follow my lead."

Tony turned to Pat and said fearfully, "Dude, we don't eat unless we burn six hundred calories? What kind of torture is this?"

With that, Tony's pace cranked up; he had a desperate look to him. Pat didn't really care if he ate or not; he wasn't really hungry. Back home he usually only ate once or twice a day. No big deal, he would just half-ass it here on the bike—so what if he missed out on the food? All the pedaling was beginning to make him nauseous, so he slowed down, praying they wouldn't have to do this for too long.

After a half hour, Tony looked over. "You've only burnt a hundred and fifty calories. Are you crazy? They're not going to feed you!"

"Like I care, man. I'm not even hungry."

"You're nuts! I bet you are gonna be wishing you had worked harder."

"Not likely."

Another half hour passed with silence between the two men. No one in the room was talking, except for Thomas barking out commands like, "harder," "faster," and "crank it." Everyone was too busy gasping for air to say anything but an occasional curse word or two. The room had gained a gamey smell from the buckets of sweat and body heat produced during the previous hour. The dome was sweltering like a sauna.

Despite his piss-poor effort, Pat was still exhausted. At least he now knew that an "orientation" at the health retreat referred to a sixty-minute bike ride. A bad sign. What would an actual workout consist of if the orientation kicked his ass? He hadn't done this much physical activity in years; every muscle in his body screamed at him in defiance.

At the end of the ride, Pat's watch said that he had burned 500 calories. No lunch for him. Tony's watch showed 830 calories, and he looked like it, too. The man was drenched head to toe with sweat.

He sat on his bike with his arms over his head gasping for air.

On stage, Thomas climbed off his bike. "Great work everyone! You all tried very hard. Now don't lose that watch. Make sure to keep it on at all times or you won't be able to get any meals."

With his food hanging in the balance, Tony clasped one hand around his watch as if to make sure it was still there.

Pat was destroyed. He tenderly climbed off the bike, wincing in pain. "My ass hurts."

Once everyone had dismounted, Thomas led them back to the sleeping hall to take showers. Like magic, a new rack of uniforms had appeared in front of the door. All their white uniforms were soaked through and sticking to their backs, giving them a flesh-colored appearance. Opposite the clothes rack, the common showers consisted of nothing more than four metal pipes sprouting out of the tile floor. The top of each pipe had a crown of showerheads designed so that five people could huddle around each one.

It was like his middle-school football locker room all over again. Pat tried to keep his eyes focused upward while he showered inches away from four other obese men who could barely fit around the shower without bumping into each other. After his brief freezing cold shower, he had seen enough fat rolls and hairy man-boobs to last him a lifetime.

After everyone had showered, Thomas led them to the cafeteria, where they lined up in front of a counter. Retreat employees were busy working blenders, shredding their prisoners' next meal.

So this was "smoothie time," thought Pat to himself.

Tony managed to force his way to the front of the line and eagerly awaited his food, even if it was just liquefied fruits and vegetables. Thomas and Mandy stood at the front with scanners.

"Now we're going to scan everybody's watch to make sure you've burnt the required calories to eat. Once we scan your calorie counter, it will reset so you can start burning calories for your next meal. If you weren't able to burn enough calories, don't worry, the next meal is in three hours."

Thomas waved the scanner over Tony's outstretched hand. He looked down at it and said, "Eight hundred and thirty calories! Great work, Tony, grab a smoothie and relax."

Tony moved quickly to the counter, where he was handed a cup. The eager look on his face disappeared when he looked into the cup and saw the frothy green liquid.

"What the hell is this? This isn't a smoothie."

Mandy laughed. "Sure it is, silly. We call it bug juice. It has carrots, wheat grass, broccoli, apple juice, and twenty grams of soy protein."

"Ugh," Tony groaned. "Oh well, down the hatch."

The big man slammed the contents of the cup in one swallow; his upper lip was covered with green froth. "That was disgusting."

Mandy ignored him and said, "Next!"

Another person stepped up to be scanned. This continued until it was Pat's turn; by the time he got to the front of the line his stomach was burning with hunger. He had made a big mistake and forgotten that physical activity had a way of making you hungry. Suddenly he was starving.

When she waved the scanner over his watch, it beeped harshly.

"I'm sorry, Pat, it says you did not burn enough calories during your workout. I'm sorry, but you're going to have to wait until the next meal. Hang in there."

He just looked blankly at Mandy in all of her hot girl magnificence.

"Just make sure you burn the correct number of calories next time."

Pat sat down alone at one of the tables and started to feel real sorry for himself.

Thomas addressed the group. "After you all finish, we're going to collect some data and run a series of tests on each of you to assess your current fitness level, body fat percentage, flexibility, and finally, your aerobic fitness. Once we establish where you are at physically, we can make realistic goals specific for each of you."

Pat shook his head. They were treating them like being overweight was a damn disability.

The tests took forever—blood pressure, max heart rate, max VMO, sit and reach flexibility testing, cholesterol, triglycerides, cardiovascular fitness, body fat percentage. It was a complete gauntlet that left Pat even more tired and hungry than when he started. He had been poked and prodded to the verge of a mental meltdown.

After the tests were finished, Mandy cheerfully gave him the results.

"According to national standards, you are in the

'poor' category of physical fitness. In six weeks time, we hope you will be up to the 'fair' level, which would put you around the fortieth percentile of men your age."

Pat didn't care what his percentile was. When he died of starvation he would be in the zero percentile, if they weren't careful.

Pat could feel himself losing weight already and it sucked.

13

"You wanted to see us, Director?" asked Mac, as he and Marnoy entered the office.

The diminutive bald man behind the desk didn't look away from his computer screen. He just nod ded and waved his hands at the two empty chairs across from him. Director Zelinski was the head of the Homeland Health Care division in Texas, a title he used with impunity to be a humongous dick.

The two agents sat down across from the director and patiently waited. Eventually, after a long si lence, Director Zelinski broke his iron gaze from his computer and locked in on the two agents instead.

"Was the airport following quarantine proce dure?"

"Yes, sir. They are currently meeting our standards. So far they have detained several hundred people. I think about half of those have already been transported to various hospitals," replied Mac.

The director rubbed his temples slowly like he was trying to ward off a headache. "I'm afraid by this time tomorrow everything will be one gigantic clusterfuck out there, and there is very little we can do about it. This thing is spreading fast. We're talking about hundreds of deaths already; it will be in the thousands tomorrow. Unbelievable. I don't know how they did it, no idea at all, but it seems those bastards have finally succeeded."

Mac and Marnoy exchanged an uneasy glance. They hadn't heard this dire prognosis yet.

"So you really think this is bioterrorism? Couldn't it just be a severe flu outbreak?" Mac questioned.

"In June? A flu outbreak in June! Really?"

Mac looked down at the floor, feeling stupid.

"The flu just doesn't break out one day in fifty major cities across the United States, Europe, and half of Asia in the middle of the summer. It isn't just babies and old people who are dying either, this thing is killing healthy young people. We're confident this is a terrorist attack, but H.H. doesn't want to induce mass hysteria. I imagine the media will do that for us. They will inevitably catch on when the death toll can no longer be covered up."

Mac whistled. "So what's the plan?"

The director laughed. "Damage control. We've declared a level-red emergency. From this point on all nonessential flights and traffic will be halted. Quarantine will be the key to stopping the spread of this until we can get ahold of a vaccine."

"Is the flu vaccine protective at all?"

"What do you think, numb nuts? No dice. No resistance to the bug has been seen so far in those who have had their flu shot. But that's not why I wanted to see you two. This new pandemic isn't the only odd thing going on out there."

Macdonald cocked one of his bushy eyebrows. "It isn't?"

"There is not a whole lot you monkeys can do about this 'supervirus.' The quarantines are up and a vaccine will hopefully be in production shortly. GeneFirm has assured us that they will have one in under a week."

Upon hearing the word "GeneFirm," Marnoy visibly bristled.

"The reason I called you two is another matter entirely. Long story short, the department received a strange letter today." The director handed a piece of paper over to the agents. Marnoy read it out loud.

"James Logan is not alone. Find Pat Henderson."

Marnoy turned the paper over. The back was blank. "That's it?"

"Certainly cryptic. What the hell does it mean?" asked Mac, scratching his chin.

"Do those names ring a bell?"

"James Logan . . ." Marnoy clicked his tongue. "I heard about this guy on the news last night. He's the GeneFirm scientist who just developed that new inheritable form of the cancer-proof genes."

The director stared at Marnoy. "Pretty exciting breakthrough, eh?"

The agent grimaced at the director's words. Marnoy busied himself with rubbing a scuff mark on one of his leather shoes. "Yes, sir," he said.

"Well it's revolutionary. This thing is going to eliminate cancer completely. Now appreciate this little coincidence: Dr. Logan collapsed from a seizure while announcing this medical marvel. He was transferred to Austin Regional Hospital, where they removed a hemorrhaging mass from his brain. Biopsy confirmed real genuine cancer."

"I had heard the rumors on the news," Marnoy said coolly. "Was he a free-birth?"

"No, no, not at all. According to his DNA sequence on file he has the cancer-proof genes just like the rest of us . . . well ninety-nine percent of us anyway. But that's when things get interesting. The hospital ran another sequencing on him just to confirm the presence of the genes, and guess what they found?"

"He didn't have them," Marnoy said without any trace of emotion.

"Bingo."

"So what happened to the genes? Could his DNA have mutated?" asked Mac with a befuddled expression.

"Of course his DNA mutated! That's how he got cancer in the first place, you moron. I thought you had to have some grasp on basic science to get a job here. If the cancer-proof genes were present in the first place, those mutations that caused his cancer couldn't have happened, could they?"

"So you think the original sequencing report was an error?"

"Very, very unlikely . . . but possible. Something we must consider is that the results were forged. It would not be the first time this has happened. Free conceivers have tried to do so before, to avoid prosecution.

"Let us return to the mysterious letter. Does the name Pat Henderson strike a bell with you two?"

The agents looked confused until Marnoy snapped his fingers. "We just sent that cow to a health retreat."

"You did indeed. I did a little research and found that Pat Henderson was engineered by the same lab as Dr. Logan. The GeneFirm conception engineering lab, to be exact."

"That is certainly an odd coincidence." Marnoy frowned.

"Frankly, I'm not ready to break down the door at GeneFirm, but I want to follow these leads. I want Pat Henderson's DNA. Then find Dr. Logan; I want another DNA sample to rule out the possibility that his hospital results were a mistake. Tomorrow morning, head west, my boys. Make sure to leave early; it's warming-storm season and there's some nasty weather in the forecast. Get caught in one of those and you won't have to worry about any supervirus because they'll be picking what's left of you out of the trees."

14

After the shower, James slipped on some shorts and went to check on the kids. By the sound of the shouts floating in from the living room, they were restless and hungry. James yelled back at his wife, "I'll start dinner."

Linda was going to take at least twenty more minutes to finish her post-shower rituals: layers of lotions to be added, hair dried, and tweezers wielded.

In the living room, he once again found the vacuum on its back, its little wheels spinning in vain. Damn that transgenic dog. He kicked the robot back over; it gave another chirp and whirled off toward kitchen. The dog's orange head peeked out from behind the couch and stared intently at the vacuum speeding away.

"Don't even think about it," warned James.

Augustus and Olivia were playing a video game that consisted of a lot of flailing limbs. It looked like they were playing tennis at the moment.

In the kitchen, James pulled out chicken breasts, wheat pasta, and some fresh vegetables. It was a meal straight out of the H.H. handbook. Just as he finished making dinner, suspiciously on cue, Linda appeared. She was wearing James' old GeneFirm softball shirt from years back, almost long enough be a dress. He put down the last plate and grabbed her as she passed by, giving her a hug; the smell of flowery soap was still fresh on her skin.

She turned around to him and said, "It smells delicious. Thank you for making dinner."

"Not a problem, dear. Kids! Take a break and come eat some dinner, will ya?"

Augustus and Olivia came running into the kitchen giggling, still energized by their tennis match.

Judging by how surprisingly easy it was to get them away from their game, the kids must have been starving.

"Daddy, your haircut is awful! They cut your head!" Olivia squealed.

James had forgotten to bandage his incision. Both of his children stared wide-eyed at the line of black crusty blood and suture that traversed its way down the side of his scalp.

"Don't worry, Olive, just got nicked by the razor," he lied. "Daddy will be okay."

Next to him, Linda was shaking her head. She mouthed silently, "Nicked by a razor?"

He shrugged his shoulders and mouthed back to

her, "Sorry." Trying to take the attention off his head wound, he turned and shouted, "TV on!"

The drone of a news anchor filled the room; the kids groaned in rebuttal.

"Do you really have to watch the news right now?" Linda asked.

"Just for a little bit," he said. "It's good to teach the kids to be interested in world events."

At the bottom of the screen, bold words exclaimed: ECO-TERRORIST GROUP DENIES RESPONSIBILITY FOR THE RELEASE OF VIRUS. PANDEMIC SPREADS.

"Don't watch this in front of the kids please. They don't need to hear about this," pleaded Linda.

"Just wait a minute, this is serious stuff. We need to know what's happening."

"We do, but your young children do not."

"Okay, okay, just let me watch five minutes more. Kids, plug your ears."

Augustus and Olivia clamped their hands over their ears.

The newsman reported soberly, "It's unclear how many deaths this new flu strain has caused, but the preliminary numbers are shocking. New York, Los Angeles, Phoenix, Dallas, Houston, and several other major cities have reported an increasing number of cases. Right now government officials are denying that this virus is the result of bioterrorism. Homeland Health Care is asking all citizens who come down with flulike symptoms to stay at home and drink plenty of fluids. This virus is incredibly infective. They warn that by coming to the hospital you are putting yourself and others at risk. Similar outbreaks are occurring throughout Europe and Asia as well. Experts say that in order for the virus to spread this fast, it must have been released in several major—"

Linda couldn't take it anymore. "TV off!"

James rolled his eyes. "You can put your hands down now, kiddos."

The children lowered their hands and continued eating, ignoring their bickering parents. Linda ate quietly, avoiding eye contact with her husband. The only sounds coming from the table were the clinking of forks and knives.

The silence of dinner was broken by the ring of Linda's phone on the kitchen counter. She got up from her chair and picked it up, looking surprised.

"Who is it?"

"Dr. Weisman."

"Why's he calling this late?"

Linda put in her earpiece and answered the call. "Hi, Dr. Weisman. Yes, James is doing much better. Thanks for asking. Really? So we're starting now? Alright, I understand. No, that's fine. I understand."

She looked annoyed as she put down her phone. "My lab is in charge of making a vaccine for the viral outbreak."

James stopped eating and put down his fork.

He stood up and hugged her. "Please be safe down there."

"We're assigned to the level four labs. Negative-pressure rooms, space suits, the whole shebang. I'll be fine."

"Just be careful," he said—almost at a whisper—as he squeezed her tightly. "Why don't you go get dressed? I can drive you up there."

Linda nodded.

James told Augustus and Olivia to wash the dishes and then brush their teeth. "By the time I get back home, I want you two in bed, is that understood?"

In the bedroom, Linda was getting dressed in their large walk-in closet. "James, are you going to be okay with the kids?"

"Of course, babe. No sweat. Just like running a goat rodeo. What could go wrong?"

"I hate to leave you right now." Linda emerged from the closet dressed in scrubs. "Are you ready?"

"Sure, let me just put on a shirt."

James went into the closet to find something to wear. On the ground was his shirt from earlier. He picked it up, and something small and black fell out of the pocket. "What the hell?" He reached down and picked it up. It was a data storage device. It didn't look like any of the ones he owned. "Where'd you come from, little fella?"

It was a short distance, but James drove slowly, holding his wife's hand, trying to lengthen the moment for as long as possible. In a minute or two, he and Linda were idling at the foot of the pyramid. "Kick some viral ass, my dear," he said, kissing her good-bye.

She replied with a big smile as she stepped out of the car.

"Attagirl."

She blew him a kiss before disappearing through the glass doors of the building.

About to pull away, James remembered the mysterious data device in his pocket.

He sat there staring up at the looming outline of the pyramid, black against the night sky. He put the car in park, got out, and walked through the glass doors; the building was eerily quiet at night, and the glass walls of the hallway reflected his silhouette all around him. It was spooky, like being followed by a horde of shadowy figures. He rode the elevator up to his lab and entered his office. James slipped the data device from his pocket and plugged it into the computer. There were only two documents stored on it. He clicked on the first one and it immediately popped onto the screen. It took him a minute to realize what he was looking at. It was a DNA sequencing study. The name at the top of the study caught his eye. This DNA sequence belonged to Molly Henderson. James instantly knew the device had come from Aunt Rose. She must have slipped this into his pocket that afternoon. Molly was her deceased daughter; she had committed suicide years ago. The girl had been suffering from depression for most of her life, but no one realized to what extent. Her death had shocked the GeneFirm community. James now scrolled quickly through the report; he knew exactly what he was looking for, and to his disbelief it wasn't there. A wave of heat flowed over him as he realized the significance. His hand trembled as he opened the second document. It was another study, this one belonging to Pat Henderson. Aunt Rose's only son had left GeneFirm around the time of his sister's death. His heart was pounding as he searched the report. The cancer-resistant genes weren't there either.

"No," James said quietly, his stomach leaping

into his throat. Jumping up from his desk, he rushed back into the lab and turned on the lights. He approached a small silver box about the size of a computer printer. Next to it was a small disposable pen that he pressed to his index finger. When he pushed the button on one end, a small needle jumped out, pricking his finger. Blood instantly blossomed from the tiny puncture. Next he held up a tiny plastic square, transferring a dot of blood onto it. He set the bloody square onto a tray that slid out from the machine.

Adrenaline surged through him as the tray slid back into the machine and a timer appeared on the display reading thirty minutes. Now he just had to wait.

15

Pat was confident that he was going to starve to death. Due to a fit he had thrown during the last exercise of the night, he had once again missed the number of calories that he needed to "burn" so that he could eat. Thus the fitness freaks had sent him to bed with a burning stomach and aching muscles. The amount of physical discomfort he was in, combined with Tony's discordant chainsaw of a snore, resulted in a long and tormenting night.

At 4:30 A.M. the sleeping hall was plunged into chaos when a high-pitched fire alarm went off. Pat bounced out of bed, half expecting the cowboys to be back, ready to manhandle him again. The ringing of the alarm was deafening; he plugged his fingers into his ears. When the noise subsided, he realized that it wasn't the fire alarm, it was just a high-powered alarm clock. Pat's hands were still shaking with adrenaline as Thomas trotted into the room, looking perky as usual.

"Good morning! So we're going to go on a short two-mile run before breakfast. Meet me outside in two minutes."

Thomas turned and jogged out of the room.

You win, thought Pat, after he found himself actually eager to work out; or, more specifically, eager to work out and then get something to eat. The health retreat had broken his will.

Thomas led them on a "slow" jog around the perimeter of the building, following a well-worn path through the forest. The long line of men and women crashed through the early dawn with Thomas at the front barking orders and a cheery Mandy at the rear of the group making sure no one stopped or got left behind. Pat was in the back of the pack with Mandy nipping at his heels. She wasn't really jogging anymore; Pat was so slow, she was basically jumping up and down in place giving him words of encouragement.

"You got it, Pat!"

"You're the man!"

"Lookin' good!"

She was filled with an enthusiasm and energy that Pat felt no human being should demonstrate this early in the morning. Thirty painful minutes later, he finished the run and was allowed to get cleaned up. After a shower, he found himself back in the cafeteria waiting for the moment of truth. This time they congratulated him on reaching his caloric goal and allowed him to proceed and get his food. His excitement diminished when he saw the plate of white shiny snot that was waiting for him.

"Blah, what is this?" Pat asked, staring with disgust at his plate.

Mandy popped up next to him, her breasts shoved into his face.

"Those are egg whites!" Her eyes filled with assurance. "I eat them every morning."

"Mandy, at this point I am so hungry that I will have to eat these boogers. Thanks for trying to make me feel better. If this is for breakfast, I'll be looking forward to the bull testicles for lunch. I hear they are also high in protein."

She laughed at this. Making sexy Mandy laugh made Pat feel a little better. He left the counter and found a spot next to Tony at one of the long cafeteria tables. Tony had already inhaled his meal and was now sadly staring at his plate, where there used to be food moments before. Despite the blandness of the meal, Pat eagerly spooned the quivering egg whites into his mouth. It wasn't much food and it only took a minute to finish it all. Afterward, he joined Tony in mourning over their empty plates.

"My stomach is so angry at me," said Tony.

Pat nodded in agreement. With no food left, he was feeling the kick of another kind of hunger. His eyes wandered over to Modest. She was sitting alone a couple tables over. He had considered taking the seat next to the dainty, pink-haired outcast, but his nerves got the best of him.

Modest sat with her head down and shoulders

slumped. Her spindly hands wielded a fork that only managed to push food around her plate. Apparently she had already had her fill of the meager meal.

After the thirty-minute breakfast and recovery time limit expired, they were rounded up and led down the corridor by Mandy. She took them to a room that reminded Pat of a dance studio. The walls were lined with mirrors so, as the group entered the room, their appearance was unavoidable.

Once everyone was inside, their Barbie doll captor clapped her hands together, her voice laced with cheerleader pep. "Okay! Is everyone ready for core ball training?"

The only response she got was a groan from Tony in the back of the room. After the small breakfast, Tony had been complaining nonstop that he was still starving and could do no further exercise without proper nutritional support.

Mandy grabbed one of many inflatable rubber balls off a shelf against the wall. She bounced it a couple times. The sound of the reverberating plastic hitting the ground made several people in the front row visibly flinch, like she was brandishing a whip or something equally painful.

"So, core strength is one of the most essential strengths we can build in the body. Everything, from biking, running, swimming, and even golf is really driven by your core. If you have weak core muscles, everything suffers and you will be more prone to injury."

Tony interrupted. "Weak core muscles? Weak core muscles? Look at this, darling, nothing but solid steel." An unashamed Tony pried his shirt over his massive belly and jiggled it like a bathtub full of gelatin.

To retort, Mandy quickly stripped off her white shirt. Underneath she was wearing a bright pink sports bra. Her sunbaked cleavage spilled out, demanding everyone's attention. Mandy had a six-pack etched out of the bronzed skin beneath her bountiful breasts. Pat couldn't help but stare. He wondered if anyone else was having conflicting feelings of inadequacy and arousal.

"Now Tony, these are core muscles!" she said. She brushed her hands down her stomach.

Tony whimpered.

She laughed and continued, "This is what all of you should shoot for. Abs just take dedication, people. Now let's have a great workout."

Mandy slipped a microphone onto her sports bra strap. Her voice boomed loudly: "Everyone grab a ball and line up. Make sure you have two arm widths of space between you and the next person."

Everyone sullenly hobbled over to the shelf that held the stability balls. One by one, they picked a ball and hugged it to their chests as they returned to the open space in front of Mandy.

"Start Mandy's Core Strength Workout Mix!" The speakers in the walls instantly started blaring a synthesized electronic beat. The repetitious pounding of the bass made Pat's ball quiver in his arms.

Oh great, Pat thought, more fucking techno.

"Okay, three sets of twenty crunches! Ready?" Mandy yelled over the music as she sat down on the ball. The question wasn't really a question because she began counting off the crunches before anyone had time to reply.

Pat grunted in agony as he leaned back and tried to lift himself. He was too weak; he just lay there splayed out over his ball unable to bring himself back up. How pathetic, he thought.

He looked around to see if anyone else was in the same dilemma. Directly to his left was Modest. She was also lying stretched over her ball, staring at the ceiling, making no attempt whatsoever to follow Mandy's lead. Her shirt had slipped up and her bleached white stomach was exposed. The view caused a surge of lust in Pat. He stared at the small mounds of Modest's breasts; she wasn't wearing a bra, her nipples clearly visible through the white cotton. Modest turned her head, catching Pat's searching eyes. A little smile crossed her lips and she blew him a kiss.

Pat whipped his head away. His gaze landed on the ceiling, lined with mirrors. Modest had probably watched him stare at her the whole time. He could feel his face flush red in embarrassment.

Stupid, stupid, stupid, he thought. Way to be a real creeper.

Getting caught ogling Modest filled him with a surge of adrenaline. He began to strain every muscle in his body; then it started to happen, like a submarine rising from the icy depths, he felt himself lifting up. His abs cramped underneath the strain of his upper body.

"One," he counted, completely out of breath.

Mandy counted off her fifteenth.

16

James woke up with a splitting headache. Rolling to his side, he noticed the sheets and pillows on Linda's side of the bed were undisturbed.

The previous night, he had waited in his office for the DNA sequencer to finish. When he sat down at his computer and read the results, James realized that everything was true. He was not cancer proof. Dizzy with disbelief, he had read the results over and over; he couldn't explain it, but he, Molly, and Pat were all missing the same set of lifesaving genes.

In the bathroom, he scooped out a couple of pills and gulped them down. His reflection was pretty frightening; his half-shaven head had a new white bandage slapped on the side of it. He got dressed in the closet, slipping on a pair of gym shorts and a t-shirt. Silently, making sure not to wake the kids, he made his way to the front door and slid out into the dawn.

The sun was beginning to edge itself over the horizon, its colors spilling across the sky. James marched down the sidewalk, headed directly for Aunt Rose's house. When he reached her street, he was disappointed to see that the windows of her house were all pitch black. Probably still sleeping, he thought; but this was serious, so he didn't mind if he had to wake her up. He rang the doorbell twice; the chime reverberated on the other side of the door. Then he waited, but no one came. He rang the doorbell twice more. After a few minutes, he sighed and stamped around to a large window on the front of the house. When he peered in, all he could see were stacks upon stacks of junk. He circled the house. Each window he came to was just another angle into the hoarder's soul; however, Aunt Rose was nowhere to be seen.

Cursing under his breath, James read the time on his watch; he had to get the kids up. With Linda at work, he would be stuck with the difficult task of getting both children ready for school. Waking them up, feeding them, and making sure they got out the front door before 8:00 A.M. would be as arduous as herding cats, and James was no cat wrangler.

Two hours later, to James' great relief, he had successfully sent his children on their way to school. Hoping to catch Aunt Rose in her lab, James got ready to head to work. Freshly shaven and dressed sharply in a business shirt and slacks, James felt like a new man. According to Dr. Paradee, he wasn't supposed to go back to work today, so he was hoping to slip in and slip out without anyone noticing him. Plus, he had one more experiment to run. Anxiously, he fingered an envelope in his pocket. He just hoped the results would be in his favor.

"I can't believe they are making us drive our asses all the way out here," Mac said, almost growling.

"At least we're out of the city. Less deadly viruses out here," replied Marnoy.

The sun was peaking above the horizon as the two agents drove west. It was already ninety degrees; the morning was steamy and the cloud cover thick. Marnoy eyed the sky suspiciously. "We should have left way earlier than this."

"Yeah, yeah, I know. I had to drive my kids to school; the wife wasn't feeling too well."

Marnoy raised an eyebrow. "Sick?"

"No, not any flu symptoms, thank goodness. She just woke up with fluids coming out both ends, if you catch my drift. Probably food poisoning. We had some killer potato salad last night."

"Morning sickness maybe?"

"Oh hell no! Two kids are enough. And to further refute your accusation, since it has obviously made me anxious, this wasn't any old morning sickness vomit; it was projectile 'everyone get the hell out of the way' kind of vomit. She'll be alright, though."

The road west was green and winding. The heavy odor of grass and pollen spilled in through the windows, reminding Marnoy of childhood and summer—memories that usually remained dormant. As they got farther away from the city, civilization was slowly consumed by sloping hills and vegetation. As a boy, Marnoy's father used to take him out on the lake nearby. It would be just the two of them sitting in their small boat, fishing until the morning sun became too brutal to withstand. Marnoy couldn't remember the last time he had gone fishing. A pity and a shame, he thought.

The demands of his job kept any notions of a woodland escape a distant thought. He enjoyed the idea of buying a fishing pole, getting a boat, and living a quiet life out here.

Eventually, they reached their first destination. Marnoy steered the car down the gravel road of the Lake Travis Health Retreat; the white domes appeared like giant golf balls that had been inadvertently hit into the rough of the tree line. The car slid to a stop and the two climbed out. A strong breeze brought along the smell of rain. Marnoy frowned and looked at Mac. "We've got to make this quick. It looks like this storm is getting closer than we would like."

Mac nodded in mute agreement.

James looked up at the shiny tip of the pyramid towering above him. Each side of the pyramid consisted of a triangular wall of glass, allowing the building to be permeated by natural light. The only place in the building where the sun could not reach was underground in the high-security areas, where Linda would be working right now. She was beneath the earth in the tomb of the level-four labs, the playground of some of the deadliest viruses and bacteria known to man. Linda would be stuffed into her yellow space suit, cut off from the world, breathing dry air delivered from a respirator hose that snaked down from the ceiling.

James put his thumb on a pad next to the doors and waited for them to slide apart. A rush of cool air swirled by him; he stood there enjoying the welcome temperature difference of the building's air conditioning.

A burly security guard named Ed greeted him. James waved as he passed by.

"Good morning."

James made his way to the expansive commons area, which served as a cafeteria, meeting hall, and occasional holiday party place. The commons took up a good portion of the east side of the pyramid; therefore, one side of the room consisted of a giant slanting wall of glass. The view was gorgeous, second only to Dr. Weisman's private office on the top floor. Opposite was the kitchen and buffet where employees could get breakfast, lunch, and dinner six days a week. At one end of the commons was a stage and podium where presentations were held.

James looked out over the emerald expanse. In the distance above the foothills, dark clouds rolled above the treetops. The commons slowly grew dark as the clouds crept in front of the sun.

"What in the hell are you doin' here?"

James jumped in surprise. He turned around and shook his head. "Dr. Paradee. You scared me for a second there."

The old man was bent over, leaning heavily on his cane. "I'm sorry, Samantha. I thought you looked like this man named James, who I specifically told not to come to work this week!"

James tried to think, not wanting to give away any information about his recent discovery.

"I bet you came up here for a free lunch, didn't you, ya cheapskate?"

"Yep. You got me." James replied in relief. He had forgotten about the Tuesday conference. Every week, the commons hosted a company-wide presentation on the state of the business and new research.

"Well, you might be stuck here for a little longer than the conference with this storm on its way."

James shook his head. "I didn't know. Someone wouldn't let me watch the news last night."

"So how's your head?"

"It's been better. The pain is well controlled, though."

Dr. Paradee squinted off in the direction of the assembling storm. "Weather's supposed to get real bad over the next couple days."

The two stood there in silence and watched the darkness grow.

17

Slate was at his desk, reviewing the morning's medical evaluations. He carefully read over each chart to make sure that none of the new arrivals would go into cardiac arrest on him.

Pounding at his office door shattered the peace of his office.

The door opened and he could hear soft footsteps approaching his desk.

Slate kept facing his computer, but his mind was on the intruder approaching his desk. "Modest, how can I help you?"

Modest stood silent.

Slate turned in his chair to face the pink-haired woman. "Now, you really had me worried with all that banging on my door. I thought you might be the fitness director here to give me shit again for my two-hour Bikram Yoga class. A couple women pass out from heat exhaustion and all of a sudden I'm a bad guy."

"You prick!"

"You're always so melodramatic."

"You are such an unbelievable prick!"

Slate mocked a look of pain. "Now those words are hurtful."

Modest started to pull off her white top. Underneath she was bare. Her pale breasts bounced as she worked the shirt over her head. Both armpits were covered with a light coat of bright pink fuzz. When she got the shirt off she let it drop onto the ground.

"What the hell are you doing?"

Without a reply, Modest wiggled out of her shorts, too, letting them fall to the ground. She wasn't wearing underwear either. She shivered and took a step toward him.

"You know you really should wear underwear with these outfits. You could get some really nasty chafing down there," said Slate as he stared at her exposed body. "I've seen it before."

"I'm sure you have you jackass."

"Ouch. Now that's no way to treat an old friend. How long has it been, a year? It feels like forever."

"A year and a half!" Modest answered. "Did you finally get bored with that new wife of yours? You've got a lot of nerve dragging me back here! You're lucky I don't report you."

Slate gave her a dumb grin and rapped his knuckles on his desk. "Again with the hurtful speech. You're still drinking, aren't you? Not taking your meds either, I suspect. I sincerely didn't want to bring you back here. Your parole doctor practically begged me. I'm worried about you."

Modest snorted, letting out a sarcastic, "Please . . ."

It was true that Slate had brought Modest back. Lately he'd been bored—and Modest, despite her many faults, had a way of keeping things interesting. On the other hand, he could only take so much of her, because she was an absolute whack job. His first memory of the chemically unstable girl was when she showed up to an afternoon workout stark naked, just as she was now. It took two fitness trainers to remove her from the room. Slate would have helped but found the sight of two husky male trainers struggling to subdue the stripped girl too entertaining. They carried her writhing, clawing, and kicking, out of the room with much difficulty.

So yes, he had personally signed the order to bring her back to the retreat for an unprecedented fourth time. The government usually limited individuals to two visits because afterward the cost benefit plummeted drastically. Slate had no idealistic notions that Modest would ever change. He liked her just the way she was.

Slate let his gaze drift down to her ghostly breasts, which hung on her chest like two fleshy moons. He could feel his arteries already routing blood flow to his necessary parts. Slate was a sucker for easy sex.

She came around the corner of Slate's desk, heading straight at him. Her breasts were now inches from his face.

"Let me go home," she said with a fierce look.

"Absolutely not. Your aggressive appeals will do you no good this time."

Modest's hand snaked around the back of his head.

"Whatever you're trying, it's not going to—" Slate stopped midsentence and grunted in pain as Modest yanked a handful of his hair, slamming his open mouth onto the hard button of her nipple.

When he managed to pull away, he looked down and saw the coarse fur of her pubic hair. Modest sat down on his lap, pressing painfully hard against him with her thighs. He briefly stared into the black chasms that were her pupils.

"Get me out of here." Modest thrust her hips into him again. Whatever willpower he had left crumbled; he grabbed the soft flesh of her butt and slammed her down roughly against the desk. She fought at the zipper of his pants, but he swiped her hands away and did it himself. His reptilian brain was craving sex like one of his famished patients did food.

Then a man cleared his throat behind them.

Slate's heart jumped as he was greeted by the smirking face of Mandy and two stunned-looking men in business suits.

Without hesitation, Slate tossed Modest off his desk. She crashed hard onto the floor. "Get the hell out of here, or I swear you'll never leave this place," he hissed.

Modest picked herself off the floor and smiled at the figures in the doorway. She leisurely strolled over to her pile of clothes. Slate could do nothing but fume as she sauntered out the door.

"If it isn't my favorite H.H. agents. How can I help you?"

The agents exchanged a set of amused glances. Mandy just looked irritated.

"Thank you, Mandy. Now please make sure that Modest gets back to her group. I would hate for her to miss any exercises."

Mandy rolled her eyes slightly and mumbled, "Looked like she was already getting her own personal exercise."

"Mandy, go!"

It wasn't the first time Mandy had caught Slate in the act. The man had no shame. But she wasn't one to judge; she'd been bent over Slate's desk more than her fair share of times, too.

"Whatever," she said, disappearing through the door.

"I'm sorry for the trouble, guys. This visit has nothing to do with the flu pandemic does it? We haven't had anyone get sick out here, but if we do they will be quarantined immediately."

"We are here on unrelated business, Slate. We need to collect a DNA sample from one of your patients."

Dr. Slate frowned. "Why would you need to do that?"

Neither agent volunteered any further explanation.

"I see. The old H.H. is up to something mischievous, eh? What's the name? I'll take you to the patient."

18

Noon came and the GeneFirm commons began to churn with people. The cafeteria staff brought out dozens of long tables and loaded them with trays of food. The sky outside had become pitch black; swirling oil-colored clouds had all but snuffed out the sun's light.

Abruptly the room broke out in beeping, buzzing, and ringing. The noisy racket was followed by a brief moment of silence as people checked their phones. James did so as well. It was an emergency text message:

SEVERE WEATHER ADVISORY: TORNADO & THUNDERSTORMS IMMINENT. SEEK COVER IMMEDIATELY.

Just as James finished reading the message, a high-pitched alarm went off in the room. When the alarm ended a calm female voice came over the intercom. "The storm shield has been activated. For your own safety, please stay away from all exits."

A loud grumbling noise followed. Then the storm-shield appeared, a set of retractable steel walls that protected GeneFirm's research facilities from the increasingly violent warming storms and tornados that plagued the area. Every time bad weather threatened, the walls were there, turning the building into an impenetrable metal spike in the landscape.

Dr. Paradee and James turned away from the rising wall. The mounting fortress left nothing else to look at but ugly metal and their own reflections in the glass.

Lunch consisted of grilled trout and a scoop each of black beans and broccoli. By the time James got his food, the reinforced wall had finished its long ascent. He parted ways with Dr. Paradee and went in search of Aunt Rose. His gaze swept over the commons, but he couldn't find the fireball of unkempt red hair that belonged to his aunt.

"James! Over here."

James saw his lab assistant waving at him. Navine was sitting in the first row of tables near the stage, nestled right in between all the corporate bigwigs. James groaned. He just wanted to find Aunt Rose and get out of there. Not wanting to be rude, James took a seat next to his assistant. Navine was a short man of Indian descent and quite possibly one of the hairiest people James had ever met.

"Hey, Navine." James tried to cover up his disappointment with the seating choice.

Navine's eyes wandered over the bandage on James skull. "So is it true?"

"Is what true?"

Around the table, other employees were listening intently. Navine noticed that he had grabbed the table's attention, so he leaned in close and said, "They say that you had a brain tumor removed back in Austin."

"Dr. Paradee doesn't think it's cancer."

Navine nodded in agreement. "Yes. That's what I've been saying this whole time. It's impossible in someone with cancer-proof genes."

James paused for a moment, wondering if he should tell Navine more. The urge to get his revelation off his chest was too strong. "But . . ."

Navine's eyes narrowed. "But what?"

"They told me my last DNA sequencing showed that the cancer-proof genes were intact, but last night I went to the lab and did a study of my own."

"And?"

The room suddenly hushed. James and Navine looked up and a woman was climbing the stairs to the stage. She was Savira Olagundoye. By the age of thirty she had become the youngest vice president in GeneFirm history. As she crossed over to the podium, you could almost hear every man in the room hold his breath. Her dense black hair fell to the midpoint of her back. She was dressed in a skintight blue Asian-looking dress with a floral pattern down one side. The dress was somewhat revealing, showing off the curves of her breasts and long mocha-colored legs. James had only talked with Savira a handful of times, but it was enough for him to know that he was completely intimidated by her.

Once at the podium, she took a hard look at her audience. "Good afternoon to you all." When she smiled, her mouth was full of perfectly straight teeth; to James it looked like a smile only a mother shark could love.

"As most of you have undoubtedly heard, Dr. Campbell's lecture on toxicology has been postponed because Dr. Weisman would like to address the company over a very important matter. So without further ado, please welcome your CEO."

Dr. Weisman, the legitimate clone of one of the most famous doctors in the history of medicine, was a legend in his own right. When people looked at him, it was like they were looking at 200 years of unbroken medical genius. Indeed, James found it hard to separate Dr. Weisman from the man who developed the cure for cancer so long ago. Dr. Weisman didn't speak at these lunches very often anymore. He was an ancient man, who at the age of 103 was a testament to the staying power of science and wealth. Despite being over a century old, he stood tall on a muscular frame with a full head of wavy brown hair. How Dr. Weisman managed to look so young was a billion-dollar question. It was a well-known fact that the clone had been searching for the scientific fountain of youth his whole life. By the looks of it, he had found something.

Dr. Weisman cleared his throat. "What I am about to say may shock you, it may even scare you, but it is the reality of the situation. It is believed that a terrorist organization has unleashed a biological weapon, a flu virus that has escalated to a worldwide pandemic. This nation will be in a very grave situation if a vaccine is not created soon. The most recent reports claim this flu virus has been confirmed in every state as well as every major country. For over one hundred years GeneFirm has been protecting humanity. Inside these walls we have eliminated cancer, diabetes, AIDS, and that's just the beginning. We have conquered biology for the betterment of man, and once again we are called upon to help." He paused for a moment as the audience gave him a brief round of applause.

"Currently one of our top molecular biologist teams, headed by Linda Logan, is busy developing a vaccine—"

A growl of thunder rumbled through the commons. Dr. Weisman paused to let it pass.

"We must rally behind them and give them whatever help they need, because billions of lives depend on it."

James hadn't put much thought into Linda's task, but now the gravity of what Dr. Weisman was saying hit him. This vaccine could be the icing on the cake of Linda's career.

"We must take the proper precautions to keep this facility safe. So from this point forward we are shutting down the complex to the outside world. No one will be allowed in or out of GeneFirm. All nonessential personnel will be sent home after the storm has passed and will not have to report to work until further notified. If the virus makes it inside our walls there will be no end to the damage it causes." He paused and scanned the stunned audience. "Remember to support your coworkers and let us hope they succeed and succeed quickly. Thank you."

With that, Dr. Weisman briskly walked down the stairs and was met by Savira. The two of them swiftly disappeared down the corridor that led to the executive offices.

◎

"The director is going to have an aneurysm," said Marnoy.

Mac nodded his head. "This will be bad for his blood pressure, for certain."

"Stuck out here in the middle of nowhere with all hell breaking loose outside."

"Slate said we can use the staff room to sleep if the storm lasts through the night. Then we can stop by GeneFirm in the morning on our way back to town."

The agents were sitting in the lobby of the retreat watching the storm unfold outside the glass doors. It had been going on for hours. Despite the offers of Slate and his staff to join them in the storm shelter underground, the men elected to stay above, hoping the storm would end quickly so they could go about their business.

Marnoy nodded to the glass doors. "Well it's not going to die down anytime soon."

The winds were so strong that the rain was flying parallel to the ground. The dome above them creaked.

"So what do you make of Pat?"

"About the fact that he's a cousin of James? That's a pretty interesting coincidence."

Unexpectedly there came a large crash outside.

"That sounded bad," Marnoy said, jumping up and running over to the door. He pressed up against the glass and looked out.

"Shit!"

"What is it?"

"I told you we should've moved the car!"

A six-foot-long tree branch was lodged right in the middle of their car's windshield.

"Oops."

"Hopefully that aneurysm will kill the director before he has the chance to fire us."

19

When Dr. Weisman exited the commons, the room erupted with conversation, mostly dwelling on the complex-wide quarantine, a drastic act unprecedented in GeneFirm's history.

Navine's voice brought his attention back to his table. "You must be excited for Linda. When she produces this vaccine she'll be famous."

But James wasn't paying attention. "Can you do something for me?"

Navine frowned. "Of course, James, anything."

Out of his pocket, James produced a white envelope. "Inside are two separately labeled samples. Can you run them through the DNA sequencer for me? I'll be up to check on it later. Right now I have to find someone."

Confused, Navine nodded, reluctantly accepting

the envelope. He left James' side and disappeared into the dwindling crowd.

James hoped he would find his aunt in her lab upstairs. He headed toward the elevators, but another lab worker bombarded him. He repeated the same old spiel: "No, Dr. Paradee doesn't think it's cancer."

He made it another ten yards before he was stopped for a second time. Annoyed, he repeated his story yet again and then quickly dashed away. He made sure to keep his eyes on the ground, taking detours around anyone who got too close. James breathed a sigh of relief when the elevator doors slid shut and a sea of disappointed faces vanished behind the sealed doors. As he began to ascend, James felt a slight throbbing in his temples that was threatening to transform into a skull-splitting headache. He dug into his pocket for the pain pills and swallowed a couple of them dry. On the sixth floor, he exited the elevator and headed to Aunt Rose's lab. Once inside, he was greeted by a sleepy-eyed woman at a computer.

"Hello, James," she said, perking up at the sight of him. Her eyes drifted toward his incision. "What brings you here?"

"Have you seen my aunt?"

The woman frowned. "No. She didn't come in today, I'm afraid. Is everything okay?"

It was James' turn to frown. "Yes, of course. I just needed to talk with her. If you see her please tell her to call me."

"Of course."

James cursed his luck, wondering where the hell

his eccentric aunt had run off to. He got back in the elevator and pressed the button marked B4. Not everyone had access to the high-security labs—just necessary personnel. He pressed his thumb on the black pad above the elevator buttons to verify his security clearance.

The elevator jolted to a stop four stories underground. When the doors parted, a narrow hallway stretched out before him; the glass walls were gone, replaced by sandpaper-rough cement. These gray walls were as thick as a bomb shelter's. He found a door marked OBSERVATION DECK #1. Once again, he pressed his fattest digit against a touch pad and the heavy locks inside the door clicked, allowing him to go inside. The observation deck consisted of a dim room with a long bench and black chairs facing a one-way mirror. On the other side of this mirror was a whitewashed lab where several yellow space suits were busily going about their work. When the door shut behind him, the room was blanketed in an eerie shroud of silence.

Through the window the lab staff looked more like astronauts on a space station than molecular biologists in a sterile laboratory. The only way for the lab workers to enter the high-security lab was through a dressing room where they had to strip down naked, throw on a pair of sterile scrubs, and then put on one of those yellow space suits. Rubber booties then had to be slipped on over the feet of the suit to protect against rubbing holes in the bottom. Finally, two layers of gloves were sealed off with tape to prevent any leaks. When the biohazard suit was properly fitted, they could enter into an air lock where they would be doused in a two minute-long decontaminating shower. All of these precautions kept them relatively safe, but accidents still happened. One tiny microtear in the suit was all it took for a virus to enter.

James would much rather work in his business casual clothes upstairs than down here. He avoided it like the plague, no pun intended. Linda, on the other hand, loved it—exactly why, he couldn't ever figure out.

She was pretty easy to pick out among the group of space suits. Despite the bulky mass of yellow covering her, she stood out tall and slender at a lab bench holding a pipette. Her hand guided the instrument back and forth between a small vial and a plate of wells, filling each one with who knows what. James could barely make out the side profile of her face through the plastic of her mask.

Sitting there in the darkness watching his wife, he remembered a company holiday party long ago. James and Linda were still in their teens and had just begun dating. They managed to escape their parents, taking refuge in a supply closet. Blind in the dark, they clumsily fumbled against each other. One of his hungry hands managed to slide up her blouse, squeezing the plump breast it found there, rolling the firm pill of her nipple between his fingers. He felt her pull down his pants and in minutes his vision was exploding with bright stars against the darkness of the closet, bringing the moment to an abrupt glorious end. That first sloppy hand job in the closet had marked the beginning of almost a decade of increasingly refined orgasms. The two were hopelessly in love with each other.

Then he thought of the night—they were both recent graduates and newly employed at GeneFirm— when James snuck into her lab, scaring her to death.

"Damnit, James! Don't sneak up on me like that."

"My bad, babe," James said with a grin spread across his face. "I just got some bizarre results. Come tell me what you think."

Linda was annoyed; it was late and she wanted to finish her work as soon as possible. It was their seven-year anniversary and for the first time it seemed he had forgotten. Annoyed was probably too weak of a word, but the man was blissfully unaware of his current doghouse status. The last thing she wanted was to walk all the way down to the UV room to look at another one of James' botched DNA amplifications.

"Ugh. Again? Why don't you just take a picture and bring it to me?"

"Nope. No way. You have to see this in person," he pleaded.

"Listen. I'm tired and grumpy. It can wait."

Standing behind her, he massaged her neck. She instantly loosened up and leaned her head back. "That feels great, James, but no thank you. I'll take a look at it tomorrow."

"Absolutely not. You need to see it now."

"You're such a baby. Just make it quick." She dragged herself off her lab bench and followed James all the way to the chemical room where they could observe the DNA gel electrophoresis results on the

UV light box. During the walk she made it a point to cross her arms and shoot James contemptuous looks.

The UV emitter was a crude box, the top of which was a black screen where UV light was projected upward. The square-shaped gel containing DNA was placed on this screen. A clear plastic lid was closed over it, shielding the user from damaging UV rays, a throwback to the days when scientists actually had to worry about developing cancer.

The DNA electrophoresis gel was a seaweed-based gelatin substance used to separate DNA based on its size and charge. The DNA was visible because it was bound to a photo-emitter called ethyl bromide, which happened to give off color under UV light.

She took one look at the square of gel sitting on the black UV screen and exhaled in frustration.

"Well, turn it on and look." His heart rate jumped and his guts flipped in anticipation. Linda reached over and hit the switch at the side of the UV box. A soft blue glow filled the room. The colorless gel before them jumped to life. Brilliant bands of light appeared, carefully arranged to form the words WILL YOU MARRY ME?

It had taken James months to find the right combination of enzymes that would cut segments of his own personal DNA into the high-tech proposal. It only took one look at Linda's face to confirm that the effort was worth it. Her face was half bathed in the blue glow of the light, the other half lost in shadows. She was beyond stunned. After a few seconds her eyes began to tear. The fluorescent orange letters cut into the gel were as strikingly beautiful as they were strangely alien.

"James . . ."

Hindered by the long lab coat, he awkwardly lowered himself onto one knee.

"Will you marry me?"

Linda's tears were picking up speed, plummeting off the sharp cliffs of her cheekbones and down the sides of her face. "Yes, of course, this is so beautiful, James," she cried, her eyes still locked onto the gel. "F.Y.I., you are the biggest nerd I've ever known. I can't believe you just proposed to me using DNA."

"Not just any DNA, my DNA."

"I love you," said Linda, almost speechless over James' creation.

◎

"Dr. Logan?" The bass of a deep male voice snapped James back to the present. He turned around on his chair to see Ed standing at the door.

"I'm sorry, but Dr. Weisman just informed me that level B4 is now closed off to all nonessential personnel. You know, just in case there is a breach or something. Hopefully, you can find a vacant couch somewhere upstairs. The storm isn't predicted to calm down until morning."

"I see. I guess I'll get out of here then."

As James got up to leave, he scanned the lab hoping to catch another glimpse of Linda. To his disappointment the lab was empty.

20

Most of the front windshield of the government car—or what used to be the front windshield—was now scattered over the car's floorboards and seats, transformed into a layer of shiny pearls of broken glass.

The storm came to a quiet end early that morning. Marnoy and Mac stepped out into the soggy dawn to assess the damage. The pieces of glass that were still left in the frame of the windshield hung like jagged teeth. Marnoy climbed into the driver's seat and proceeded to kick out the rest of the windshield. When they pulled out of the health retreat's parking lot they left behind a pile of tinted glass and a large tree branch lying in the gravel.

They headed toward GeneFirm, hoping to get the DNA sample from Dr. Logan before returning back to Austin. Without a windshield, the ride was cool. The smell of grass and rain whipped through the car as they sped up and down the serpentine roads. The asphalt was covered with the limp branches of trees that had been dismembered in the storm. Marnoy weaved back and forth to avoid the bigger chunks of debris.

Soon the entrance to GeneFirm loomed ahead. In front of a white brick guardhouse, a massive fountain separated the incoming and outgoing traffic lanes. In the middle of the fountain a twelve-foot-tall silver DNA strand wound its way up from the water. Marnoy pulled into the entrance, coming to a stop next to the doors of the guardhouse. After a moment, the glass door slid back and a man emerged in a guard uniform. The man was thin and his clothes hung off his body as loose as trash bags. His name tag simply read ABE.

"Looks like ya'll had a little accident," said the security guard with a smirk as he eyed the remnants of their windshield.

Marnoy sighed. "We're with the Department of Homeland Health Care and we need to meet with Dr. James Logan for a minute or two."

Abe scratched his head, squinting his eyes into the light of the rising sun. "Well, I'd like to help ya'll out but GeneFirm is unfortunately under a quarantine at the moment."

Agent Marnoy stared blankly into Abe's eyes. "Quarantine? Why is that?"

"The vaccine, I guess. I just know I'm not allowed to let anyone in."

"We have a warrant, so quarantine or not, you're

letting us in. You don't want to interfere with a government investigation. I suggest you call your boss and make this happen."

The guard clicked his tongue as he weighed the situation in his mind, finding himself stuck between the law and his paycheck. "Hold on for a sec." Abe disappeared back inside the guardhouse.

"We must be cursed, Marnoy." Mac leaned back and sighed.

After a minute, Abe reappeared. "I'm sorry but the answer is still no. According to my boss, due to the fact we are currently under a government contract to develop a vaccine, we have the legal right to take all necessary measures to ensure its success. It would be better for you boys to come back in a few days after this quarantine mess is over."

Marnoy's temper flared. "You have to be kidding me!" He turned to Mac. "Can they do that?"

Mac shrugged his shoulders.

"Now ya'll be safe driving back to Austin."

"Wait—"

But Abe had already ducked back into the building. The door slid shut.

"Damnit to hell!" Marnoy slammed the steering wheel with his fist. He grabbed the door handle, and was about to climb out and kick in the guard's door if he had to. Mac intervened before Marnoy could get out.

"Listen, he's right. They're under government contract and we shouldn't interfere. Think about it. We could get in serious shit for jeopardizing the vaccine. The trip wasn't a complete loss. We got Pat's sample, so the director can at least check his DNA. When we get back I can check out the laws and make sure that Abe over there didn't just feed us a load of horseshit. If he did, we can come back here tomorrow and force our way in."

Marnoy revved the engine and rocketed backward toward the street, leaving a black streak of tire marks on the pavement. The rest of the drive back to Austin they sat in silence, lost in their own thoughts. Later the car took a sharp curve, bringing Austin into view. The tall peaks of its buildings stretched out over the horizon. More storm clouds were already gathering, hanging like smoke above the city, as if panic had set the town ablaze.

21

James' neck ached like hell.

"That's the last time I sleep in my desk chair," he mumbled under his breath as he stood up and stretched.

From the windows in his office he could see that the storm-shields were down. Outside the sky was blue and dotted with clouds.

James walked out of his office to find Navine busy at the lab bench.

"Navine, did you even sleep last night?"

"A little. I couldn't sleep very well. Anyway, I decided that if I was going to be stuck in here all night, I might as well get my work done early."

"Good for you. What time did the storm-shields go down?"

"Around four a.m.—I'm not exactly sure."

"Did you finish sequencing those samples I gave you?"

Navine set down the plastic tubing he was working with and pulled off his latex gloves.

"Oh yeah, boss. They should be uploaded to the system already." He scooped up an envelope from the lab bench. "I didn't use all of the samples you gave me, if you'd like them back."

James took the envelope and thanked him.

"So what is this all about?"

"I'll explain after I see the results."

James turned away, headed for his office. Nervously, he opened up the sequencing program: two new results. He took a deep breath. As he read the contents his stomach began to turn. The second round of sequencing held the same grim news; now he was certain it was true.

James leaned back and felt the smooth paper of the envelope in his hands. When he opened it up, his mind raced as he stared at the two short bundles of shiny black hair, each held together by a rubber band, hair that had been carefully trimmed from his children's heads the previous day.

Thomas led Pat and his band of merry chubbies into the domed auditorium after breakfast, where they found Slate once again hammering away on his spin bike. Like usual, the doctor was shirtless. Slate looked up at the sound of the entering group and smiled. "Ah, Thomas and the gang, welcome!"

Slate hopped off the bike, the pedals still turning furiously as he walked toward them. He used a white towel to wipe the sweat from his face and chest. With one hand he motioned them toward the stationary bikes.

"Please, everyone take a seat and keep a nice easy pace while I talk with you." The doctor jumped back on stage, mounted his bike, and clipped on a small microphone. "First I would like to apologize for your interrupted workouts yesterday. The severity of the storm forced us to move you to the underground shelter for your safety. We are currently working on making a gym down there so this doesn't happen in the future. Now let's get back to business. Over the last few days we've been observing you at night to determine if any of you suffer from a sleeping disorder. Most overweight people do. Even a mild sleeping disorder can lead to severe long-term medical complications.

"There has been a lot of research on sleeping disorders and their effects. You see, in an overweight person, the buildup of soft tissue in the neck and chest area results in blocked airflow. This blockage of air may or may not wake the person, but it does cause a neurological arousal that interrupts the deeper stages of sleep that are essential for many of the body's normal functions."

Blah, blah, blah, Pat thought. He couldn't move his feet anymore, so he just sat there, motionless and defeated, on his bike. Slate was still spinning his pedals without any sign of exhaustion.

"There are several stages of sleep, including stages one through four and REM. During the deep stages of sleep, consisting of stages three and four and REM, sleep's restorative properties kick in, releasing essential hormones and chemicals. These stages are necessary to give a person that feeling of a great night's sleep. Is everyone following what I'm saying? I know I'm getting a little technical."

The only reply Slate got was the deep huffing and puffing of his audience, who were desperately trying to keep up.

"Screw this. I can't take it," Pat said to no one in particular.

Right on cue, Thomas appeared besides him. "In order to eat dinner you must burn seven hundred calories in the next hour. You've got to keep going! I believe in you, Pat!"

"I hate this shit!"

Despite his whining, Pat started to move his feet again. Hunger drove him on.

"In someone afflicted with sleep apnea, these sleep stages are interrupted over and over again, resulting in low blood oxygen levels and negative side effects on growth patterns, immunity, and the body's ability to heal itself. It's just another perfect example of how obesity leads to an accumulation of ailments."

Please stop, thought Pat, wanting to cry in frustration.

Slate hopped off the bike and walked over to a cart covered with a white sheet.

"Symptoms of sleep apnea include daytime drowsiness, irritability, inability to focus, and decreased sex drive. Over the years here, we have found that our campers have greater success when they are treated for their sleep disorders. By restoring a good night's sleep, you will have increased energy, better immune systems, and bodies that will recover faster from your workouts. So without further ado"—Slate paused to rip off the sheet, exposing what looked like a little white shoebox—"I would like to introduce everyone to your new best friend, the Continuous Positive Airway Pressure machine, also known as a CPAP. Around here we call it 'Pappy.' Basically, this wonderful device delivers a continuous flow of pressurized air through this mask, which will be worn at night. Pappy will make sure that you receive more than enough oxygen while you sleep."

Slate picked up the plastic mask and held it up toward his captive audience. He pressed a button on the side of the machine and the mask began to hiss. The noise stopped when he pushed the button again.

"This little device will give you the best sleep you have ever had. By the time you return to your beds tonight, everyone that has been diagnosed with an obstructive sleeping disorder will find one of these babies next to your bed. Its use is mandatory."

With that, Slate clasped his hands together, closed his eyes, and rolled his head in a small circle, stretching his neck. After a full circle of his head, he opened his eyes slowly and looked around the room. Silence crept over everyone as they waited to hear what his next words would be.

"Now, who feels like a run?"

22

What James had discovered about his children's DNA kicked and screamed at the back of his mind. Aunt Rose was still nowhere to be found; the answers that she held in this mystery still evaded him. Whatever was going on, he didn't know why or who was responsible. Why were he, his cousins, and his children all missing the cancer-resistant genes? The genes. He cursed himself for not thinking of this before. What kind of luck is that, he thought, that he and his wife had literally just developed a virus that could cure him and his children.

It was almost four o'clock, so the kids were about to be released from school. He imagined they would be relieved to come home after spending more than twenty-four hours locked up inside there, a kid's worst nightmare.

The school had undergone extensive remodeling since he was a kid, and was now pretentiously dubbed GeneFirm Academy. The number of students these days had to be more than a thousand; most of them were the second or third generation to attend the school. As James could testify, the company worked very hard to recruit its employees' children to come back and work there. It was Dr. Weisman's belief that GeneFirm was a close-knit family business, an odd goal for a sprawling multibillion-dollar biotech company.

James reached the school just as the bell rang the day's end. The doors opened and a sea of little sneakers and backpacks poured out. Olivia was easy to pick out with her shiny black hair pulled into two tiny and slightly uneven pigtails. She was wearing her favorite neon pink-and-purple outfit.

Olivia caught sight of him and bounded over to give his leg a vicelike hug. "Hello, Daddy! I missed you. I was so scared."

"Was the storm that bad?"

She nodded. "I cried. I wanted to go home."

"I missed you last night, too. How was your day?"

Olivia's face brightened. "We played dodgeball in P.E.; I got hit right here," she said, pointing to the bridge of her nose, which was still slightly red and puffy. "It's okay though, I didn't cry."

"Oh my! I'm glad you're okay. You should be more careful with that pretty little nose of yours." James pushed her nose flat with his finger. "It would be a shame if it got squished."

Olivia giggled and pushed his finger away. With the other hand she gingerly felt her swollen nose.

"So what did you learn today?"

Olivia raised one eyebrow and wrinkled her forehead. This was her "thinking hard" face. James knew it well because it was the exact same face Linda made when she was deep in thought. His daughter was so similar to her mother, it was excessively adorable.

"Oh! Mrs. Dickinson taught us about global warming!" Olivia said.

"She did? So what is that?"

"Um . . ." She scratched her ear. "It's what happens when humans pollute! It makes the earth hotter. It melts all the ice, causing cities to sink."

"Is that it?"

"No, it also makes really bad weather happen. Like the storm last night."

"Right again. So how do we stop it?"

Olivia leaned back proudly because she knew the answer to this one: "We can't! It's too late."

It was ten minutes past four and Augustus was still nowhere to be seen. James slipped his phone out of his pocket and, sure enough, a new text message and a voice mail awaited him. The text confirmed his suspicions that Augustus was safely stowed away in after-school detention.

Olivia was still straining her eyes into the afternoon sunlight, trying to pick out her brother from the thinning crowd.

"Your brother is in detention, Olivia. You don't have to look for him anymore."

"Uh oh," she gasped, putting her hand over her mouth. "He's in trouble."

"Like usual." James picked her up and swung her onto his shoulders. She squealed the entire way up.

"Well, let's go find your troublemaker of a brother, shall we?"

As they walked toward the school he listened to the voice mail: "Dr. Logan, Augustus will be in after-school detention today until five p.m. I would like to meet with you and your wife in my office as soon as possible so we can discuss your son's behavior. Thank you."

James laughed with a mixture of frustration and amusement.

Principal Coker was infamous for her frequent and bizarre citations. Parents traded a seemingly endless list of offenses that warranted detentions in the warped mind of the principal. This included everything from "not having a nutritionally balanced lunch" to "not making eye contact while speaking."

He ducked as he entered the school so that Olivia, who was still perched on his shoulders, wouldn't smack her head. The school was in great shape, no surprise considering Dr. Weisman's hard-on for philanthropy. He made sure that the school always had more than enough money to go around. The hallways were lined with glossy oak lockers that looked like they had just been installed. They were definitely an improvement over the rusty blue metal ones James remembered from decades ago. Overall, the school was incredibly successful, with some of the highest test scores in the country. Now, whether this was due to its progressive teaching practices, bottomless funding, or merely the fact that all the children were the progeny of doctors and researchers was up for debate; most likely, it was a combination of all three. The academy itself was usually all the convincing most employees needed to move onto company property and join the neighborhood.

After a few minutes of walking through hallways covered with frescos of finger paint and macaroni art, they finally reached the administration offices. A sleepy-looking secretary looked up from her desk and gave an exhausted smile. James recognized her as Allison, the wife of a scientist that worked in the lab with him.

"Hi, Allison."

The secretary looked a little shocked when she saw him. "James! What happened to you? Are you alright?"

He didn't want to explain the whole ordeal again, so he lied. "Just a minor surgery. Nothing serious."

Her eyes stared with disbelief at his not-so-freshly shaven head, where thick stubble had already begun to sprout.

"I'm sorry to hear that. It looks like you're doing great, though. And I'm sure all that hair will grow back soon."

"Thanks, Allison. I think it's a good look. I might keep it. No? So do I dare ask what my son did this time?"

"Surprise, surprise right? We usually don't see you in here. Where's Linda?"

"Working late," which was sort of true, James thought.

"Ah, I see. Principal Coker has been waiting for

you." Allison rolled her eyes, conveying exactly how she felt about the principal's endless stream of parent conferences.

"Oh, she has? I hope I haven't kept her waiting too long. Should I head back now or is she busy?"

"I'm sure she is very busy, but due to the severity of your son's misdemeanor, I suggest you go back immediately," she said with a wink.

"Hey, Olivia, sweetie. Do you mind staying here with Allison while I go and talk to the principal? This could get ugly."

Olivia shrugged and said, "Alright."

James popped her off his shoulders and sat her on a chair across from Allison's desk. "You don't mind, do you?"

"Not at all."

23

A short walk down the hall brought James to a familiar doorway. The edgy voice of Principal Coker beckoned him inside. "Come in."

James stepped into the office and glanced around. Countless awards and certificates crowded the walls; each rectangular frame was geometrically arranged to an anal perfection as if aligned with the precision of a laser.

Principal Coker was a short wisp of a woman who kept her hair constrained in a knot at the back of her head, each hair as tightly wound as she was. Her thin body could not have weighed more than a hundred pounds. A skinny storklike neck protruded from underneath the black collar of her blouse. Behind her boxy black glasses, her pupils darted around like eager flies. James didn't think she was a beautiful woman, but she wasn't exactly unattractive either. She definitely had a certain naughty librarian look going on.

At the sight of James' head wound, Principal Coker's face grimaced briefly. "Ah, Dr. Logan! So what, dare I ask, happened to you? It looks pretty bad."

"It's nothing. I had a slight procedure recently. Nothing serious."

"Really?" she said, furrowing her eyebrows. James could tell she didn't believe him. It was possible that she had already heard the rumors.

"So what did Augustus do this time?"

"Dr. Logan, it's not what Augustus did, it's what he didn't do!"

"Which was?"

"Today we had an emergency lecture for the entire school about the most effective ways to stop the spread of the flu. It was my idea," she said with a large smile. "I wanted to stress the importance of hand washing, covering your mouth when you cough, and not sharing utensils or drinks with anyone. It is my top priority to make sure this school does not become a breeding ground for this supervirus."

Her tone was becoming more curt and unwelcoming as she went on. She spoke as if each sentence was building toward some sort of climax. If she continued on much longer, she would be yelling at him.

"And what does your son do right there in the middle of my lecture? Do you know what he did?"

"No idea."

Coker pursed her lips and looked James dead in

the eye. "He sneezed! Dr. Logan, a completely unrestrained, high-pressure, disease-spreading sneeze. Only moments after I explained not to do this. A classic act of insubordination."

James reflexively laughed, which was cut short by the all-too-serious look on the principal's face. He straightened up. "Is that it?"

"Your son was either making light of a very serious situation or he just neglected to remember what had just been taught to him moments before. He must cover his mouth and nose when he sneezes. Either way, he had to learn his lesson. Perhaps it will save a life or two in the long run," said the principal, crossing her arms and leaning back, looking rather satisfied with herself.

Out of all the crazy scenarios he had gone over in his head, James hadn't expected this.

"So you gave my son detention for sneezing?"

"Of course not! Everyone must sneeze from time to time, Dr. Logan. It is only natural. However, I gave your son detention for not covering his face while performing this reflex."

"Well, thank you very much, Principal Coker. I thought I taught my son better than that. Thank you so, so, so much for teaching him a lesson. This flu pandemic is indeed very serious and you did the right thing," James said, mustering up all the dry sarcasm that he could possibly pack into each word. Sadly, it was lost on the principal. She had been temporarily blinded by the joy of having a parent finally agree with her.

"I'm so glad you think so, Dr. Logan! Perhaps there is hope for Augustus yet with such a great role model like you around the house," she said, leaning closer over her desk, with a gleam in her eye that made James feel uneasy.

"Okay, well if that settles it, I will just go and pick up Augustus from detention now. And don't you worry, I will make sure to sit him down tonight and have a long talk about the birds and the sneeze."

Principal Coker's smile grew wider. "Oh, Dr. Logan! You are so clever. Thank you for understanding. You can now go if you want. . . ."

If he wanted? That was an odd choice of words, he thought. As James got out of his chair to leave, Coker called out to him, "Actually, could you wait for a second, Dr. Logan? I would like to show you something."

Like a rabbit trapped in a snare, he painfully lowered himself back into the chair. Principal Coker reached into a drawer and pulled out a computer pad that looked like a black clipboard.

"What's this?"

Principal Coker got up and walked over behind him where she could see the screen as well. Her hands dug into his shoulders like talons. Her hot breath tickled the hairs on the back of his neck.

"This is your son's file, Dr. Logan, his test scores, eye exams, physical fitness, evaluations, etcetera."

James tried to focus back on the screen despite the uncomfortable feeling that he was about to be eaten by a black widow. "And what am I supposed to be looking at?"

"Do you see anything slightly odd about your son's records?"

"Not particularly, everything looks perfect to me.

Maybe he has a few too many detentions. No idea why."

"Everything looks perfect," she repeated. "Exactly! Your son is smart, far above the average, as are most of the kids at this school. What strikes me as odd is the widespread consistency. Almost every single child at this school is above the national average in both intelligence and fitness. You don't think any of that is unusual? Look at your son's physical fitness evaluations for this year."

Across the board his son's scores were in the ninety-ninth percentile. The sheet had several categories, including cardiovascular fitness, dynamic strength, absolute strength, and flexibility. Homeland Health Care mandated these yearly fitness exams in order to monitor the health of the population.

James smiled, glad to see that his son was excelling. "What can I say?"

Principal Coker squeezed her small hands down on James' shoulders, each finger digging like a claw into his trapezius muscles. He winced in pain.

"These scores aren't unique to your son, Dr. Logan. Almost the entire student body of this school ranks in the top ninety-ninth percentile in everything imaginable."

Coker's grasp on his neck was getting tighter. Is she trying to strangle me or just draw blood? thought James.

"We have the best teachers and a well-run fitness program, but let me tell you, our curriculum compared to other top-notch schools is not significantly different enough to account for these dramatically increased scores."

"I'm not sure what you are getting at. . . ."

"Why are these students so exceptional?"

He shook his head. "No idea."

"Why are you so exceptional?"

"What are you trying to say?" asked James, shaking his head, confused as hell.

"I think GeneFirm is genetically enhancing its own people."

"That's insane! You're suggesting something highly illegal. Only medically related genetic modifications are allowed. You know that."

"The children at this school that weren't born here at GeneFirm are not nearly as competitive as the rest. Maybe they aren't strictly altering any DNA. What about gene doping? By simply screening the embryos from a couple, you could easily select the ones that would maximize the future child's potential."

"Nothing like that is going on, I can assure you."

"Can you? This is about the upper class once again speeding up their own evolution—the ultimate form of artificial selection, each embryo selected for the best genes possible."

For most of human history, parents had to roll the dice when it came time to conceive. This gamble could be sidestepped by what Principal Coker was suggesting, giving the wealthy a winning hand every time.

"Gene doping is unethical, and I can guarantee that nothing like it is going on here."

James jumped up from his seat and rubbed his shoulders, which now had ten fingernail-shaped indentations in them. "My daughter is waiting for me outside. You know you should let go of this gene doping idea. It's ludicrous." He laughed nervously, backing toward the door. "You're not giving enough credit to this school and its achievements. These students all come from great people; success breeds success. Doesn't seem like much of a problem to me."

When James shut the door behind him, he instantly felt relieved. He walked away quickly, almost jogging, relieved to be free from the mad principal. From now on he would let Linda take care of any parent conferences with that woman.

"Come on, Olivia. Let's go get your brother."

Olivia hopped off the chair and trotted over to him. They turned right and continued down the hall to find his son. Augustus wasn't a social deviant or anything, but he had been punished to the point where both of his parents were well versed in the path to the detention hall. After winding around a few more corners, they came to a classroom with its lights still on. The room was filled to the brink with kids, which made James wonder if Principal Coker had some sort of detention quota she was trying to reach every afternoon. If she did, it looked like she was fulfilling it.

A teacher watched over the kids from a desk at the front of the class. Mrs. Golembiewski had been around so long that James could remember serving his own detentions under her watchful eyes. In the back of the room sat Augustus, recognizable only as a shaggy mass of black hair resting on the desk. When James entered, Mrs. Golembiewski looked up from her desk and squinted in the direction of the door. "Well, well, well. Little James is back again. The apple doesn't fall far from the tree, does it?"

"What a pleasure it must be for you, Mrs. Golembiewski, to spend so much quality time with two generations of Logan men."

He turned to Augustus; his son's head shot up at the sound of his father's voice. "Get your stuff, son, I'm taking you home."

"Excuse me, James, but detention isn't over for another half an hour," Mrs. Golembiewski cut in.

"Unfortunately, I must take Augustus home early. Family emergency, I'm afraid." As James said this, he pointed to his head wound.

Mrs. Golembiewski snorted and whispered something unintelligibly hostile under her breath.

His son got up from the desk and walked over to his father's side, still rubbing the sleep out of his eyes. As James escorted his children out of the room, he heard Mrs. Golembiewski shout behind them, "See you soon, James!" This was followed by the dry cackle of the old hag's laughter. He slammed the door behind them, cutting off the terrible hyenalike sound.

Augustus looked up at James. "What emergency, Dad?"

"Oh, there is no emergency. I just made that up to get you out of there. You're getting detentions for sneezing now?"

Augustus threw his hands up in the air. "My nose itched. I couldn't help it. Principal Coker is nuts!"

"You have no idea," said James, rubbing the back of his neck. But as he stared down at his two perfect children, he heard the principal's words echoing in his head. A week ago he would've never given any merit to her assertions, but now . . .

"Looks like it's just going to be us tonight, kids. Mom is still working down in the lab."

James scratched his kids' heads in sympathy as they stepped outside. Suddenly a high-pitched shrieking made both kids jump. The intensity of the scream steadily grew louder until a fire truck swerved into view, its sirens earsplittingly loud as it raced past the school and down the street.

"Let's go." James quickly threw Olivia up onto his shoulders and took Augustus' hand and followed the path of the fire truck. That's when James noticed the smoke billowing up above the neighborhood, black against the blue sky. Someone's house was on fire. When he realized what street the smoke was coming from, he broke into a sprint, his son struggling to keep up behind him. The house had been completely swallowed in flames, the crackle of fire audible from the end of the block as the wood buckled and popped under the extreme heat. It was Aunt Rose's house.

"No . . ." James cried. He sat down on the curb, pulling his two wide-eyed children into his arms. There they watched as the firemen began to douse the structure with jetting streams of water, hoping to quench the hungry flames that licked violently up at the sky.

24

"They told you what?"

"That since they were operating under a government contract they had the legal right to maintain a quarantine to protect vaccine production," mumbled Marnoy. Now the statement sounded so stupid he didn't even believe what he was saying. He wished he hadn't listened to Mac.

"What does that even mean? That they are above the law? That's complete horseshit. I can't believe you two accepted that answer. I should have Logan's DNA sample on my desk right now. Fuck!"

A thick worm of a vein sprouted on the director's forehead.

Mac interjected, "Director Zelinski, it was a legitimate reason. If we broke the quarantine we could have jeopardized the vaccine that we're in desperate need of. I didn't think it would be prudent to disrupt GeneFirm unless absolutely necessary."

The director grimaced and ground his fingertips into his forehead. "It can't wait! I told you already, a man has cancer and I have a hunch that medical record fraud is behind it. There is no 'quarantine immunity' law. You have a warrant, therefore, you have the legal right to enter GeneFirm property and get my damn samples! So tomorrow morning Tweedledee and Tweedledum, that would be you two numb-nutted assholes, are going to march back over there and get me a DNA sample."

"Yes, sir," chimed both agents.

"The only thing keeping me from firing both of you right now is this one sample you managed to bring back to me."

The director turned to Mac. "Could you please leave us for a moment?"

Confused, Mac said, "Alright," and left the room, making sure to shut the door securely behind him.

The director stared intensely at Marnoy. "I expected better from you. You know as well as I do that you're lucky to have a job here on the account of your 'condition.' This is your one and only shot at a decent government job and you're about to blow it. Do you understand?"

Marnoy nodded slowly.

"Here is one little piece of advice. Don't let that buffoon Mac persuade you against your better judgment or your career will be over before it ever began. I suggest you follow your instincts and keep Mac in line. Got it?"

Marnoy nodded slowly, chin dipping ever so slightly, his neck stiff with hate.

"Good," said the director, who waved him out of the room like he was a mosquito. Marnoy did his best not to slam the door behind him. Outside, Mac was waiting for him.

"Shit, man, I'm sorry."

Without acknowledging the statement, Marnoy walked right past his partner, headed for the elevators.

"Listen, Marnoy, don't worry. I'll go talk to Director Zelinski tomorrow when he's cooled off. You're not going to be blamed for any of this." Mac couldn't help but feel like a layer of ice had just frozen over their relationship as they took an empty elevator down to the garage. The two stood there facing the doors, shiny and metallic, their distorted forms reflected in front of them.

The elevator came to a halt and the doors parted. Mac gave a sincere "goodnight" but still got no reply from the mute Marnoy. The click-clack of their footsteps grew farther and farther apart until each man was alone.

Marnoy's car was a child's toy of a machine, tiny and compact. To get into the car, he had to stoop low and squeeze into the driver's seat. He pushed the ignition button and the engine quietly purred to life. On the radio, a woman from the BBC was describing grisly scenes of the growing international pandemic. He pulled out of the garage onto the dimly lit streets of downtown Austin and listened as the radio described a story of unfolding havoc. In Britain thousands of cases had sprouted up overnight.

The flu seemed to be sneaking its way around quarantines. Hospitals were being hit the hardest. Here in Austin they were being shut down left and right due to the virus' devastation. With all of this bad news on his mind, his foot became heavier, accelerating the car forward. He zipped beneath passing streetlights that filled his car with pulses of unnaturally orange light. Unlike Macdonald, no wife, kids, nor cold dinner awaited his return, only the maddening solitude of an empty apartment.

To Pat's relief, he did not have sleep apnea, but he was the exception. When they returned to the sleeping hall to shower after another grueling ninety-minute run, most of the campers discovered the shoe-box-sized machine named "Pappy" sitting next to their beds. At lights-out, the sleeping hall was alive with the soft whirl of the machines keeping all of those fat-encroached airways wide. At least two-thirds of the room's passengers were hooked up to machines. The hulking mound next to Pat, also known as Tony, was among those using the CPAP device; the racket of his painful midnight gasping had finally come to an end. Yet Pat still couldn't sleep. The guy in the cot on his other side seemed to be coming down with a cold or something. The man started violently coughing every five minutes for what seemed like the whole night. Pat finally resorted to concocting a pair of homemade toilet-paper earplugs. This brought the cough down to a subdued hiccup, but still sleep evaded him.

25

Marnoy waved his key card past his apartment door. The light on the lock blinked green and the door popped open. The apartment was located between a group of run-down buildings west of the interstate. The rent was dirt cheap, as the area's best days were far behind it. The poverty here on the east side amplified the violence tenfold like a magnifying glass aimed at a dry leaf on a sunny day. None of this bothered Marnoy though; he was so intimidating that the troublemakers of the east side did their best to avoid him.

The sickly light from the streetlamps spilled into the apartment, cutting an unwelcoming yellow wedge through the complete darkness inside.

"Lights on."

A row of harsh lights in the ceiling coughed and

sputtered to life, illuminating a small underfurnished apartment. The tiny living room before him contained an old lawn chair and a glass coffee table. The sole item on the table was a small computer. Little milky circles tracked their way across the glass tabletop like alien footprints; coasters seemed like a moot point.

He dropped his keys and phone on the table and plopped onto the couch, kicking off his shoes with a sigh of relief. Another day, another paycheck. The familiar pain in his head had started just on time—his postwork migraine. His life had become so routine that even his damn headaches had developed their own unyielding schedule.

A bottle of aspirin awaited him underneath the table and he swallowed the pills dry. On his computer, he checked the news again: more hysteria about the rampaging virus. Another headline warned of more severe weather predicted for tomorrow across the South and Midwest: tornados, floods, thunderstorms; the misgivings of a disgruntled planet.

Marnoy went to his bedroom and dumped the contents of his pockets on the nightstand as he loosened his tie. After tugging off his tie, slacks, and stiff white-collar shirt, he felt like a new man, his clothes were so boxy and uncomfortable. In the mirror on his wall, he caught a peculiar sight: Marnoy's face, arms, and neck down to the collarbone were much darker than the rest of his body, which was a light mulatto brown. It looked like the black equivalent of a redneck farmer's tan. With another depressed sigh, he hunched over and pulled off his socks, leaving deep lines of indentation in his shins where the socks had been squeezing him all day.

Goose bumps sprouted across his skin in the cold morgue of a bathroom. When he twisted the shower knob, ice water blasted his skin like the spray of a riot hose. The pandemic, the director, the human blobs he dealt with everyday at work, were all violently sheared from his skin by the sting of the freezing water. He grabbed a bottle from the shower ledge, lathered up his hands, and started to wash himself. Then a weird thing started to happen. The water running off Marnoy's feet became licorice black. The color of his face began to melt away and the blackness of his skin ran down his legs and face like crude oil. In a few seconds his unusually extra-dark face, neck, and forearms were back to the same light brown color as the rest of his body. The filthy water swirled down the drain like coffee.

He finished the shower and dried off. In the mirror a different person greeted him; he hated putting that paint on, but he had no choice. As he stared in the mirror, he wondered what it would be like if he stopped putting on his daily camouflage. Would he be able to find a woman? He doubted it. Up to this point in his life he didn't have much luck in that department. In all the years he had lived in this apartment he hadn't had one guest, especially not a female one. How could he expect to get close to someone when he was hiding behind a layer of gloom? For every day he covered himself, he felt himself becoming more impatient and hostile, as if the thick makeup was trapping his emotions inside him. There was no other option. He had to keep doing it; if not he would be out of a job.

Still naked, he went back into his room to get dressed. When he opened the drawer filled with underwear, he paused, as if lost in deep thought. He dug deep beneath his undergarments and extracted a black folder hidden below. It had been years since he had flipped through the pages inside, but maybe it was time to read it again. He sat on the edge of his bed and flipped open the binder. On the inside, the name Alex Jurgen was written in bold black letters.

The first page was a tattered and worn science article on camouflage in the animal kingdom. At the bottom of the paper there was a picture of a chameleon and an octopus. The article explained how the reptile's color-changing ability is very rudimentary, but the camouflage of cephalopods was much more advanced. The octopus and cuttlefish can disappear almost instantaneously against any background. Not only can cephalopods change the colors of their skin, but they can change its visible texture as well, whether it be the pebbled rocks of the ocean's floor or the ruffled swaying arms of a sea anemone. Cephalopods could even cross between two different backgrounds while blending in the entire time. According to the article, this complexity came from the millions of nerves that directly attached to the chromatophore skin cells, giving the brain a direct line of communication with the skin. These specialized skin cells were just sacs of pigments that could be squeezed to change shape and thus color. The cell also manipulated reflective plates within to control the appearance of the skin's texture. Marnoy had read the article thousands of times; he flipped the page.

On the second page was a newspaper clipping dated sixty years ago, with the headline, "First Transgenic Human Chameleon." The article continued on to say how scientists at GeneFirm had successfully inserted cephalopod genes into a human child, who now had the unique ability to change the color of his skin. The article stated how the child belonged to a wealthy octopus enthusiast, John Jurgen, who had funded the research. Human genetic rights organizations had been up in arms over these aesthetic transgenic modifications for years. Religious and antitransgenic groups called the existence of such children a grievous injustice against God and man. The article explained how a bill was stalled in Washington that would ban these kinds of superfluous genetic alterations; however, many legislators feared the bill would end the transgenic alterations used to create their own gene-doped "super kids."

The legislation was in response to the increasingly bizarre transgenic humans that were popping up everywhere. The market was a free-for-all, with parents playing God with their children's genome. If someone was rich enough, most genetic engineers weren't going to question their motives.

Marnoy hated his skin, he hated crooked government officials, he hated ignorant parents, but most of all he hated the unethical scientists at GeneFirm. He had more in common with cephalopods than he cared for; his grandfather, John Jurgen, was that billionaire nut job of an octopus enthusiast. Sam

Marnoy was not his real name. He was born Alex Jurgen.

Reading all this was intensifying his headache, but he kept on. The next page was an article on his father, Paul, the stocky bodybuilder and first human chameleon. His dad lived an abnormal life in the spotlight of the media. His color-changing ability was a breakthrough in genetic modification. Sam's father loved every minute of it. Thanks to his brand new "trait," he was famous. Paul was the life of any party when he would strip naked and effortlessly blend into the wallpaper, jumping out and scaring the living shit out of his fellow intoxicated revelers. Marnoy's father loved his unique ability about as much as his son hated his. By the time he was ready to have kids, laws had been passed so those genetic aesthetic modifications would be removed in any future progeny. Paul Jurgen didn't want this. So what did he do? He had a free conception, the only way to pass on his transgenic DNA without it being removed by the government. Thus Alex Jurgen was born just like his dad, a human chameleon, a despised free birth, a genetic leper with no cancer-proof genes. To make matters worse, young Alex never lived up to his father's expectations. Like the octopus, he and his father's color-changing ability was linked to their emotional state. When they were mad they turned a blotchy dark red. When they were happy their skins would pulse with bright colors, such as yellow, orange, and blue. For whatever the reason, Alex had trouble controlling the link between his emotions and his skin; this inability to control his color-changing led to many complications in his day-to-day life. For him the cephalopod genes were a crippling lie detector and a blowhole for his temper. His childhood consisted of a constant stream of punishment for letting his true emotions run wild over his flesh.

"Did you break the garage window, Alex?" his father once asked.

Young Alex didn't have to say a word. His skin rippled in waves of red, giving him away. He hadn't grown up with his heart on his sleeve; his heart covered the surface of his entire body, exposed to anyone who cared to look.

Marnoy appreciated more than most the importance of hiding your true feelings. Losing the ability to do so was an incredible disadvantage in this world. Emotional deception, it seemed, was a staple of human culture; without it, human civilization would be crippled by honesty. Whether it is talking to a boss or a girlfriend, people must hide their feelings daily in order to keep the peace. He never had this luxury. During college he had a job at the school's newspaper. One day he was told by the editor that his article wasn't good enough to be a feature. Marnoy's skin immediately flushed red and rippled with displeasure, alerting his boss to the contempt he felt. The editor asked if Marnoy had a problem with his decision, and that was the end. He lost his temper and the next day he was jobless. His life had been filled with so much heartache and grief as a result of his transgenic burden. It was nearly impossible to get a job as Alex. No one wanted to hire a transgenic freak, especially a free birth with a susceptibility to cancer. His unstable skin was a liability. Legally, no one could officially reject him for his genes, thanks to transgenic equal opportunity laws, but since his genes could interfere with his actual job, he was screwed.

It was only after he started using his dark cover-up that he was able to land a real job. Thus Alex Jurgen became Sam Marnoy. Every morning he applied the dark mask, covering his face, neck, and arms. He had begged Director Zelinski for the job, who, in a rare moment of compassion, agreed to hire him as long as he promised to keep his disguise. So far it had worked. Life had suddenly become a great deal easier, with a sense of normality that had been out of his grasp for so long.

Frustrated and angry, Marnoy threw the pages down on his bed and stood up. He walked into the bathroom and looked at himself again in the mirror. This time he was no longer that light chocolate brown. Instead his flesh had transformed into rippling waves of bright red, like a flashing beacon, as if to warn him of some unforeseen danger.

26

Soft music began to push its way through the earplugs. Pat opened up his eyes to the dawn sky peering through the octagonal windows above; the realization that it was morning hit him like a sucker punch. He was still extremely tired. Speakers that invisibly impregnated the walls were getting louder with each passing second. This wasn't the usual shrieking wake-up alarm. A piano and an assortment of string instruments serenaded the room. Over the music spoke the familiar voice of Dr. Slate; however, there was something strange about his voice. It sounded a bit nasally.

"Good morning, everyone. It's a beautiful day here in the hill country and I hope you—" In mid-sentence Dr. Slate burst into a hacking cough. Pat could almost hear the phlegm flying through the speakers and raining down on him from above.

Slate regrouped: "Excuse me. I'm feeling a bit under the weather. Anyway, I hope you all are ready for a great day of recuperation."

A man a few beds away beat his pillow in frustration, yelling "shut up, shut up, shut up" into it. He rolled over and tried to smother himself with the pillow to block out Slate's voice.

Unaware of the cries echoing throughout the room, Slate's voice continued. "I'm sure all of you are feeling pretty beat down at this point."

"No shit!" screamed a camper.

"That's why today is a recovery day. You will have a few light workouts later in the afternoon, but besides that, we want to give you plenty of time for your aching muscles to get a much-needed rest. There will be no morning workout, so breakfast is now being served in the dining hall. After breakfast Mandy will lead you all in a group stretch to loosen up those tight muscles."

The sleeping hall burst out in cheers.

Pat couldn't believe it. He jumped off his cot in joy. A recovery day! Thank you! Thank you!

The news had struck a chord of motivation within many. The room started to crawl with people eager to get to breakfast. Tony, for one, quickly unhooked himself from Pappy. Metal ground and springs groaned as the big man rolled off the cot and the two meat loaves that were his feet slapped the floor. He stretched out his arms and rubbed his stomach sorely.

"This is too good to be true! I'm starving."

Tony pulled up his white shorts to the bottom of his bulging gut. "You coming to eat, Pat? That was the best night's sleep ever."

Annoyed, Pat agreed. "Yeah let's go. But I slept like shit. I wonder if they would give me a Pappy, too?"

"You should ask, man! I love it. It has changed my life overnight. I feel like a billion bucks."

Pat bent down to grab his shirt. As he did, he noticed the coughing guy who had been on his left side was gone, vanished into the night. The man had coughed himself into oblivion, thought Pat.

A surge of jealousy hit him; he bet the guy was probably off relaxing in the infirmary, taken care of by a nurse with rocking tits decked out in one of Slate's pornographic health-retreat uniforms. Lucky bastard.

James woke up to a bright orange mound of fur in his face. For an instant, he thought he was being smothered by a fluorescent feather boa, but then realized Clementine had forced herself into his room and was frantically trying to wake him up.

"Alright. Alright, you freak, let's go," James said, rolling slowly out of bed. The long night's sleep had left him feeling groggy; his eyes felt like they had been glued shut. Throwing on a pair of flip-flops, he stumbled his way out the back door. Clementine sprinted past and almost knocked him over in the process. The dog galloped into the middle of the lawn and just stood there in the dew-laced grass.

With a sigh, James said, "Well, I'm not going to wait all day. Go ahead and do it already."

Clementine just stared back at him, her floppy tongue hanging out of the side of her mouth. The dog then busied herself with sniffing the grass, walking farther and farther away from the house. Not caring to wait on the dog any longer, James shut the door and went back inside. He pulled a container of cereal out of the pantry and made himself a bowl.

The image of Aunt Rose's burning house was unshakable, her loss hung heavy on his shoulders. It was too many coincidences for his liking. His brain tumor, the data drive, the missing genes, and now Aunt Rose—the only woman with answers—was dead. In his mind he replayed how the firefighters had carried the body bag out of the charred remains of the house, a group of yellow-emblazoned fire-retardant pallbearers. If he was right and that fire wasn't a mistake, he needed to be very careful. He considered reporting his suspicions to the H.H.; was he just being paranoid? No answers came to him, so he just sat down at the kitchen table.

"TV on."

The rectangular screen instantly appeared on the wall. What he saw made him choke, spew milk out his nose, and scatter flakes of oat bran all over the table.

A reporter was standing outside of Seton Hospital in Austin explaining that a newly developed vaccine was being distributed as quickly as possible.

"What the . . ."

The reporter said that the supply of vaccinations

was extremely limited, so only government and health care workers were currently eligible. James sat with his jaw open as the reporter declared that GeneFirm had begun to release the first deliveries of the vaccine late last night. Other divisions of Gene-Firm around the world were already producing the vaccine in order to meet the demand. The news claimed that death tolls were extremely high, in the hundreds of thousands.

But it was so soon, he thought. It was too good to be true. James felt his face flush with heat and his eyes start to water. This would be another huge accomplishment for his wife and the company. Feeling the need to confirm this miracle, he whipped out his phone's earpiece and said her name. After a few seconds, the phone rang once and went straight to voice mail. Frowning, he hung up. With the vaccine finished, she shouldn't be underground in the labs anymore.

The bowl of cereal looked unappetizing now. There was too much excitement coursing through him to eat. He didn't know quite what to believe. There was only one way to find out.

27

The elevator came to a halt and softly dinged twice as the doors slid apart. Marnoy and Macdonald stepped out and stopped, surprised by what was unfolding in the H.H. office.

"What the hell?"

The normal drudgery of the agency had morphed into an excited ruckus. A long line of employees stretched along the far wall, ending in the break room.

"What is this?" Mac asked. He thumped his potbelly with his hand and turned to Marnoy.

"No idea."

The two of them wound their way through the maze of desks to the back of the line. A young intern stood at the very end, looking more wide-eyed than usual. His skinny frame jumped as Marnoy belted out, "So what's the deal with the line?"

The intern's face flushed red as he stuttered, "It's a line for the vac-vac-vaccine."

"No shit!" gasped Mac.

Marnoy looked confused. "Already? That was fast?"

"GeneFirm announced the vaccine last night and it was delivered here thirty minutes ago. The director says that vaccination is mandatory for all government and health care workers," squeaked the intern.

Marnoy felt a surge of bitterness rise up in him. He cursed, "Damn government, protecting its own ass first."

"Please Marnoy, you know that priority vaccinations make sense," Mac retorted. "Imagine if there were no more doctors, policeman, or government officials left during a crisis like this. It would be a total shit show."

"Yeah, yeah. I understand. I still don't like it."

Marnoy understood the clusterfuck that would unfold if the flu took down the government, leaving the country vulnerable to instability and panic. Priority vaccinations were best supported by the lesson of the Spanish Flu of 1918. During this epidemic, all of the grave diggers fell ill and died, leaving Europe with mounds of decaying bodies rotting out in the open, thus worsening the public health nightmare and leading to even more disease. A similar situation occurred in European hospitals as doctors and nurses died by the dozens, leaving no one else to take care of the ill. So yes, priority vaccinations were justifiable, but it didn't mean that Marnoy had to feel good about it.

Somehow, the intern's eyes got even wider as he

pointed to the TV on the wall behind them. "Oh look!"

The news was showing images of National Guard troops standing around the Austin hospital. The reporter explained how riots were already breaking out around the country as desperate citizens demanded the vaccine.

"Damn! Riots at eight in the morning?"

"They have a right to be pissed," grumbled Marnoy.

Despite his misgiving about priority vaccinations, Marnoy was not going to lose his spot in line. He knew how nasty the virus was, and he wasn't going to skip an opportunity to prevent a very painful and early end. It might be unjust, but there were very few things about survival that weren't.

The three of them continued to watch the news in silence, waiting for their government-mandated salvation.

James tried not to look conspicuous as he almost ran through the main doors of GeneFirm. He was wearing nice slacks and a white business shirt that he had managed to throw on before rushing out of the house.

Ed waved to him from behind the guard desk with one Frisbee-sized hand; his other hand cradled a cup of coffee.

"Good morning, Dr. Logan. You're looking sharp."

"Thanks, Ed."

"So I assume you've heard the news?"

"Is it true?"

"Unfortunately, yes."

"What do you mean, 'unfortunately'?"

Ed's brow wrinkled. "Sir?"

"The vaccine."

"Oh, the vaccine," said Ed, who finally realized the misunderstanding. "Yes, we are lucky they were able to make it in such a short time. But that's not the news I was speaking of. No one called you?" He paused as if searching for the right words. "I hate to be the bearer of bad news, but there was an accident."

The words hit James hard. He felt like his stomach had been slit open, sending his spaghetti entrails to the floor. "What kind of accident?"

"A leak. A sensor picked it up this morning. Your wife is fine. No one was harmed. But until we make sure that no one has been contaminated, level B4 has been sealed off."

"So she is safe?"

"Completely."

Feeling somewhat relieved, James shook his head. "You really scared me there, Ed."

"My apologies, sir. I promise I will let you know as soon as the quarantine has been lifted on the lab."

"Thanks, Ed." James turned to leave but stopped as he debated whether or not to ask a question. Finally he nodded, leaning back over the desk.

"Is Dr. Weisman available? I need to meet with him. Now."

Twenty minutes later, a massive figure appeared in the lobby. It was Ari, Dr. Weisman's son, a man shrouded in GeneFirm lore. Ari was wearing his usual dark suit. His crew-cut blond hair looked almost white in the sunlight spilling in from outside. He looked down at James; his blue ice-cube eyes peered out from behind a facial structure built like the Berlin Wall.

James and Ari were the same age and had briefly shared the same class in the first grade; however, for unknown but heavily hypothesized reasons, Ari disappeared and wasn't seen again on GeneFirm property for another twenty years. Many believed that Ari was the product of illegal genetic tampering. This theory was supported heavily by the fact that Ari was a large muscular blond-haired boy with blue eyes, while his parents, Dr. Weisman and his wife, were both slim, average-sized, and of Jewish descent with stereotypically dark features. Due to the unique arrangement of employees living and working within an isolated complex, GeneFirm had the tendency to become a rumor mill. Every week nasty allegations and other scandals about its employees would run the gauntlet of the company's hallways, and no one seemed immune. The birth of Dr. Weisman's little Aryan baby launched a number of rumors about how he must have illegally genetically enhanced his spawn. Many believed it was fear of an H.H. investigation that drove Dr. Weisman to send his son to a European boarding school.

"Dr. Weisman is ready to see you," said Ari with his deep, monotone voice.

"Oh, I'm sorry, Ari, I didn't need you to come down here to get me. I could have walked up there myself."

Ari shook his head. "My father insisted," he said, without any further explanation. "Follow me."

Ari led James down several corridors into the heart of the building.

"So what have you been up to, Ari?" James asked. "I hardly ever see you around here."

The colossal man tossed a bored look back at him. "Oh, you know, saving the world one day at a time." Ari laughed and then continued, "But really, I've just been doing a lot of traveling, working on side projects for my dad."

"What kind of projects exactly?" James asked as they passed through the empty cafeteria to the first set of security doors separating the executive offices from the rest of the building.

"You know how my father is, always the great humanitarian."

James thought he caught a hint of sarcasm in the last comment.

They stopped in front of the thick glass doors and Ari pressed his thumb to a scanner. The doors beeped and split open.

Ari continued, "Now that he's reached the twilight of his life, him being a century old and all, I believe he has been thinking a lot about his legacy."

The two came to a stop in front of the executive elevators that would take them upward to the pinnacle of the building, the gateway to Dr. Weisman's renowned office in the sky.

28

During lunch the whispers started. People were getting sick. The news spread among the campers in hushed voices, only pausing between desperate bites of food. Tony followed Pat to a cafeteria table after they got their small plates of sustenance.

Shaking his head, Pat asked, "Did you hear that guy coughing last night?"

Big Tony only nodded as he devoured the pita bread sprouting with green vegetation. After he finished swallowing a mouthful of food, he said, "I did indeed. Poor dude was having a tough time."

"We need to find out what's going on . . ." said a feminine voice behind them.

Both men turned to see Modest standing there with her breakfast tray. This was the first time Pat had seen those brilliant green cat eyes up close. Pat hoped they were just bizarre contacts and not her real eyes, but he highly doubted it.

"Why?" asked Pat.

"Look around. There are definitely at least ten people missing."

Tony shrugged. He tenderly picked up a piece of lettuce that had fallen onto his plate and plunged it between his greedy lips. "You're exaggerating?"

Pat looked around. "No, she's right. I hadn't noticed, but it seems like there are a lot less of us today, doesn't it?"

"And did you hear Slate this morning. He sounded pretty sick, too. Listen, Thomas told me there's a viral pandemic out there right now; they haven't told us because they don't want us to panic. But we deserve to know what's going on outside this hellhole. Have you seen Slate or Thomas today? No, you haven't, just Mandy and a few others."

People at the table began to ignore the seemingly crazy girl. Frustrated, Modest saw that Pat was still paying attention. She slid into the seat next to him, making his heart almost stop; sweat sprouted on his palms as he felt his skin flush. This was his usual reaction to a female presence. He watched her frail hands manipulate her fork, but she didn't touch her food.

"Speaking of Mandy, where did she go?" Pat asked as he searched the room for the tiny tanned bombshell.

Modest's head whipped around the room; not finding Mandy, her eyes narrowed.

"No, that's not right. They never leave us alone in the cafeteria. You see, something serious is going on."

As if to answer her, the intercom speakers in the ceiling beeped to life. The conversations, laughter, and even the clinking of silverware immediately silenced as everyone froze, hoping to hear some kind of explanation for the rumors of sickness that were circulating about. Mandy's bubbly voice spilled into the room: "Hello, everyone," she cheered. "As part of your recovery day you will have the rest of the afternoon to relax. Dinner will be served at six p.m. We hope you will all choose to spend your free time bettering yourself, and don't forget to stretch!"

The cafeteria exploded with chatter.

"Sweet! Is she kidding?" Tony shouted.

Modest was the only one not smiling. She shook her head. "No, no, no! I've been here three times and never, ever have they given us any free time."

But her words fell on deaf ears. Tony and the rest of the campers at the table had suddenly forgotten about the rumors, excited by the thought of having some time to themselves. Several people, including Tony, got up with their trays to go beg for seconds.

"I believe you," said Pat, leaning over toward Modest.

She smiled. "Good. Let's go then, shall we?" Modest got up and walked swiftly toward the cafeteria exit. Unsure if he should follow, Pat watched the pink vixen glide away.

Fuck it, he thought, pushing himself up and trotting after her. When he caught up with her, he asked, "So where are we going?"

"The only TV in this building is in Slate's office, but his door is locked."

"How do you know that?"

"Because I tried to open it already. I need your help to kick in the door."

"So you're just using me?"

"Technically."

"I'm not kicking in any doors. Can you imagine what they'll do to me if they find out?"

"Oh please."

Pat stopped. "I'm going back to the cafeteria. I can't do this."

Modest rolled her cat eyes at him. "Fine, go back. But what if there really is a pandemic out there? How long will you last? It's a death trap here. People are sick; you know it's true."

The fear of punishment and the fear of the mysterious illness had a tug-of-war in Pat's brain as Modest continued down the hallway without him. Standing there conflicted, he watched her slim hips sway farther and farther out of his reach. He rubbed the palms of his hands on his white shorts, wiping off a layer of sweat. The thought of being alone with the odd girl was too enticing, even if it was going to get him in trouble.

"So where is Slate's office?" he shouted.

She turned toward him. With a smile, she pointed down the hall.

"How do you know Slate isn't there?"

"Well, number one, the door is locked. If he were there, it wouldn't be. Number two, his bike isn't in the lobby."

The hallways were unusually quiet. To Pat's relief, they did not see a single white-clad employee during their trek to Slate's office.

When they reached the office, Modest stopped and tried the doorknob.

"Still locked." She pointed at the door. "This is all you, big guy. Be a manly man now and break down this door."

Pat sighed. "I can't believe I'm trying this. I'm not going to guarantee that I can."

"Give me your best shot."

Pat slowly approached the door. When he knocked on it, he was disappointed to hear that the door sounded pretty dense. Gritting his teeth, he reared back and threw his shoulder into it.

"Fuck!" he yelled.

When his body connected with the door, it didn't budge an inch. It felt like he had dislocated his shoulder instead. A blinding pain shot through his deltoid.

"There is no way I can do this, Modest. This door is solid as a rock."

"Try again."

He desperately wanted to impress the girl, so he took a step back, readying himself for another try. Pat threw himself at the door much harder this time; and there was a thud as he bounced off it like a tennis ball. His shoulder lit up with pain again.

"Oh shit! Damn it, that smarts!" He cringed. "I can't do this, Modest. I'm sorry."

"No, that was good. I saw the door give a little that time. Try again, I know you can do it. You're a human battering ram."

Was she being sarcastic? He was only succeeding at inflicting pain on himself.

Modest put her hand gently on his shoulder. She

leaned over and gave him a peck on the cheek, her lips hard, like two Jolly Ranchers against his face. "Do it again. Please."

This unexpected kiss energized him; a surge of adrenaline ran its way down his spine. Pat backed up, shaking his head in disbelief over what he was willing to do for a woman. This time he got a running start and barreled toward the door like an enraged bull. A millisecond before impact, he closed his eyes, preparing for the painful blow. But none came. Instead he opened his eyes in time to see the tile floor approaching as he crash-landed inside the office.

"What the hell?" screamed a very frightened Slate, who had opened the door just before Pat had reached it.

"Slate!" yelled a shocked Modest. "What are you doing here? Your door was locked and your bike wasn't here. I thought you were gone."

Slate was not looking himself. His long blond hair looked unwashed and disheveled, hanging down in front of his face like dirty rags. A thick blanket was wrapped around his shoulders. He broke into a painful-sounding coughing fit, then took a few seconds to recover.

"I'm obviously sick, so I didn't ride my bike today. The next thing I know someone is trying to break down my door."

The sick doctor slowly walked back to his desk, ignoring the man sprawled out on his office floor. Slate dragged his feet the whole way and then sunk down into his chair, looking exhausted.

"Don't come any closer please. I'm dying."

"Slate, you are being a drama queen," laughed Modest.

"Usually yes, but today I'm afraid not. I've caught it. If you don't believe me, see for yourself."

He punched a button at his desk and a TV on the wall blinked to life. Sure enough, the news headlines were scrolling, TERRORISTS UNLEASH DEADLY VIRUS. A sleepy-eyed reporter wearing a mask was explaining how there were a limited number of vaccinations.

Slate punched the button again and the TV died.

"They claim that the virus kills everyone that it infects. The most lethal in history."

In shock, Pat had lost the ability to speak. He tried to say, "No way," as he stared at the doctor, but the words got stuck in his throat like a splintered chicken bone.

Upon hearing Slate's prognosis, Modest's already pale skin got even whiter. "I . . . I . . . I'm sorry Slate," she said, her voice cracking.

Slate struggled to smile as he looked at the girl. "Modest, get the hell out of here. No need to cry over me. I just hope you haven't been infected yet."

"I'm sorry, Slate," she repeated.

"No, I am sorry. I confess I was the one who brought you back here. I like you, Modest, and maybe, I might have even missed you."

Modest nodded. "I know."

He broke into another horrible fit of coughing. With a hand, he waved them out of the room, finally managing to say, "Just leave already!"

Modest and Pat reluctantly retreated from the

room, leaving behind the droopy shell of the once-vibrant Dr. Slate.

Out in the hallway, Pat looked at Modest with interest. "You and Slate?"

"It's a long story."

He looked at her with doubt.

"Well, I guess it's not that long of a story. He screwed me a couple dozen times" —She paused, looking like her mind was still back in Slate's of-fice—"both literally and metaphorically, it seems."

Very briefly, a look of sadness swept across her face, a brief glimpse beneath the pink-haired girl's frosty armor.

29

The director appeared in the doorway of Marnoy and Mac's shared office. "You two, come," he said before disappearing back into the hallway.

The agents wearily followed the director back to his office. The familiar view of the state capital's dome could be seen in the distance from the window behind the director's desk.

The room felt different to Marnoy. He scanned it briefly to discover that they were not alone. Two square-faced men in stiff suits sat in one corner of the room; they both cocked their heads at Marnoy and Macdonald. Their faces remained expressionless.

"Mac. Marnoy. Meet Agents Wells and Crimmins from Homeland Security," said the director with a sweeping of his hand. The two sets of men exchanged a series of handshakes that were about as friendly as a python's death grip.

Oh shit, Marnoy thought. What the hell was the H.S. doing here?

The director sat down. "Now, despite you two turds screwing up yesterday, we have had a bit of good fortune."

"How so?"

"I received a phone call this morning from a very disturbed James Logan."

Marnoy sat up straight in his chair.

"Dr. Logan claimed that his aunt had passed on evidence to him that her two children were also born without the cancer-proof genes. One of those children was Pat Henderson. Naturally, this got Dr. Logan worried. He did a little research of his own and discovered that he and his children were also missing the genes. That's not all: apparently his aunt perished in a mysterious house fire yesterday before he could question her."

The director paused as the agents absorbed the news. "Gentlemen, we have something significant on our hands here. Who knows how many people are running around without these genes? We ran Mr. Henderson's DNA sequencing last night and confirmed what Dr. Logan told us. I can safely say that someone over at GeneFirm is purposely failing to insert the cancer-proof genes and then altering the DNA sequencing reports to cover it up. Due to the severity of these accusations, Homeland Security is now investigating this case."

The director stood up and walked over to the window. Looking out into the hazy sky, he almost grinned as he said, "We have the chance to blow GeneFirm right out of the water, my friends—one of the last privately owned medical-research facilities."

"Listen, I know what you're saying," Mac responded, looking a little doubtful. "I just find this all a little hard to believe."

The director shook his head. "Not at all, Mac. It's not hard to believe at all. Private industry lacks adequate government oversight and control."

The director clapped his hands as he looked at the two sets of men in front of him. "Mac and Marnoy, you will assist the Homeland Security agents in the arrest of the GeneFirm CEO, Dr. Weisman, as well as the search and seizure of all information that could help with this investigation."

"Yes, sir." Mac tapped his foot nervously on the floor.

Marnoy glanced suspiciously at the two H.S. agents and then back to his boss. He couldn't explain the slight feeling of unease that had just crept over him, but these emotions were quickly overtaken by the excitement of the impending shit they were about to bring to GeneFirm's doorstep. He was about to grab by the balls the company responsible for all of his fucking misery. Yes, GeneFirm might have just created a vaccine that was going to save billions of lives, but it was still an evil corporation in his mind. This was not only a chance to have his revenge on the people responsible for his devastating genome, but it was also a chance to get his career moving in the right direction. An opportunity to finally to get what he deserved.

The director dropped back into his leather desk

chair, rapping the table with his knuckles, signaling that this meeting was now over. "Now go make it happen!"

Marnoy and Macdonald nodded in unison.

"And one more thing, Agent Macdonald," the director said, eyeing the agent's midline. "We have a gym downstairs. I would highly suggest you use it, otherwise you're going to land yourself at a retreat sooner or later."

Cracking a fake smile Mac said, "Gladly, boss."

As soon as they were out of sight, Macdonald's smile turned into a scowl. He leaned over to Marnoy and whispered, "Screw that man. What a piece of shit!"

Marnoy nodded.

Looking down at his paunch, Mac continued to shake his head. "Does this tie make me look fat?"

Ignoring the comment, Marnoy headed toward the exit sign that glowed promisingly at the end of the hallway.

30

The executive offices of GeneFirm stood at the very peak of the pyramid. Ari walked ahead of James at a good clip, the sharp click-clack of his hard leather shoes the only audible sound in the silent corridor. James struggled to keep up.

The walls around them were busy with awards and plaques racked up by the company over 100-plus years of scientific breakthroughs. They climbed one more flight of stairs and found themselves at a desk where a lean-looking secretary sat with short red hair and swollen pink lips that matched her even more swollen cleavage. The secretary looked up at the sound of Ari's footsteps; she smiled, her lips parting to show two rows of perfectly straight bleach-white teeth. She nodded toward the double-doors of Dr. Weisman's office. "He's ready to see you."

Ari went first, pushing open both doors, making no attempt to hold them open for James, who had to sidestep as they swung back at him like punching bags. He snorted to show his disapproval of Ari's rudeness, but the man showed no sign of hearing it.

James had never seen Dr. Weisman's office with his own eyes, only heard stories. It was incredible. Above them loomed the four corners of the building, touching together to form the mighty point of the pyramid. The horizon was visible in every direction; from here the earth was just a gigantic stretch of green, dotted here and there with wind turbines and other signs of humanity that stood out like pock-marked scars. James felt like he was standing on a cloud.

Considering its size, the room was basically empty, looking more like a high school gymnasium than an executive office. In fact, a one-lane running track circled the perimeter of the room. The only indication of an "office" was a bovine of an oak desk. Behind it, Dr. Weisman casually leaned back in a chair, looking like royalty. There was a single chair positioned across from the desk, giving the impression that the CEO only met with one person at a time. Next to the desk was a stand with a television playing the news with the volume muted, leaving only flashing images of men in hazmat suits. As they approached the desk, Dr. Weisman jumped up from his seat and stretched out his arms to give James a hug.

"James, so good to see you." He pulled back and examined James' incision. "How are you feeling?"

Embarrassed, James threw up his hands. "I'm doing better now. I feel like I just crossed through St. Peter's pearly gates," said James. "It's beautiful up here."

Weisman laughed. "So what can I do for you?"

"Well, uh," James stuttered, briefly looking over at the imposing Ari. "It's quite serious actually. Do you mind if we talk alone?"

Dr. Weisman paused for a second and glanced at his son. "Ari, I believe Savira is looking for you. She needs your help preparing for our guests."

Ari nodded, but James caught the brief flash of protest that crossed the man's face as he left James and his father alone. Over Dr. Weisman's shoulder, James saw that the TV was showing a row of bodies covered in white sheets. The CEO turned to look at the morbid scene and then back to James.

"Guests?" asked James.

"Oh, no worry of yours. Now, tell me, what is on your mind?"

For being well over a hundred years old, James was shocked at how remarkably fit this man was. His arms and legs were laced with pinky-sized veins and tough ropey muscle.

"Sir, I need to tell you something. It's only right I tell you firsthand."

"And what's that?"

"To state it simply, my children, my two cousins, and myself are all missing the cancer-proof genes."

Dr. Weisman frowned. "And how do you know this?"

"After my alleged brain tumor, my aunt gave me a DNA sequencing study that showed her kids were missing the cancer-proof genes. I grew suspicious and personally sequenced my DNA as well as my children's. Someone inside GeneFirm must be creating people without these genes, and we need to find out who. The death of my aunt was not an accident. It's too coincidental; she was the only other person who knew about the missing genes and someone killed her because of it. I didn't know what to do, so I contacted Homeland Health Care and told them everything."

Dr. Weisman looked concerned. He stood up and walked toward the glass walls behind him. He waved for James to follow.

The CEO looked out over the world below; his eyes drifted over the scenery, looking lost for a moment. After an awkward pause, he cleared his throat, apologized, and then started to speak.

"This is not news to me, James. I wish you had come to me first—getting the government involved will only make things . . . messy."

"Sir?"

Dr. Weisman swept his hand around his office. "One hundred and sixty years ago, my father changed the course of humanity forever. The cancer-proof genes were arguably the biggest medical breakthrough of all time. In the old days, heart disease and cancer were the leading two causes of death. They bagged heart disease easily enough with prevention, so cancer was the last big killer. So what now? Was it a good idea to eliminate death? Many people, including myself, question the logic of ridding humanity of these plagues that some would argue are completely natural. Was what my father developed really a cure?"

Silence settled around them, and James suddenly had a horrible sinking feeling.

Dr. Weisman continued, "As a civilization, we are not winning the battle on overcrowding. Birth control and limited conception laws are helping, but these will leave nothing but a black skid mark on the pavement as we hurtle over the edge. You see, ironically, by curing these diseases we have shortened the ultimate lifespan of our species. Our planet is overpopulated, natural resources are dwindling, and I can honestly say this very company, my father's brainchild, is the damn engineer of it all.

"He didn't save us." Dr. Weisman turned toward James and locked his fierce eyes upon him, his face as serious as stone. "He doomed us. My father, my clone, me—it's hard to see a difference between us now. What we thought was a blessing was really a curse. Individuals aren't supposed to live forever, James. Every parent must leave this planet in order to make room for his grandchildren. Do you understand what I'm saying?"

"Of course, Dr. Weisman, but you can't blame humans for wanting to live long, healthy lives. You can't stop progress."

"Progress!" snorted Dr. Weisman. "Fire was progress! What we have now is far different." A dark tone had crept into Dr. Weisman's voice.

"Listen, you can't blame yourself for the ills of the world. We will struggle on. Conservation and technology will make our species sustainable. . . ."

"You are an optimist, James! I have been studying this issue for most of my career. The statistics all point in one direction, and that is a fast approaching demise of the great human experiment. I'm talking about the end of our species. The dinosaurs had their time and we high-minded chimps have just about finished ours. Overpopulation isn't even the biggest problem."

"So what is it, then?"

"Those little organisms that my father found in the Ganges, they are the real problem. The parasite whose genes prevent cancer in almost every man, woman, and child in this country, an organism that can no longer mutate. That species has the exact same genetic material today as it did when my father studied it. That's over a hundred and fifty years with each organism replicating a hundred times a day. During that time, any normal species would have accumulated over three million mutations. Three million! I'm talking about evolution, James. Thanks to that parasite, the human race is now the evolutionary equivalent of stagnant water. Evolution is the driving force behind nature; without it we are condemned to failure. Mutations can lead to cancer, this is true, but mutations to our genetic code are essential in defending our species against infectious plagues. Over a lifetime, bacteria and viruses develop resistances to the human immune system only to be thwarted by a mutating human genetic code. Mutation is the weapon by which we fight this never-ending arms race. Today we rely almost exclusively on our vaccines and medicines because the bugs have bested our natural defenses. My father was a foolish, overconfident man!"

Dr. Weisman smiled and put a hand on James' shoulder. "And that is where you come in."

31

"I'm leaving," Modest said as she looked back at the white domes of the retreat.

"You can't leave! Where are you going to go? You heard what the news said. The cities will be worse; you won't be safe," Pat pleaded.

Modest pointed a finger back at the building. "Like we're safe! It's already here. Forget about the news, this place is a death warrant and I'm leaving. If I were you, I would come along."

The image of Slate, wrecked and feverish, flashed in Pat's mind. He took one last look at the retreat and, shedding no tears over the place, he shuffled on after Modest. She was, unfortunately, right.

The thought of sleeping next to the man with the coughing fits the previous night made him shudder. Was he already infected?

"Let's go. You're right, there's no point in staying here. If people are already sick, it won't be long until we are all sick."

"Smart move, buddy. But let me say this. If I, for one moment, think you're infected, if you show any signs of it, I'll be gone faster than you can blink."

He nodded solemnly.

For a fleeting moment, he fantasized about the two of them on the run. Maybe they would find a secluded lake house. Safe from the virus, hot nude summer nights would follow, pungent with the smell of sex. He wouldn't mind that at all.

"And same goes for me," he lied.

Pat thought he wouldn't leave Modest if she had the bubonic plague and was covered in festering boils. But maybe these were just the untested thoughts of chivalry. Good intentions tend to faint in the blank stare of death. He wanted to be a hero, but he had this nagging feeling that his spine was the consistency of papier-mâché.

Abe felt like shit. The security guard lounged back in his chair, sweat shimmering on his brow. He was running a fever, his body unable to decide if it was hot or cold. He was brought out of his stupor by the sharp sound of brake pads grinding together outside. Through the window he saw a familiar government car. They were back.

Oh brother, he thought, not wanting to deal with this now.

Ed had made it perfectly clear to him: no one comes in or goes out of the complex, no matter what.

The two men from yesterday were climbing out of the car. Their facial expressions were that of men who had recently had a very large and unpleasant object shoved up their rectums. Abe was surprised to see a second car directly behind the first. Inside were two more unpleasant-looking agent types, looking like they belonged at the back of a funeral procession.

Abe cussed under his breath and tried to summon the energy to deal with the situation. He slid open the door.

"Back so—" The guard's sentence was interrupted by a coughing fit that made both agents cringe and take a step back. After a few hacking coughs, Abe regained control and apologized. "Forgive me. What can I do for y'all?"

Marnoy and Mac looked at each other, both thinking the exact same thing—this guy was done for. "You don't sound so great. Did you get the vaccine?" asked Mac.

"Oh, no, this isn't that supervirus. Just a little cold, that's all." Abe tried to laugh, but all that managed to escape was the deep throaty cough of a man who had just inhaled a cup of water.

"Alright, if you say so. We have our warrant and I'm afraid you're going to have to let us in this time," said Mac. He pulled out the warrant and held it in front of Abe.

With drops of sweat rolling down his face, the security guard squinted at the paper. "I see," Abe sighed. "Well, we are still under a quarantine, but I'll call up and see what they say."

"You can call, but 'no' isn't an option at this point."

Abe slipped back inside and shut the door behind

him. He picked up the phone and pressed a button; a second later he heard Ed's gruff voice.

"Are they here?"

Shocked, Abe responded, "Yes, sir, and they have a warrant."

"Let them in."

"What?"

"Just let them."

"What about the quarantine?"

"Don't worry. I'll take care of it."

With a trembling hand, Abe hung up, relieved that he wouldn't have to deny the agents again. He pushed a button on his desk and heard the sound of the metal gates rolling open. The agents were already back in their respective cars waiting.

With a great deal of effort, Abe stood up and went outside. "Okay, you guys have the all-clear. Once you enter, keep to the left, and it will take you all the way to the main building." As he finished his last statement, the security guard busted into another episode of violent coughing. After a brief wave to the men, he disappeared from sight. Marnoy and Mac exchanged another look.

"That sucks for that guy," Marnoy said under his breath.

"I'd say, you're right about that," Mac chimed in as the car slid past the gates and onto a heavily forested road, the dense canopy of trees blocking out most of the sunlight.

"Let's just get this done fast. This place is giving me the creeps."

32

It took James a few seconds to process all the information Dr. Weisman had just told him. "What do you mean 'this is where I come in'?"

"Come on, James. You're brighter than this. That brain tumor was no mistake. Well, I guess 'technically' it was a mistake, but a completely natural one."

All the air felt like it had been sucked out of the room. He meditated on the words, saying them over and over. "*It was no mistake?*"

Dr. Weisman's tirade finally made sense. James stepped away from the man in disgust.

"You are responsible for this!" he yelled, the words spewing out like fire.

Weisman smiled and nodded. "Since the year you were born, not a single embryo at GeneFirm has been given the cancer-resistant genes. We're bringing back evolution. And yes, sadly, cancer is the price we have to pay."

"A price we have to pay? You mean, a price that I'm paying. This is illegal. I could die of cancer! And my children!"

James was as disturbed as he was angry. He put one hand on the glass in front of him and leaned against it, holding his head in the other hand. The thought of losing his wife or his children to a preventable disease made him want to vomit.

"James, you must calm down. Humanity coexisted for a million years with mutations, and if we are to survive another million, we cannot have a mutation-free genome. Without mutations, we would still be chimps hanging from branches. Evolution is essential for progress, and progress is a long-term commitment. Progress takes sacrifice."

James glared in anger at the old man. "You're fucking insane! You can't take up the duty of saving humanity from something that may or may not happen! You don't have the right to subjugate us to cancer because of a nutty apocalyptical prediction."

"It is no prediction! I have done what's best for your family and every one of your future ancestors. Don't you see? You should be thrilled. I have chosen you and the employees of this company to continue mankind's legacy," Dr. Weisman said with a smile. "GeneFirm's children are the smartest, brightest, and fittest group of individuals on the planet. I have worked to ensure that. Look at your wife; she is a goddess, a near-perfect woman."

"What are you trying to say?"

"You, your wife, your kids, almost every employee that works here has been genetically engineered to be smarter, fitter, and more beautiful. Random chance rarely produces such specimens like you and your wife, such very high quality."

Oh, God, Principal Coker was right, thought James. His voice cracked with anger and accusation: "You're gene-doping?"

"The word 'doping' has such negative connotations. I've been bettering my employees, nothing more."

"I can't believe this," James said.

"Believe it, my friend. Now, you are not the first case of cancer we've had here."

"I'm not?"

"Oh, no. Not at all. We have thousands of people here without cancer-proof genes, so it happens from time to time. So far we have been able to take care of them surreptitiously. We just say we removed a benign lesion and that's it. Unfortunately, you went to an outside hospital, so we couldn't cover it up this time, and now the government is asking questions. And the timing of your incident. I don't believe in fate, James, but sometimes I think it believes in me.

"Your aunt's situation was truly unfortunate. It was beyond my control."

"What situation?" asked James, his hands trembling with fury.

"Her daughter, Molly, developed a particularly malignant form of cancer. A suicide was arranged before the cancer could devastate her body. We saved her from an immense amount of pain, I assure you. However, we were unaware that your aunt had grown skeptical and had her children's DNA sequenced without us knowing. She kept it quiet for all these years. We only discovered it when she leaked some information to the department of Homeland Health Care a few days ago. Then she made the mistake of passing on her children's DNA sequences to you."

"You didn't . . ."

"She left us no choice. Come, take a seat," Dr. Weisman said, motioning toward his desk.

Too angry to speak, James watched as Dr. Weisman sat down in his leather chair.

"Did you have something to do with that fire?"

"Please, James, sit down."

"No, I will not fucking sit down. Now tell me, was that fire an accident?"

"You already know the answer to that question," Weisman said sternly. "My father created GeneFirm with humanity's best interest in mind. His goal was to build a state-of-the-art research institution, not the whimsical idea we have these days about curing death itself. He told me his fears right before he died. It was a powerful moment in my life, sitting there, staring into the eyes of my father, watching a piece of me die. I refuse to repeat history. Your aunt's death was necessary. Do you understand?"

After a tense pause, James finally understood and whispered, "You son of a bitch."

Dr. Weisman dropped his head in exhaustion, disappointment etched across his face. He nodded toward the TV playing near his desk; the news caption SUPERFLU INFECTING MILLIONS scrolled the bottom of the screen.

"Tomorrow, the caption will be hundreds of millions, then billions, then there won't be any more captions, only silence." Dr. Weisman said coldly, "You don't have to agree with me or what I've done—it's happening and there is nothing you can do to stop it."

James looked away from the screen like he had just seen his whole family murdered in front of him. A sick feeling crawled up his esophagus, stopping just short of his throat.

"You didn't," repeated James painfully.

"It is the only thing that can save us! Surely you understand that," shot back Weisman, leaning both elbows on his desk, creeping closer to James.

"Killing innocent people? You bastard!" James shouted as he jumped to his feet. He lunged at Dr. Weisman, but before reaching him a sharp pain stabbed into his lower back and every muscle in his body contracted tightly. Next thing he knew he was on his side, shaking on the floor. After a few agonizing seconds, the pain subsided, and his muscles finally relaxed. He could see Ari towering above him, a black Taser in hand.

"I'm the only one committing violent acts today," he assured James.

33

Marnoy stopped in front of GeneFirm's entrance. The shadow of yet another looming DNA statue cast itself over the parked car. He got out of the vehicle and the others followed suit. As they all walked toward the entryway, the shorter H.S. agent finally broke his silence.

"We are going to arrest Dr. Weisman. You two will search medical records and collect DNA samples. When you're done, we will meet you back here. Let's try and keep this under an hour."

The agent's voice was dry and booming. Neither Marnoy nor Mac questioned his authority; they just nodded with resentment.

"Fuck these guys," Marnoy whispered under his breath.

Mac chuckled, but cut it short when the beady eyes of the H.S. agents shot his way.

When the little troop of suits and hard demeanors entered the front door, a mountain in a security uniform greeted them. The big man sat up and stared at them from behind the front desk.

"Hello, how can I help you?"

"The Department of Homeland Health Care has a warrant to investigate GeneFirm. We need to see Dr. Weisman and obtain DNA samples from several employees," said the shorter agent.

There wasn't even a glimmer of surprise in the security guard's expression. Without missing a beat the man stood up.

"Certainly. I'll do my best to assist you."

Dr. Weisman gazed down at James with a sympathetic look. "James has every right to be angry. He doesn't understand the significance of what we're doing. Now please get him back into his seat and pull those damn prongs out."

Ari stooped down and pulled a very stunned and disoriented James off the floor. Before setting James in a chair, Ari yanked out the two sharp Taser prongs lodged into the scientist's back.

James felt no pain; however, his mind was lost in a hurricane of tragedies—his niece's and aunt's needless murders, the cancer that threatened his family, the viral pandemic that had been unleashed on the world.

"So you are a terrorist as well!"

Dr. Weisman clasped his hands together. "Now, James, if you will open your mind, I'm sure you will begin to see my reasons."

"I will never understand how a man could take it upon himself to kill millions of innocent people," James shot back.

Dr. Weisman continued unabashed. "Billions of people, not millions. Now hear me out. This is a precise culling. The virus has been designed to be both potent and effective, but it doesn't infect everyone. It only targets those transgenic humans with the cancer-proof genes."

"How did you make a virus that only infects those people?" interrupted James.

"The secret to the virus' specificity lies in the transgenic genes themselves. When the cancer-proof genes are inserted into human cells, they produce specific proteins that are then expressed on the outside of the cell. These proteins act as a docking station for our virus. The virus can then bind to the cell and slip in discreetly. So you see, only the cancer-proof humans can be infected. From our studies, we believe that within the month all cancer-proof humans on this planet will be dead. The people of GeneFirm, including you and your family, people living in third world countries, as well as the few remaining free conceptions, will be spared. If you don't have the genes, the virus is completely harmless."

James said, with more than a hint of sarcasm in his voice, "What about Linda's vaccine? Will it not stop the virus?"

"Linda and her lab haven't produced a functional

vaccine yet. They've been locked in the lower level labs since this morning. I'm sure they would all be very surprised to see that a vaccine was released to the public. No, what we released today wasn't a vaccine at all, but just the second phase of our plan. They will soon find out that each vaccine contains our active virus."

"Oh my God," James whispered, shaking his head at Dr. Weisman's incredible madness.

"But even if someone managed to make a vaccine, there isn't just one virus out there. Right now the superflu spreading around the globe is actually caused by thirteen different versions of the virus. Therefore, in order to stop it you would need thirteen vaccines. Each of these viruses is an unstoppable killing machine; they make smallpox look like the common cold."

"You unbelievable bastard," James whispered, realizing the difficulty of trying to reverse what Dr. Weisman had done.

Dr. Weisman shot James a look of disdain.

"All influenza viruses have two proteins on their surface, hemagglutinin and neuraminidase. In the past, when flu vaccines were made, different versions of these two antigenic markers were used to bolster the immunological memory. Originally there were only sixteen types of hemagglutinin and nine types of neuraminidase. We have created multiple completely novel types of each, so the cancer-proof population is facing a molecular attack on multiple fronts. Each virus is a deadly sucker punch to the immune system. No one will realize that there are multiple viruses floating around until it's too late."

James stared down at the dark wooden floor. A sense of helplessness swept over him; Dr. Weisman had engineered a plague to end all plagues.

The CEO placed a reassuring hand on James' slumped shoulders. "There is no reason to mourn, James. I have assured that our children will live on for centuries to come. In a year, a new frontier will once again be opened. Trees and grasslands will crack through cement; the skies will return to blue and the rising oceans will recede. Perhaps even global warming will halt and the temperatures will crawl back down to some degree of normality."

"It won't work! I told you I called Homeland Health Care. They are on their way here and will soon put an end to all of this."

Dr. Weisman laughed. "James, you are a comedian. Thanks to our source inside the H.H. I knew about your phone call minutes after you made it. We are all too aware of the government agents headed our way."

After he finished speaking, an odd silence fell over the room as James sat dazed and outwitted. The hush was finally broken by the chirp of Ari's phone behind them.

"Speak of the devil. James, it's your lucky day. Your government has come to save you!"

The Homeland Security agents were led away by a tall black woman to Dr. Weisman's office, while Marnoy went with the hulking security guard to collect DNA samples from a list of employees born around the same time as Dr. Logan.

Mac had lucked out with the least intimidating

escort, an extremely old man named Dr. Paradee. The doctor had volunteered to help him access the electronic DNA sequencing records. Mac liked the crumbling old man, with his watery blue eyes and dry creased skin, who had introduced himself with all the warmth of a long-lost grandfather.

The two men had just entered the expansive cafeteria when shrill alarms filled the room. Both men nearly jumped out of their skin at the unexpected noise. A few seconds later, the alarm ceased and the lights went out, leaving the room bathed only in the sunlight. Red emergency lights started to glow around the room and an electronic female voice emanated from speakers in the wall.

"The quarantine breach alarm system has been activated. Repeat, the quarantine breach alarm system has been activated. Stay calm and remain where you are until further notice."

As the woman's voice finished speaking, tremors began to shake the room.

"Earthquake!" yelled a frightened Mac.

Dr. Paradee gave a hearty laugh. "Earthquake in Texas? Now I've heard everything. It's just the storm shields going up."

Dr. Paradee pointed at the glass wall and Mac saw a solid piece of metal inching upward, blocking their outside view. The wall extended until all sunlight had been choked out of the building, leaving only the blood red glow of emergency lights. Mac looked over at Dr. Paradee, covered in shadows, the old man's facial expression obscured from view.

"What is the quarantine alarm system?" Mac asked.

Dr. Paradee took a few steps toward Mac as rows of LED lights in the ceiling switched on, restoring light. The new metal barrier was making Mac feel a little claustrophobic; he felt like he had just been entombed to serve in the afterlife as some pharaoh's unlucky slave.

"The quarantine alarms go off when the building's security system detects exposure of noxious or lethal materials. Nine times out of ten it's a false alarm. Earlier this morning we had a quarantine breach in one of our labs, which has been locked down since. This alarm could be related to that one."

The security scanners next to all the doors in the room had turned to an unfriendly red. They were locked in.

"What kind of security measures are we talking about?" Mac questioned.

Dr. Paradee shuffled his feet. "Well, for starters, you've become acquainted with our storm shields." He pointed toward the vast wall of metal that had risen from the ground. "Second, a quarantine breach results in all exits, doors, and vents being sealed. I hope that virus wasn't able to escape, eh?"

Mac shook his head. "Escape? Are we in danger?"

"Possibly."

"Is there any way out?"

"No. My security clearance won't work on any of these doors now."

"So you're telling me we're stuck in here?"

The old man nodded his head slowly. "Yes, high-level clearance is needed to get around the building now. I'm afraid I don't have that. We will just have to wait until it is over."

"How long will it take?" Mac scoffed.

"Sometimes minutes. Sometimes days. About a decade ago, some poor bastard got quarantined in the primate lab for an entire week. By the time we got him out he had developed a disturbing relationship with one of the chimps. So don't get any ideas, Agent Macdonald. I'm a married man."

Despite the dire situation, Mac still had to laugh at that one. It was a nervous laugh, however.

"If the virus did get out, the vaccine will protect us, right?"

There was a long pause of silence after Mac asked this. Dr. Paradee stared off at nothing in particular while Mac waited for an answer. Eventually the doctor shook his head like he was coming out of a dream.

"What? Aw, yes, the vaccine. Yes, we're perfectly safe. But precautions are precautions."

The doctor's response did not instill much faith in Mac, who breathed out in frustration, shrugged his shoulders, and then lowered himself into a nearby chair at a lunch table.

"Good idea. No reason for us to be standing around; my feet are killing me," Dr. Paradee said.

Mac's eyes wandered around the room but stopped when he saw snacks over by the buffet area. He stood back up and patted his belly.

"Well, as long as we're stuck, I don't think anyone will mind if we have something to eat, right? I'm starving."

34

It had all happened so fast. One minute Marnoy had been walking down the corridor with that Godzilla of a guard, the next minute he was on his back in a dark room.

The back of his head burned in pain; he tenderly rubbed the knot developing there. It felt like he had been tossed down a flight of stairs or hit by a small vehicle. He sat up and scanned the room, finding nothing remarkable. It looked like your typical break room; there was a table, sink, coffeemaker, refrigerator, microwave, and even a toaster.

Marnoy had been following the guard when some kind of fire alarm went off. With his hands clamped over his ears, he looked at the guard in confusion. The lights shut off, temporarily plunging them into darkness. A second later a single red light on the ceiling cast the hallway in hazy red. The guard had disappeared; Marnoy looked in disbelief at the spot where the guard should have been. How could a man as big as a fridge just disappear? He heard a sound behind him and managed to spout off the words "What the—" before something was smashed over his head.

The agent slid a hand down to the holster on his waist and was embarrassed to find that his Taser was gone. After a minute, he gathered himself and clambered to his feet. First he checked the door and confirmed that he was locked in. The weight of the situation started to press itself upon him; there was something big going on here. What would push a company to commit such a desperate act?

Marnoy didn't have the answer, but it was easy enough to conclude that this was his big chance. Maybe he could get promoted or—even better—get a job with Homeland Security, a career that had remained out of his grasp until now. This was the opportunity he had been waiting for; but first he had to get out of that room.

The office doors swung open and Savira and Ari strutted up the stairs. Two intimidating men in suits followed them. James almost cheered with joy; the government had come to the rescue. At first, he was tempted to jump up and shout out what was going on, that GeneFirm was part of a misguided terrorist plot to destroy the civilized world. But he had to admit that sounded crazy. For now he would have to wait and see what happened.

Savira strode over the hardwood floor toward them, but it wasn't her normal catwalk strut. She was looking a little unbalanced, wobbling as she approached the desk. James could easily see that the woman was not feeling well.

Savira led the agents over to the desk and presented the men to Dr. Weisman. "These two are from Homeland Security." She paused to suppress a cough. A wheezing could be heard deep in her chest. "They would like to ask you a few questions."

Dr. Weisman smiled, his perfect set of teeth gleamed in the sun. "Of course."

The shorter agent nodded. "Your are under arrest for suspicion of conspiring to intentionally engineer humans that are susceptible to cancer and the fraudulent falsification of government medical records."

"Oh my," Dr. Weisman said, rubbing his chin. "I can assure the two of you that this company has done nothing illegal."

"He's lying!" interrupted James. "GeneFirm is behind the viral pandemic, too! You have to sto—"

The agents, distracted by the sudden outburst, didn't notice Dr. Weisman's fingers discreetly pressing his computer's screen. Instantly the rest of James' words were drowned out by the piercing scream of an alarm.

The intercom in the ceiling squawked to life. James recognized the familiar voice of the quarantine breach alarm. After the voice had subsided, the walls of the room began to vibrate softly; far below, the storm shield had begun to climb its way upward.

Dr. Weisman had tripped the alarm. James felt his

heart sink at realization that there would be no escape for any of them.

"What's going on?" the short agent asked.

"The alarm means there has been a breach in our security. The virus could be loose inside this building."

"Are we in danger?" asked the tall agent.

"Simply put, yes," Dr. Weisman said. He stood up slowly and looked up at the blue sky above him. The agents followed his gaze upward.

Then it happened. The agents grunted in unison at the electric crack of Tasers sprung to life. Behind them, Ari and Savira were both holding Taser guns; wires were stuck into the backs of the agents now convulsing on the ground. Ari and Savira whipped out plastic zip-ties and proceeded to bind the agent's arms and legs together.

"Stop it!" James jumped out of his seat. Ari quickly turned toward him with another Taser in his hand and pointed it right at James' chest.

35

In the dark security room, bathed in the glow of the video monitors, Ed was looking puzzled. The screen showed the break room where he had locked up the black H.H. agent.

The room was empty. That is, almost empty; mysteriously, the agent's clothes were lying in a pile on the floor like the man had evaporated into thin air. The thought of a naked and angry government agent prowling the corridors of the building made him cringe. The boss would surely not like that. A quick scan of the screens from other parts of the building gave him no clue as to where the guy could have disappeared to. Without security access, the agent wasn't going very far, he assured himself. Dr. Weisman had been very specific about that; right now only Ed and Dr. Weisman's thumbprints could open the doors locked by the quarantine.

"Where the hell is he?"

Ed had to investigate. Before leaving the room, he went over to a large safe built into the wall. He placed his thumb to the touch pad and the door popped open; inside the safe was an assortment of guns. This was his secret stash of contraband weapons, barrels shining heavy and black. After he strapped several of them to his belt, he walked out into the empty hallway, feeling strong and deadly with the weapons at his side. He thumbed one of the gun's heavy handles; its power surged through him like electricity. With a smile, he took off at a swift jog.

With all the employees locked down by quarantine, the corridors were an eerie quiet. Ed's black boots slapped the ground. Periodically, he would stop at a thick glass door and unlock it by pressing his thumb against the touch pad. As he approached the break room, he slowed down to a walk, catching his breath. Eventually, he came to a halt in front of the door. He used one of his meaty fingers to pop open the holster at his side. With his left hand aiming the gun at the door, he placed his right thumb on the door's scanner, which instantly chirped as the door slid aside. The soft gurgle of running water greeted him as he cautiously entered the room. There was a slight movement in the corner of his eye. He whipped the gun to the right but found himself aiming at a tiny waterfall running down from the overflowing sink. Ed's eyes scanned the rest of the room. There was no one there; nothing was out of the ordinary, except for the lump of clothes in front of the sink. He hesitantly approached the sink, kicking the clothes with his foot, as if the agent was the victim of some form of magical witchcraft. Ed's boot came away shiny with wetness. He raised an eyebrow and bent down to examine them closer. Not only were they wet, they were also smeared with dirt or something.

"What the hell?" Ed's fingers were stained with what looked like black ink. He inspected the sink further; curiously it, too, was slimed with the black substance. Ed was baffled. He didn't know what to make of the disappearing agent, the mysterious black mess, and the wet clothes. He walked out of the room at a loss for words. The agent had escaped and he needed to find him quick.

Only Dr. Weisman could have let the man out, but that was unlikely. As he reached for his phone to call the CEO, he heard it—directly behind him, a small sniffle, a sucking of air. In a flash of movement he spun around, his gun drawn. To his further bewilderment, he found himself aiming the gun down a long silent hallway. No sign of the disappearing agent.

Ed scratched his chin. "Fuck me," he said, embarrassed by his jumpiness. A feeling of uneasiness slipped through his guts like a large worm. Fearful for the safety of Dr. Weisman, he put in his earpiece and called his boss' office. After several rings, there was no answer. His uneasiness was now full-blown fear; things were not going according to plan. The thunder of his boots picked up again as he broke into a full-on sprint toward the executive offices.

The triangular tips of the ascending storm shields finally came into view. They continued climbing until only a pinpoint of sunlight was visible above, replacing the blue skies with gunmetal gray.

Bathed in shadow and the red glow of the emergency lights, James shuddered. Ari had bound his legs and arms with duct tape to the chair he was sitting in.

When the regular lights came on, James saw Dr. Weisman standing over the two bound H.S. agents. The agents looked back with fear.

"No need to worry about arresting me, because, regrettably, you both will soon be dead, along with most of the—"

"We are going to put you away for a long time," the short agent interrupted.

Dr. Weisman looked at Ari. "Son, use more of that tape, please."

Ari proceeded to wrap tape around the short agent's mouth; the man squirmed in protest, but eventually his yells were muffled, and he lay there as a mute observer.

"That's much better," Dr. Weisman said. "Now, before you interrupted me, I was about to explain that the vaccine you received was actually filled with an active form of the superflu virus. So you will soon be dead, along with every government employee who has received it."

The agents' eyes opened wider. Their cries were unintelligible, underneath the tape covering their mouths.

Dr. Weisman went on, "The vaccine will decimate the government, leaving no one between my virus and the billions of people it will infect. I have just sent out an emergency message to the Department of Homeland Health Care that a new mutant version of the virus has escaped within these walls and many of our employees have fallen terribly ill. I also explained that, unfortunately, four of their agents have been exposed and are now under our watchful care. There will be no one coming to your rescue."

At that moment, a thought occured to James: "Weren't you born with the cancer-proof genes? You should be vulnerable to the virus like everyone else!"

Dr. Weisman sighed and eased himself back into his chair slowly. "Yes, unfortunately for me, I was born with the genes. But in our new future, we will need a strong leader—"

"What? Are you serious?"

"Imagine a world where fantastic men could pass on the best parts of themselves to their children—or even better, just re-create themselves as a clones. What would have happened if Alexander the Great had the ability to duplicate himself over and over again? But to answer your question, I am immune to the virus. I had a vaccine made for me and me only."

"You're a narcissistic sociopath! Do you even hear the words that are coming out of your mouth?"

"If other cancer-proof individuals survive, they will want their children to be cancer-proof, too. I can trust myself not to spread any more diseased genes into future generations; I cannot bring myself to trust anyone else." As he said that, he glanced toward Ari and Savira, both of whom turned their heads shyly away.

"You're out of your mind. You have no right to decide who lives and dies," James pleaded, his voice breaking. He turned around and faced Savira, who was looking pale; her feverish skin had begun to glisten with sweat.

"And what about you, Savira? You weren't born here at GeneFirm. That means you have the cancer-proof genes, too. Are you ready to die for Dr. Weisman's crazy plan?"

Savira gave an unconvincing nod and then burst into a violent coughing fit. She did her best to regain her composure. The black voids of her eyes avoided James.

Dr. Weisman nodded sadly. "We did plan to spare Savira, but our quarantine was not effective in preventing the spread of the flu virus. I know that she will face her death courageously. Now"—He pointed to the agents bound on the floor—"Ari, why don't you go lock up our visitors in one of the boardrooms? Make sure they're tied up tight."

Ari bent down and grabbed the feet of the two agents; with surprising ease he dragged them toward the door like bags of trash. He stamped down the stairs—the thud, thud, thud of the agents' heads smacking each step made James cringe.

36

After Ed sprinted off and disappeared around the corner, a very peculiar thing happened. The wall outside the break room breathed a sigh of relief. Then the wall began to melt and ripple as colors washed together until, miraculously, the outline of a man formed. The colors condensed together to form hands and feet, nipples, a shriveled scrotum, and then finally, an entire body.

That was a close one, thought Marnoy as he stepped away from the wall and rubbed his cold hands up and down the goose bumps on his arms. He took a much-needed breath and sighed. For the last fifteen minutes, he had been pressed up against the break room wall, taking only very shallow breaths to cut down on any movement that might give him away. When the big guard had unexpectedly entered the break room, he had reflexively jumped, almost giving away his location. For an incredibly suspenseful moment, the two men had stared directly at one another. Luckily for him, he was able to control his skin for just long enough. When the guard was looking at his clothes, he had managed to slip out into the hallway. He was impressed with himself; even after all these unpracticed years, he was still able to pull off some decent camouflage.

He decided to follow the security guard and see where it would take him. Naked, unarmed, and freezing, Marnoy was in a precarious position, but he had no choice. He took off, a nude blur streaking down the hallway. Clothing wasn't an option, his camouflage being his only defense at the moment.

It had been years since he had used his ability, and by doing so he had inadvertently opened up a floodgate of memories. Thoughts entered his head like long-lost enemies, tearing open old wounds that he had not felt in decades. His skin color began to pulse blood red.

He remembered the cold sweat of a night terror, waking up screaming and stricken with fear. But no one came to check on him. Then he heard the sound of voices stalking into his room like battling ghosts. In horror, he found himself rolling out of bed. Down the hallway he tiptoed, the wood floor creaking beneath him. He heard breaking glass, the familiar cries, shouting hatreds, but he still pressed on, some invisible force drawing him closer to danger. As he moved outside of the door there was a loud grunt, followed by a bang as something heavy hit the ground.

He remembered how he cringed at the sound of a woman's weeping. The bedroom door was slightly cracked; a vertical slit of light spilled out, cutting a line of light down the middle of his face. Still drawn to the room, he forced himself to peek inside. The large mirror over the dresser had been punched, turning the glass into a spider's web of cracks. His mother lay motionless on her back with a dark red line across her forehead. Blood. At the sight of his battered mother, he had cried out, instantly clamping his hand over his mouth. Suddenly, the bedroom became too quiet.

Did they hear him?

He backed up farther into the darkness of the hallway, kicked off his shorts and threw them behind the couch. His dark skin became even darker, blending into the shadows. The bedroom door swung open and he held back a cry. The outline of his father against the light of the room stood stout and blocky in the doorway. His father's skin throbbed dark red, a color that he associated with his father's drunken fits of rage. The scared young boy held his breath, keeping completely still in the shadows. "Alex! Are you there, boy? Show yourself!"

Then to his horror, it started to happen. Too scared to control it any longer, first his hands started throbbing yellow, and then it spread inward, making him instantly noticeable. He had turned into a flashing light at the end of the hall; his dad recognized his naked son instantly. The boy pressed up against the wall with tears, wet warmth flooding down his cheeks.

"You little bastard," his father growled as he moved toward him.

Marnoy shook his head clear of the memory, bringing him back to the silent hallways of GeneFirm. The feeling of inadequacy and terror lingered for a moment; his skin still rippled with color. The dark memories receded like a dense fog as he tried to focus on the present. Soon he disappeared from sight again, leaving only the slight specter of his outline gliding down the corridor.

Marnoy reasoned that if they had attacked and locked him up, no doubt they had tried to do the same with Mac and the H.S. agents. He bet this guard would lead him straight to them.

37

■r. Weisman walked past James, looking intently at the TV screen: flashing images of hospitals wrapped in yellow caution tape, orange hazmat suits, and truck beds filled to the brim with body bags looking like black cocoons. The scene then switched to Chinese riot police on a gray city street and images of scrawny men throwing glass bottles and rocks that smashed harmlessly into bulletproof shields. Another scene followed, this one of an old homeless lady, dressed in rags and squatting on the street, coughing up blood into her leathery hands.

James found his eyes glued to the unfolding vision of death and chaos. For a brief period, he watched the fruits of Dr. Weisman's cruel labor, the terrible sights filling him with nausea. Turning back to Dr. Weisman, he yelled, "So what's your plan?

Are you going to rule over mankind with an endless line of clones?"

"That's not a bad plan. But thanks to you, I might be around for a much longer period of time. You and your wife, my lovely geniuses, have given me a way to potentially live forever."

"Excuse me?"

"That wonderful little viral vector you two created, so potent it can deliver inheritable copies of the cancer-proof genes to every cell in the body—obviously we will never use it for that purpose, but with a little modification, think about the possibilities. What if we inserted into your miracle virus a recipe of genes that could make a man immortal?"

"Please, there are no such genes."

"Oh no?"

"There is no way that would work. Aging is much more complicated than that."

"Perhaps, but it won't stop me from trying."

Dr. Weisman reached into his desk drawer and pulled out a syringe filled with clear fluid.

"What is that?"

"Exactly what you think it is, the impossible. In mouse models, this virus eliminates the aging process. We are now ready for the second phase of this trial. A human subject."

"You're lying . . ." But James had a feeling he wasn't. His palms became sweaty at the thought of his scientific contribution to this disaster. The last ten years of his life had been devoted to a false idea; he was a pawn in a mass murdering CEO's quest for immortality. The word "betrayal" reverberated around in his head.

"James, it is decision time. Are you for our cause or against it? A man of your caliber will be useful in the post-viral reconstruction."

"Never!" bellowed James, his chest burning. "I will never support what you have done here."

"You should really wait to make up your mind until after I tell you the consequences."

"I will never help you."

Dr. Weisman hung his head and rubbed his eyes. When he stood up, James was acutely aware that he had the syringe in his hand.

"That is unfortunate. You realize we cannot allow you to live. My role in the viral pandemic must be kept secret. However, since I cannot stomach the thought of wasting such a wonderful asset like you, before you die I will give you the opportunity to be a part of one last experiment. It seems only right considering you helped make this virus. This will be your final contribution to that great abstraction—science!"

Dr. Weisman grew closer, the menacing syringe poised to strike.

"Last chance?"

"Just do it, you bastard."

Dr. Weisman plunged the needle deep into James' shoulder.

38

When Pat woke up, everything was sore. Even muscles he had never known existed were tight and cramping. A breeze drifted lightly over his skin and there was a gentle rustle of leaves above him, sounding like newspapers blowing down a street. Panic surged through him as his mind recalled why he was lying in the middle of the woods.

The viral pandemic. Modest. The escape. But where was Modest? They stopped to rest for a while and he had fallen asleep.

"Modest?" yelled Pat. No sound of her. Rising to his feet, he scanned the area around him. Panic boiled up and out of him when he discovered that he was alone. The spot where Modest had sat down across from him was empty, nothing but a thin Modest-sized area of matted-down grass.

She had left him, he thought.

Not able to believe that she was gone, he crumpled to the ground and bowed his head. To his surprise, he found himself on the verge of tears. The idea of being alone, maybe even dying alone, was now very real. Pat admitted that he did not feel well. He assumed the virus had already infected him and he was dying slowly. His temperature had to be high. He was sweating bullets. His breathing was labored.

In the fetal position underneath the tree, he waited for death to come. In his delirium he just lay there and said her name, as if she were curled up right next to him.

"Modest," he whimpered. "Modest."

"What?" yelled an irritated voice.

Pat stopped rocking and sat up looking confused. "Modest?"

"What the hell do you want, Pat?"

"Where are you?"

"Over here."

Pat saw a pale stick of an arm emerge from behind a tree about twenty yards away.

Embarrassment replaced mortal fear.

"What are you doing over there?" Pat asked.

"I'm taking a shit! What does it look like I'm doing?"

"Oh," said Pat, a little grossed out. "What are you using to wipe?"

"These leaves, of course. The skinny arm dipped down into a pile of foliage next to the tree. Pat looked away, his face getting very red.

"Why didn't you answer when I first called you? I thought you had left me."

A laugh floated to him on the forest's air. "Because I was pooping and I didn't want you to know about it," Modest replied.

A minute later, Modest appeared from behind the huge oak tree. She was still pulling up her skimpy white pants as she came back to where he was. "You ready to keep moving? It looks like there is another storm coming," Modest said as she looked off in the distance. "We might be screwed if that's a warming storm."

Pat looked and saw an ominous mass of darkness heading their way over the tree line.

"I have to tell you something."

Modest rolled her eyes. "Damnit, what now?"

"I think I'm infected. You should leave me behind."

"Whatever. You're not infected."

"I have a fever. It's hard to breathe. I'm all sore."

She placed one of her hands on his forehead, catching him off guard. He was excited to be touched by her, but, on second thought, she hadn't washed those hands.

"You don't have a fever. You're hot because you've been lying in the sun. It's hard to breathe because you're fat and we've been hiking all day. Finally, you're sore because we've been forced to exercise like dogs for the last couple days at that shit hole of a retreat."

"Oh, that all makes sense," Pat said, feeling stupid, wishing that Modest was still touching him.

"We've got to hurry. How much farther did you say it was?"

Walking after her, Pat thought for a second. "I

don't know for sure, I haven't been there in years. Probably a couple more miles if we keep following this road."

"So you used to live at this GeneFirm place? I've never heard of it."

"GeneFirm? The company that cured cancer? AIDS? Diabetes? You've never heard of it?"

"Cured cancer, huh? That was like a century ago, ancient history. Why would I know that?"

Pat looked at her incredulously. "You never learned about it in school? It seems like you learn about GeneFirm in every history and science class starting from the second grade."

"I was never a big fan of school," said Modest, shrugging. "So your dad was a scientist or something?"

"No. My mom is a researcher there."

They heard a car coming down the road. The two retreated back into the trees and kept walking.

"When's the last time you went home?"

"I haven't been back there in eight years. Not since my sister died."

"What happened to her?"

"Suicide. She had been really sick."

Modest wrapped an arm around Pat and gave him a squeeze. "I'm so sorry."

"After my sister died, my mom forced me to leave. Sent me to a private school in the city, separated from all my family and friends. The whole thing sent my mom over the deep end, honestly. When she came to visit me, she would rant about how my sister's death was a conspiracy or something. She claimed that my sister had developed cancer, which is impossible, and that her suicide was just a cover-up. When I left, she made me promise to never come back."

"Wow. So you haven't been back since?"

Pat did not have time to answer; he was staring at the road with a look of panic on his face. When Modest saw it, they both dashed behind the nearest tree and froze. They pressed up against the sandpaper-rough bark, waiting.

It was a white van. Its two passengers were wearing cowboy hats. As it passed by them, the van slowed down almost to a crawl.

Pat let out a little squeak.

"Those cowboy assholes," Modest seethed.

To their relief, the van picked up speed again and continued on down the road.

"You think they're looking for us?" Pat asked.

"Let's just keep our distance from the road from now on," Modest said.

The two walked in silence until the van disappeared behind a bend.

"Anyway, enough about my sad life. What's your story?"

Modest sighed. "I drink too much, I'm bipolar, and I was having an affair with Slate."

"Oh . . ." Pat said, not knowing how to respond. He felt a surge of jealousy when she said Slate's name.

"Car!" Again they jumped behind a tree and crouched down. Pat found himself staring face-to-face with Modest as they pressed closely together to fit behind the tree's trunk. From this close, he could smell her; not a girly perfume scent, but the smell of sweat and pheromones, just a few degrees shy of the musty smell of sex. She leaned out from behind the tree to watch the car as it zipped by. Pat was busy staring at her. To him, she was skinny pale perfection.

"Is it the van?"

She shook her head. After the car was gone, she turned and looked at him from behind her long pink eyelashes, which were almost translucent in the sunlight.

"Okay, it's gone. Let's go."

"I love your eyes. They're beautiful," Pat blurted out, shocked at his own directness. His face grew red again.

"Well, that makes one of us. You can thank my asshole grandfather, Skull Fucker."

"Skull Fucker! Your grandfather was Skull Fucker."

Modest popped up, swiftly walking back toward the road. He quickly chased after, eager to hear more.

"I can't believe it! I loved Skull Fucker in college. That man is a death metal legend. I have every album."

"Good for you. I would be excited by that fact if I got any of the royalties, but since I didn't, let's just pretend I didn't bring him up. I'm not his biggest fan."

"So he had this done to you? How?" Pat asked.

"Not me, exactly. He had his daughter, my mother, genetically engineered while it was still legal, before they banned that shit. My mom wanted her child to look like her, so what did she do? She had a free conception. Thanks, bitch. . . ."

"So you are a natural birth? Jesus, that's dangerous. And you're not happy with how you look?"

"Look at me, Pat. I'm a freak—thanks to my family. What they did is a crime. You know how hard high school is when you've got pink hair and cat eyes? I'm cursed."

A lump formed in Pat's throat. She was obviously sensitive about this topic.

"I can imagine. If it's any consolation, I think you're beautiful. But I'm sorry you had to deal with that."

"Thanks, but I don't care. Don't be such a sensitive pussy."

The words stung Pat like a baseball to the ear. He shut up, hoping to sidestep any more of Modest's wrath.

Pat and Modest kept on following the road, trudging through the woods, on the run from a virus, their bitter memories, and an overwhelming sense of disillusionment.

39

James' shoulder was still burning from the needle when Ari reappeared at the top of the stairs. As the giant approached he yelled from across the room, "Father, we need to talk!"

Dr. Weisman looked up with concerned interest. "About what?"

"I need the vaccine. I can't let her die!" he said, coming to a halt by Savira's side. Thick veins coursed over the top of his hands as he cracked his knuckles together.

James noticed that Ari now had a gun as well as a Taser stuck into the waistband of his pants. The gun must have been stolen from one of the agents. Ari almost stroked the weapon as he stared down his father.

Looking slightly hurt, Dr. Weisman sat down and crossed his legs before addressing his son.

"Savira agreed to this plan. It's unfortunate that she will die, but the vaccine was made for me alone. Besides, look at her. It is too late."

This time it was Savira who spoke. "I never had any intention of dying for this 'cause.' I didn't work my ass off my whole life to die like this. Give us the vaccine!"

The expression on Dr. Weisman's face didn't change. With a calm demeanor, he merely leaned back in his chair. His slender lips smirked. Something told James that Dr. Weisman had been half expecting this treachery all along.

"And you are going to help her, are you?" Dr. Weisman asked, while nodding toward Ari.

His son pulled out the gun and pointed it at him. Ari nodded.

"There's no reason for her to die. Please . . ."

Dr. Weisman stood up from his desk. "I'm sorry. There's nothing you can do. I had the real vaccines destroyed after I received them, anyway. There is no turning back. Accept that."

"I don't believe you!" screamed Savira, who immediately burst into another coughing fit.

"The answer is no."

"I'm sorry to hear that," Ari said, tucking the gun back into his pants and pulling out the Taser. Unceremoniously, he shot the Taser straight into Dr. Weisman's chest. The clicking of electricity filled the room. A shocked Dr. Weisman cried out, crashing to the floor, where he jerked violently as wave after wave of electricity coursed through him. After a few seconds, Ari let go of the trigger and Dr. Weisman lay there motionless.

"Give us security clearance so we can go get the vaccine."

"Not a chance, son. You're wasting your time."

The sound of the Taser came to life again as Ari held down the trigger. The old man convulsed on the ground, but this time Ari went for a few seconds longer. When he stopped, the room was quiet except for the hard breathing of Dr. Weisman. With hurt in his voice, he softly said, "You are going to ruin everything."

Ari ignored his father's pleas, electrocuting him again. Dr. Weisman's body writhed on the floor, his face contorted in pain.

James couldn't bear to watch this go on any longer. "You're going to kill him!"

Ari held the trigger down until the Taser ran out of juice. When the electric rattle stopped, the room went dead quiet. Dr. Weisman lay motionless. Ari walked over to the lifeless body and squatted down. He pressed his two fingers into his father's neck, looking for a pulse.

"Fuck," Ari whispered. His massive frame hovered over the body. Unexpectedly, Ari stooped down, pinching Dr. Weisman's nose and puffing into his mouth. For the next five minutes Ari pumped furiously on his father's chest. James could hear Weisman's ribs breaking like toothpicks underneath the powerful chest compressions. Finally Ari stopped. Huffing and puffing for air, he leaned back on his haunches and rubbed one hand across his face, which was red and puffy with tears, wiping a trail of shiny snot from his nose to his cheek. The monster was sobbing.

Savira walked up and put a hand on Ari's shoulder.

She bent down and slid something out of her pocket. Grabbing Ari's hand, she placed the object there, closing his fingers around it.

Realizing what was about to happen, James cried out. In Ari's hand, a knife blade flashed in the light as he brought it down to the base of his father's thumb and proceeded to saw it off. There was a final crunch of bone and it was over. Ari stood up, dismembered digit in hand.

When James looked back down at Dr. Weisman's mutilated hand and the pool of blood spreading around it, he became sick. He leaned over in his chair and forcefully contributed his fair share of bodily fluids to the now-soiled floor.

40

Mac finished checking every door in the room and, as Dr. Paradee predicted, they all were locked. He returned to the cafeteria table where Dr. Paradee was slouched in a chair looking completely at ease. The old quack didn't seem to be worrying at all. The idea that there might be a deadly virus floating around somewhere within this building had Mac rattled even though he was vaccinated against it.

On the table in front of Dr. Paradee were a couple bags of baked potato chips and a few bottles of water sweaty with condensation.

Dr. Paradee took a sip from the water bottle in his hand.

"Agent Macdonald, stop being such a pain in the ass and come sit down and relax for a little bit. You pacing back and forth won't accomplish anything but exhausting yourself and annoying me. There is no way out of this room."

"How long will we have to wait?" Mac asked.

"They won't open up a quarantined section of the building until they know there is no longer any risk. So I'd say within twenty-four hours they will either give us an all clear or keep us here longer if we happen to get sick."

The doctor's last words were somewhat ominous to Mac, echoing off the glass walls of the cavernous room around them, leaving the two of them in hushed silence.

"Sit down. We are far removed from the dangerous parts of this building. You are much safer than you would be back in the city anyway."

"My family is in the city."

Dr. Paradee's face softened. "Sorry to hear that. I'm sure they are perfectly safe, wherever they are."

"I hope so," Mac said dejectedly.

Dr. Paradee nodded slowly. "I know so."

"If I'm stuck in here for too long, they are going to worry to death. I just wish my phone had reception so I could let them know."

Hearing the agent talk about his family made Dr. Paradee depressed.

The sudden sound of a lock beeping and a door whooshing open alerted both men in time to see two people walking through the doorway. Dr. Paradee jumped up and pushed Mac aside, limping toward the two with surprising speed.

Confused, Mac yelled after him, "What's going on?"

The doctor ignored Mac's question and headed

straight for Ari and Savira. "What are you two doing?" Dr. Paradee bellowed. "You're not supposed
to be here!"

"There has been a change of plans."

"Ari, what the hell are you talking about?"

"I need the vaccine," Ari said, nodding toward
Savira. "For her."

"Ari, you know that can't happen."

"Bullshit! It can and it will! You can tell me where
the vaccine is or I can make you tell me."

"Are you threatening me?" laughed Dr. Paradee.

Mac slowly inched toward them, trying to listen
to what they were saying.

Ari gritted his long white teeth. "Suit yourself,"
he said as he pulled out the Taser and aimed it at a
suddenly very nervous Dr. Paradee.

When Ari pulled out the weapon, Mac took off at
a sprint toward them. He armed himself with his
Taser. "Stop it right there!"

Savira started coughing violently. She clutched on
to Ari's shoulder to keep herself from falling to the
floor. Both men briefly glanced at her. The cough
sounded awful to Mac.

"You hear that?" Ari said to Mac. "She is infected
and so are you. So why don't you do yourself a favor and help me find the vaccine?"

Mac's eyes widened, almost popping out in fear.
"What do you mean, I'm infected? I received the
vaccine earlier today."

"That vaccine was a fake. You were injected with
the live virus, so you're infected whether you know
it or not."

"A fake? Live virus? I don't understan—"

Ari roared, *"Dr. Paradee is going to tell us where
the* real *vaccine is because you, like me, need to find
it very soon."*

Mac turned to the old man and asked, "Is any of
this true?"

Dr. Paradee nodded his head reluctantly. "I'm
afraid so. But there is no vaccine—it was destroyed."

Mac's eyes settled on the woman. She did look
sick. Her mane of black hair was still tossed in front
of her face from her last bout of coughing. As if to
confirm his suspicions, she doubled over and began
to forcefully cough again.

"There is no vaccine!" Dr. Paradee yelled again.
"There is no stopping it!"

When Savira finished coughing, she stared down
into her cupped hands, now dotted with bright red
droplets of blood. "Fuck," she whispered as she held
her hands in front of her shocked face.

In a flurry of movement, an utterly horrified Mac
stepped forward and grabbed Dr. Paradee by the
collar.

Ari spoke: "This man is one of the masterminds
behind this virus. Will you help me?"

"Damn right I will!" Mac pulled Dr. Paradee
down to the ground. Leaning over him, he wagged
his fist in front of the doctor's face. "You bastard!
Where is the vaccine?"

"For the last time, it no longer exists. You don't
think Ari and Savira played a role in any of this? We
are all guilty."

Mac pointed his Taser at Ari again.

Calmly, Ari looked the agent in the eyes. "We're
on the same team now. I need the vaccine. You need

the vaccine. The sooner we find it, the better for the both of us."

Agent Macdonald hesitated for a moment. Slowly he lowered his Taser and put it back in its holster.

"I knew you would see things my way." Ari turned back to Dr. Paradee. "One last chance to start talking."

The doctor remained silent.

Ari nodded. "Alright then. Let's see if I can get you to talk."

"Ari, there is no vaccine anymore. I swear it," he pleaded.

Ari rolled his eyes. "So you keep telling me."

Without warning, the prongs of Ari's Taser sprung forth, straight through Dr. Paradee's white coat, lodging into the man's sternum. Mac winced as the harsh sound of electricity filled the room. Dr. Paradee shook around on the checkered floor until Ari released the trigger, leaving the doctor on his back, chest heaving up and down.

Dr. Paradee began to chuckle sinisterly between deep breaths. "You're pathetic, Ari!"

Savira leapt toward him, the sharp hammer of her high heels loudly striking the ground. She bent down next to Paradee and grabbed his tie, yanking it upward until his head lifted off the ground. "Tell me where the vaccine is or I will tear your eyes out!"

She followed this with a vicious backhanded slap across the doctor's face. Her grip on his tie was strangling him, his face turning dark purple. Before he could pass out, she let go of his tie and his head landed with a smack on the hard ground, making him groan painfully.

"Tell us where the vaccine is, damn it! Then this can stop," Mac begged.

Dr. Paradee was no longer responding. Ari leaned over the body and saw a dark wet spot spreading quickly across the front of the old man's slacks. He checked for a pulse.

"He's alive. Pissed himself though," Ari growled. "Well, shit! That was useless."

"What now?" Mac asked.

"We go downstairs to the labs and find the people who make vaccines."

Ari put one of Savira's slender arms around his shoulder and began to help her move toward the next locked door.

Mac's nerves were shaken. Not knowing what to do or who to believe, he followed them.

Ari removed a fleshy red stump from his pocket and pressed it to the touch pad. The door beeped and slid open. Mac swore to himself that the object looked suspiciously like a human thumb.

41

To Pat's relief, there had been no further sign of the white van. Storm clouds had swept in and a suffocating silence, thick as the humid air, had followed.

Pat and Modest had not spoken for a while now. He was too busy trying to breathe. Both were feeling the aftermath of the health retreat. The long hike had just exacerbated their blistered feet and angry hip flexors.

Modest was on the verge of throwing a tantrum. She toyed with the idea of lying down on the road in hopes a car would take the turn too quickly and end all of her suffering. Pat, shouting up ahead, interrupted her thoughts.

"What?" she yelled back.

"We're here! Look," he said, pointing down the road to a grandiose white guardhouse.

In front of the guardhouse was a circular fountain with a metal sculpture of a DNA double helix spiraling out of the water. This left little doubt in her mind that they had finally arrived at GeneFirm.

When they reached that guardhouse, Pat knocked a few times on the glass door. "Hello? Is anybody there?"

Nothing.

The door was unlocked and slid open easily. Cautiously, he stuck his head in and looked around. "Hello? Abe?"

The room was empty, but he could hear voices coming from above. Abe, the front gate guard, had worked there for decades. Pat assumed he still did.

"Wait outside for a second, I'll be right back," Pat said to Modest.

Against his better judgment, he made his way over to the stairs. He slowly ascended, with each step straining to hear the voices. The source of the noise was a large TV on the far wall. In front, Abe's familiar form, albeit a little skinnier and with a coat of gray hair, sat watching the blaring TV. His back was facing Pat.

No wonder he couldn't hear me, thought Pat. The volume on the television was on full blast.

"Abe," Pat said loudly.

Still the man did not hear him. Maybe he was asleep. Pat crossed the room and put a hand on the man's shoulder.

"Abe, wake up!" The man slumped over; this sudden movement made Pat jump back in surprise. There was a sinking feeling in Pat's stomach. His hands went up to his face in dread as he carefully stepped around to look at Abe from the front. A thin layer of blood caked everything—his white shirt, his hands, the TV remote. He was dead alright. Beneath his mouth, his chin was painted with dried blood, more black than red.

Pat felt weak. With his hands still cupped over his face he quickly went back down the stairs. If he didn't get fresh air immediately, he was going to be sick. He didn't make it. As soon as he stepped out of the guardhouse he spewed vomit onto the driveway. With his hands on his knees, he retched a few more times. When he straightened up, he found himself looking into Modest's shocked face.

"Are you okay?"

He nodded. "I've been better."

"What did you find?"

"Nothing." He paused. "Wait here a second, I forgot something."

He went back inside, leaving a stunned Modest outside. After a quick search, he was unable to find any keys to the small car parked at the back of the house. There was no way he was going back up the stairs to look for them. Instead he settled for hitting the red button that would open the gate. Immediately he heard the metal clanking of the great gates rumbling apart outside.

When he stepped back out, Modest was looking concerned.

"No one was there. Let's keeping going. Only a mile left."

"A mile!" she complained.

The trees in front of them arched above the road like a gaping mouth. Pat hesitated for a moment; it had been years since he had been inside these gates.

Unexpectedly, something cold and soft slid into his hand. Surprised, he looked down to see one of Modest's limp hands had wiggled its way into his grasp.

Feeling braver, he took a step forward, pulling her along into the cool shadows of the forest. The gate growled behind them as it slid shut.

◎

James lay facedown on the floor with his eyes closed. His arms and legs were still securely fastened to the chair. In an attempt to free himself, he had knocked the chair over and was now lying uncomfortably on the floor.

Something wet touched his cheek. When he opened his eyes, he saw that a small pool of blood had oozed its way over to him from Dr. Weisman's body a few feet away.

"Ugh." He struggled to move away from the bloody lake inching toward him.

Dr. Weisman's death seemed unreal. He could not believe any of this was happening. The old man had become one part delusional messiah and two parts homicidal terrorist.

The office doors at the bottom of the stairs slammed open. Heavy footsteps were approaching. "Shit," whispered James. Desperately, he attempted to free one of his limbs to defend himself from Ari, who was no doubt back to inflict some new form of torture.

"Dr. Weisman, are you okay?" said a deep baritone voice, but it wasn't Ari.

"Ed! Thank God. You've got to help me," James shouted.

The security guard galloped over to James but stopped short when he saw the broken mess that was Dr. Weisman.

"Dr. Weisman, are you okay?"

"He's dead, Ed. Ari killed him."

"Ari did this! But why?" Ed kneeled down and felt for a pulse. When he didn't find one, he just sat there kneeling, head in hand.

"Ed, can you please untie me?"

Snapping out of his trance, Ed looked over at James' bound form. "Of course. I'm sorry."

Ed whipped out a knife and cut the duct tape. Deep red indentations were cut into James' wrists, which he rubbed tenderly.

"Ed, you may not believe this, but Dr. Weisman was behind the viral pandemic."

"Dr. Weisman would never do such a thing." Ed shook his head, trying to act as surprised as possible. Now that Dr. Weisman was dead, he was going to make damn sure that no one discovered his involvement. "That's impossible!"

"Believe it," said James. "Ari wanted a vaccine and Weisman wouldn't give it to him. So Ari killed him and took his thumb. They went off to look for the vaccine."

Ed thought about an enraged and homicidal Ari running loose inside the building. "Your wife could be in danger."

"What? Why?"

"She was downstairs making the vaccine, wasn't she?"

James trembled at the thought of Ari, unstable and desperate, demanding a cure that didn't exist from his wife.

"We've got to get to Linda before Ari does."

Ed nodded and grasped the gun holster at his side. "I will take care of it."

"No. I'm coming with you."

"You're going to need this, then," Ed said as he took out another gun and handed it to him.

The gun felt foreign in James' hand. He had never seen a real gun, much less held one.

"I have no idea how to use this."

"It's simple. Aim and pull the trigger. Just not at me, okay?"

Ed began to jog to the stairs. James followed a couple steps behind, the gun grasped firmly in his sweaty hand.

It was raining lightly, more of a fine mist than actual water droplets. When Modest saw the massive metal spike of the pyramid framed against the gray anvil clouds, she gasped.

"That is beautiful."

"Shit," Pat cursed.

"What?"

"The storm shield is up."

"Um, I have no idea what you just said."

With his finger he pointed at the pyramid. "Underneath all that metal is a lot of glass. They put up those metal walls for only a couple of reasons."

"Like what?"

"Warming storms, for one."

"Oh . . ." Modest sighed, tilting her head upward as the sky spit moisture down onto her forehead.

"We should get inside as soon as we can. My mom's place isn't far from here."

Modest could see that the GeneFirm neighborhood was filled with street after street of cookiecutter two-story houses. The closer she got, the more bizarre the whole scene was—a suburban paradise. Not a single unmowed lawn. All the hedges, gardens, and yards were perfectly manicured. She didn't believe any of it was real, just a giant plastic replica of the American dream.

Beside her, Pat was busy swimming through his past. The houses, the streets, the smell of rain, everywhere he looked he was drowning in childhood memories.

They turned down the first street they came to, but were greeted only by more oppressive silence. Pat had the terrible thought that each of these perfect houses were now doubling as oversized caskets for the perfect families laying cold and motionless inside.

A little ways down, there was a blue car parked awkwardly. The owner of the car had decided to block the entire street off. As they approached, Pat knew what they were about to see, but it was too late to warn Modest.

Another corpse.

It was an older Hispanic woman; her skin was pale and blood encircled her mouth. This time it was Modest's turn to lose her lunch. She spun around from the grisly scene, ran to the nearest lawn, and began to hack up her guts onto the green grass.

With her hands on her knees, she puked until her throat burned and her eyes watered. Meanwhile, Pat peered into the car to get a closer look, sighing with relief when he saw an unfamiliar face.

When Modest had emptied her scant stomach contents, she stood up and wiped the tears from her swollen eyes. The lawn she had thrown up on belonged to a cute red house with white shutters. She was surprised to find herself thinking how nice it would be to live in this house, maybe even with a husband and kids of her own. These brief thoughts of domestication turned on her quickly, unsettling her stomach. She got sick again, retching onto the lawn once more. An arm wrapped around Modest's shoulders, making her cry out.

"Jesus Christ, Pat! You scared me."

"Sorry. We don't have much time. My house is right around the block."

She followed him without protest away from the grisly scene in the car.

"Almost home," said Pat as they turned onto the next street.

Then he stopped.

"What's wrong, Pat?" Modest noticed his face had turned white as he looked down the street. Without warning, he began to run.

"Pat!" she yelled.

He didn't turn around, so she began to jog after him. That's when she saw it, the burnt wreckage of a house. When she finally caught up to him, he was standing motionless on the lawn in front of what she could only assume were the charcoal remains of his childhood home. At his feet was a framed photo of a red-haired woman. Bouquets of flaccid flowers surrounded the picture, a tiny impromptu memorial. Pat dropped to his knees on the wet grass. Modest knelt down, wrapping her scrawny arms around him; his shoulders shook in her grasp as he began to cry.

42

The first thing James saw upon entering the commons was a body sprawled out on the floor. Ed rushed toward it while James followed closely behind. As he got closer, he was appalled to see that it was Dr. Paradee, lying on his back, eyes closed, dead still.

Kneeling down, Ed put two fingers to Dr. Paradee's neck. As soon as his fingers touched the wrinkled folds of skin, the old man's eyes opened.

"Ah!" screamed Dr. Paradee at the top of his lungs.

"Shit!" yelled Ed, the miraculous reanimation of the doctor taking him by surprise.

"Whoa, whoa, Dr. Paradee. It's just us," said James, trying to calm the old man down.

The fear in Dr. Paradee's features faded when he

recognized the two friendly faces above. The doctor relaxed and tried to smile.

"James! Ed! I'm glad to see you. I thought he had come back."

"Ari?"

"Yes. I'm afraid so."

"Are you okay?"

"Oh, yes, I will be fine. Ari, the bastard, electrocuted the piss out of me. As you can see." Paradee glanced down at the dark area of saturation on his trousers. "They were looking for a vaccine." He laughed at this.

"So you are involved with this virus, too?" asked a disappointed James.

Dr. Paradee smiled and started to say something but was cut off by Ed's thundering voice, "There's no time for questions. We need to find Ari now! Linda is in danger."

The old man broke eye contact with James. "I'm afraid Ed's right. Ari is probably headed toward her lab as we speak. One of the homeland agents is with him. Be careful."

A wave of unease surged in James; he wondered how many GeneFirm employees were involved in Weisman's terrorist plot. Shaking the thought from his mind, he focused on his more pressing concern—Linda.

"Ed, we have to get to her now."

"Agreed. Dr. Paradee will you be okay?"

"Boys, I'll be as okay as a man can be with a death sentence. I don't have long till the virus does its dirty work. I'd like to have a little peace and quiet, so you can just leave me here."

"Let us help you up into a chair," James pleaded.

"No. I'm comfortable here. That, and from the incredible pain that I'm feeling in my groin, I suspect that I might have a hip fracture. Best to stay down here for the moment."

He winced and waved them on. "Now go!"

James couldn't help but feel sorry for Dr. Paradee, despite his involvement with the virus. He had known the doctor his entire life. The effects of the virus would be nasty, and he wished there was more he could do for him. Paradee knew damn well what was approaching. First, the virus would enter the body, infecting and multiplying in the respiratory tract. The lungs would be the site of the most lethal damage. Paradee's immune system would respond to the virus by releasing molecular signals that cause inflammation and the release of additional inflammatory signals. This exaggerated immune response would cause so much swelling in the lungs that the airways would become blocked. As he coughed harder and harder, his lung tissue would be traumatized to the point where his lungs would hemorrhage and deteriorate like wet paper bags. In twenty-four hours, a sweaty and shivering Dr. Paradee would be blue in the face, mouth sticky with rust-flavored blood, unable to get any oxygen through his destroyed lungs. Suffocation would follow, death shortly thereafter.

James tried not to think about the billions of other people who would suffer the same fate. First and foremost, he had to stop Ari and make damn sure that Linda got out of this alive—easier said than done with that violent genetically enhanced sociopath on the loose.

"Go on! I'm an old man. Dying is the only thing I'm good for now. Get the hell out of here and go stop Ari from messing everything up," yelled Dr. Paradee.

Ed and James jogged toward the door, leaving the ailing Dr. Paradee lying on the ground. The two men were almost there when they heard the loud swoosh of sliding doors opening behind them. James was shocked to see the Homeland Security agents sprinting into the room, guns drawn and pointing directly at them. The shorter agent was holding something bloody in his hand, which could only be Dr. Weisman's other thumb, explaining how they managed to open the door in the first place.

"Stop! Put your hands in the air!" screamed the short agent.

Without a moment of hesitation, Ed rolled to his right, coming to a halt down on one knee, gun drawn.

James dived behind a table as the crack of a gunshot split the air. Ed fired on the agents. Another gunshot rang, followed by an explosion of blood from Ed's right thigh. He grunted, crashing down next to James, his blood-splattered hands gripping his thigh so tightly his fingers went white.

"Holy shit! Holy shit!" James repeated.

He whipped off his belt and pulled it tight around Ed's bleeding thigh.

Meanwhile the agents cautiously approached. Ed and James huddled underneath the table and out of sight.

"You're trapped!" hollered the short agent from across the room. "Get facedown on the ground and put your arms behind your back."

"What do we do?" shouted James between deep gasps for breath. His heart felt like it was seconds away from leaping out of his chest.

"You have to get to Linda." Ed's face contorted in pain as he moved his leg. "These guys know they're infected. They don't want to arrest us. They want revenge. I'll do my best to hold them off. Just stop Ari."

"I can't leave you. You've been shot! And I don't have security access."

Reaching into his pocket, Ed procured a key card and threw it to James. He then reached down and pulled out another gun from a holster hidden around his leg.

"Christ! How many of those do you have?"

"More than necessary. Now go!"

From underneath the table, Ed spotted the legs of the approaching agents across the room. He opened fire. Following the pops from his gun, a piercing shriek cut through the room. The tall agent dropped to the ground, clutching his leg.

"Fuck, okay, I'm going," James said, scrambling on his hands and knees toward the door, using the tables as protection. More shots were fired as he scrambled near the exit. He heard bullets whizzing past his head, slamming not so harmlessly against the wall. Ed fired back at the agents, making them take cover behind the tables, which gave James enough time to get to the door. He swiped the key card in front of the touch pad. To his relief, the door slid open, and he rolled through the doorway. The bangs of gunshots echoed loudly back in the commons. Peeking around the corner, James could see the short agent crouching behind Dr. Paradee, using the old man as a human shield.

Ed, who was not going to fire on the agent with Dr. Paradee right in front of him, had stopped shooting and was hunkered down behind an over-turned table.

There was another gunshot and blood burst out the back of Ed's right shoulder, which he had not managed to hide behind the table.

"No!" James cried, slamming the glass door.

Ed's face contorted in pain. He dropped his gun and clenched his shoulder with his opposite hand, then collapsed on the spot. The tall agent had re-gained his composure and was now inching toward Ed. A shred of his shirt was wrapped around his leg as a makeshift tourniquet. Both agents were now converging on the spot where Ed lay wounded.

James instinctively reached for the key card to open the door back up. He could not leave Ed to die. The shorter agent was slowly approaching, gun raised, ready to deliver a final shot.

With speed he wasn't aware he possessed, James swiped his key card across the sensor and the door in front of him opened. Both agents cocked their heads toward the door. Their menacing glares landed on James, who now stood dumbfounded in the doorway. He instantly regretted his decision to open the door.

"What are you doing?" Ed yelled.

But James didn't have time to respond. He watched as the short agent drew a bead on him with his gun. James could already feel the bullet ripping through his rib cage, puncturing his lungs, and lacerating his aorta.

James reflexively shut his eyes and a gunshot rang out. He bit his lip as he waited for impact, but no bullet wound appeared in his chest. When he opened his eyes, he was surprised to see the short agent falling backward. The agent's limp body slapped the tile floor—a bloody bullet hole had been drilled into his forehead.

The source of the bullet was evident. Ed lay prone on the ground, his left hand still aiming the gun.

"Now get out of here!" Ed shouted through clenched teeth dyed red with blood.

Picking himself up off the floor James dashed back down the hallway. The clatter of gunfire rang out behind him. By the time the glass doors slid shut, James was in a mad sprint toward the elevators. With his right hand, he pulled the gun from his waistband and squeezed the pistol until his hand cramped. The solid handle of the gun was a small comfort in the face of an imminent confrontation with Ari. He just hoped that Linda was still safe. He would kill Ari if he had to; he was no hero, but with his family's lives on the line he would find the courage to do anything.

Pat had not moved. He sat, head hanging, on his knees in front of his mother's memorial. Above them, the sky looked menacing. Modest didn't want to interrupt Pat's mourning, but they needed to find shelter soon.

That's when she heard the desperate barking of a dog somewhere nearby. Modest's heart jumped at the sound of life. The animal sounded incredibly frantic to her. By the edginess in the bark, she assumed the dog had been locked up somewhere for quite some time, its owners most likely dead.

With a burning need to rescue the dog, she stepped up and put a hand on Pat. "I'm really sorry. But I think we need to go soon. The storm is getting close."

The only response she got was a slow nod.

"I'm going to go find this dog. I don't want it to stay outside during this storm. You can stay here if you want. I can come back for you."

Pat shook his head. "No, it's fine. Sitting here isn't going to change anything."

A couple blocks away, they found the source of the barking. The dog was in the backyard of a pretty blue house with white trim. The front of the house was lined with rosebushes. A short white picket fence marked the front yard's boundaries. From behind the backyard fence, the dog continued to bark incessantly.

"I'm going in to get it."

"I can't see any more death today. Do you mind if I wait out here?"

"Not at all. I'll be right back." Modest walked up to the front door and rang the doorbell twice, just in case.

She couldn't help but imagine what unpleasant images awaited her. After waiting a minute, she peered through the narrow windows on each side of the door. She saw nothing but an empty living room. Finally working up the courage to open the door, she turned the knob. Her heart skipped a beat as the unlocked door swung open. They hadn't even bothered to lock the front door, something unfathomable to her, a woman who lived among strung-out addicts and criminals.

In the living room, the couch was void of any angelic child's body. She breathed a sigh of relief. Next she checked the master bedroom. Empty. The bedroom was normal: a perfectly made bed, candles, and a plethora of picture frames filled with smiling faces. She picked up one of the frames off the dresser and stared longingly at the happy family sitting in a field of bluebonnet flowers. Modest could not control her tears. Her eyes were watering; teardrops began to trickle off her long eyelashes and roll down her cheeks while she fought back the sobbing.

Upstairs, there was an empty boy's room lined with sports posters, video games, and action figures. Down the hall she found a little girl's room that was empty, too: brightly colored walls, tea sets, and dolls. No dead family here.

The barking of the dog in the backyard once again caught her attention. In the back of her mind she knew that it was she who needed the company of the dog more than the dog needed her. She found the back door and opened it. From the side of the house, she heard the swiftly approaching jingle-jangle of a dog collar. Modest was unprepared for what bounded around the corner. A mass of fluorescence sprang up onto her, wet paws staining her white shirt. It took a second to comprehend that the neon fur belonged to an orange Labrador. She had never seen a GloPet quite like it, big and brilliant.

The dog wagged its tail as she scratched the animal's bright belly.

"Good dog! We have something in common, don't we? Those bastards made you a freak, too. What's your name?" she asked as she patted its side.

No stranger to the unfairness of genetic modifications, Modest already felt like she had a bond with the animal. She slipped her hand around its collar and looked at the tag. "Clementine. That's a good name. Are you hungry? Let's find some food."

In the pantry, she found the dog food and poured a couple scoops into the food bowl in the kitchen and filled up another bowl with water. The dog greedily attacked the bowls, splashing water everywhere and scattering dry dog food across the floor.

Next it was her turn. She was famished. In the pantry she found some granola bars, which she took back to the kitchen table. She scratched Clementine's back and then collapsed into a chair. After she unwrapped the rectangles of oats, she greedily crammed them into her mouth. The blisters on her feet throbbed painfully.

She was finally home, she thought, but whose home she did not know.

43

"**H**ow long is this quarantine going to last?"

Linda exhaled in frustration inside her biohazard suit after hearing the woman's voice in her earpiece. After being locked down in the level four labs for the past few days, Linda's coworker was getting edgy.

Linda leaned back in her office chair. "I have no idea, Kim. You know as well as I do that these things take some time."

"I haven't seen the sun in days! I need to get out of here before I stick this pipette in my eye."

"Ow—my ears! No need to yell, Kim. You're using a radio. I can hear you perfectly fine. Just relax? We're quarantined and there's nothing we can do about it."

Kim snorted in frustration. "What are the reasons

for the quarantine again? We've had no accidents down here. Everything is fine."

"Perhaps one of the lab sensors is faulty. It wouldn't be the first time we had a false alarm. Remember when the sensors falsely detected the airborne herpes virus in the air system? People were trapped down here for days. We just have to be patient and continue working on this vaccine."

"Arggh," Kim cried.

Linda returned her attention to the computer screen. She waved a gloved finger across it to turn to the next page. Instead of looking at the latest test results for the vaccine, she was reading *Brave New World* for the umpteenth time to ward off complete boredom. She was halfway down the page when she heard the characteristic beep of the air lock, odd considering they were under lockdown. On cue, the radio crackled to life again.

"Someone is in the air lock!" Kim exclaimed over the radio.

Linda swiveled around in her chair. Perplexed, she stared at the large steel door, waiting for something to happen. When the door finally popped opened, Linda felt the pressure in the room change. The papers on her wall fluttered briefly in the newly created breeze. She gasped when the unmistakable form of Ari strode into the room. The slender body of Savira hung at his side. They were both soaking wet from the air lock's decontamination shower.

Linda was stunned, but it only took a second to realize what was going on here—classic human themes of love and betrayal. Following them was a man in a drenched business suit. He had a thick mustache and a bulging stomach, giving him the look of a detective from a cheesy police movie. She was almost certain he was with Homeland, there could be no other explanation.

None of them were wearing biohazard suits, and they had left both air lock doors wide open. Whatever bugs that were floating around in the room were now free to roam the corridors.

Kim boldly ran toward the group of intruders screaming, "Ari! What do you think you're doing here? You're not wearing any suits? You left the air lock doors—"

The woman's voice was cut off when Ari planted his thick boot into her stomach. With his arms busy holding up Savira, he elected to give Kim a swift high kick to get her out of his way. The tiny woman was launched backward, toppling over the lab bench and disappearing over the opposite side. This sent the rest of the lab workers scurrying into their offices, slamming the doors behind them.

Calmly, Linda stood up and walked out into the lab area.

"Ari what the hell are you doing?"

"I'm here for the vaccine—the real one. She needs it," Ari snarled.

The giant was clearly very pissed off. Linda could see the rabid look in his eyes as he looked over Savira's shivering figure.

Linda inspected Savira more closely. The woman was obviously in the earlier stages of the viral infection. It was hard to tell if she was sweating profusely or if it was just water from the decontamination shower that had soaked her blouse. The amount of heat coming off the both of them was impressive; Linda could feel it from a yard away.

Ari repeated himself. This time there was a disconcerting crack his voice. "I need that vaccine now!"

"We aren't done with it yet, Ari."

"Shut up and give me the *real* vaccine," he bellowed. "Don't play games with me."

"The real vaccine? I have no idea what you are talking about. Like I said, we are not done making it yet."

"You're lying! Give me the one my father used."

Ari took Savira's arm off his shoulder and made a long stride toward Linda. He brought the back of one of his big hands across the hood of her suit, hitting her like a boat paddle. The momentum of the blow lifted her off her feet. She hit the ground hard and lay there groaning and holding the side of her face.

Slowly, she stood back up with a look of disheveled pride.

"Fine, Ari," she said, eyeing him angrily. "You want a vaccine?"

Linda walked over to a large fridge in the back of the lab and opened it. She pulled out a small glass vial and a syringe. She tipped the vial up and stuck the needle in, pulling back the plunger. The clear liquid rushed into the syringe.

"I'm afraid there's only enough for one dose," she said, throwing a glance over to the Homeland agent standing motionless behind Ari.

"Give it to me," Ari demanded.

Mac looked at Ari in protest. Desperate thoughts

ran through his mind, converging on the small syringe that Linda was holding. He knew it was his only chance for survival. Linda saw the look on the agent's face. Her ploy had worked. Ari was moving toward Linda when she heard Mac's voice from behind him.

"Don't move!"

Ari put his hands in the air and slowly turned around. Mac had drawn his Taser.

"This is a really bad idea," Ari said coldly.

"Just give me the vaccine."

Ari stood motionless, glaring at Mac. "Go on, Linda. Give it to him."

Hesitantly, she walked over, keeping one eye on Ari. She placed the syringe into Mac's open palm and quickly backed away. Mac clenched the vaccine to his chest. He felt a brief sense of comfort radiate from the syringe. It wouldn't last. The reality of the situation was that he was still locked in a building with a very violent and increasingly frantic man who would have no trouble killing him.

"I'm sorry, I have a family. I need this vaccine."

Ari remained silent and motionless, like a tiger ready to pounce. The man fumed with anger like heat rippling off desert asphalt. Mac knew the only way to safely inject himself without being attacked was to get out of the lab. The Taser in his hands trembled as he slowly backed up. Mac was almost to the door when there was an inexplicable blur of motion—a glass flask rocketed through the air and struck the retreating agent in the temple. It shattered over Mac's head, causing him to grunt in pain as sparkling shards sprinkled down around him. He collapsed to the ground. When he touched the side of his head, his fingers came away sticky and warm with blood.

Everyone turned to see where the flask had come from, but there was nobody there, just an empty lab.

The distraction was enough. Taking advantage of the situation, Ari raised his gun.

Bang. Bang. Bang.

Linda screamed. The three gunshots tore through Mac's chest. Thoroughly baffled, Mac wrenched back in pain. The blood ran down his white shirt and he made a strange gurgling sound, giving one last pained look to the side of the room where the glass had come from. His confused eyes caught Linda's as he fell backward. Mac's body lay motionless in a river of broken glass and blood. Ari smirked, sweeping his gun back toward the side of the lab where the glass bottle had come from.

"Come out. Come out," Ari said playfully. "I believe we have a stowaway on this ship, Linda. Which one of your lab rats is out there? That little woman I kicked earlier? Show yourself!" Ari yelled.

He carefully inched toward the end of the lab bench where the dead agent lay. He quickly glanced down and discovered that the syringe was gone. Ari briefly panicked. Did the agent drop the syringe? Did it lie with all the other broken glass on the ground? He bent down and desperately searched among remnants of the flask for signs of the needle. Nothing. With one foot, he stepped onto Mac's lifeless body, using him as a stepping-stone to cross the expanding red tributary below. When he shifted his weight to the man's body, the room filled with the sickening crack of bones. He needed to find the person who threw that flask. Maybe they had managed to grab the syringe as the agent fell.

Watching Ari unceremoniously step on the agent made Linda feel ill. She heard the sick snapping sound of breaking bones underneath Ari's heavy boot.

Ari stalked down the row of lab benches with the silent grace of a predator.

Linda saw the movement first; another flurry of motion above the body of the agent. Then something strange happened. The agent's hand opened up, and his Taser floated upward as if by magic. The air above the body wavered. She gasped. Ari whipped around just in time to see the Taser hovering in the air, pointing right at him. Then he saw it. The faint outline of a man, the Taser in one hand, in the other, the syringe. It was hard to make out, but he could see the distortions in the air created by the man's presence. A hush fell over the lab.

Without warning, Ari lunged. The invisible man managed to squeeze off a shot. The prongs caught Ari in the thigh.

Linda took the opportunity to hide underneath her lab bench, covering her head with her arms.

Despite the electricity coursing through his body, Ari miraculously managed to reach down with his violently shaking hands and rip out the Taser prongs. He popped up behind the lab bench with his pistol drawn.

"Fuck," he cursed as he panted for breath. The man had disappeared again. Ari forced himself to control his breathing; the lab grew quiet as he listened intently for any sound that might give away his camouflaged prey.

The crunch of glass a few yards away drew his attention. Ari shot in the direction of the sound. To avoid the bullets, the chameleon was forced to dive to the ground. Miscalculating the landing, he ended up rolling through the dark pool of blood and glass, painting a red streak down his side. With his skin marred with blood, he was no longer invisible. He swiftly took cover behind the opposite side of the bench from Ari. From the safety of the lab bench, Agent Marnoy materialized out of thin air. He gingerly laid the syringe down and then launched himself over the bench toward Ari. In midair his skin flashed red, transforming him into a bloody naked flash rifling through the air. He slammed into Ari, who was momentarily caught off guard by the sight of a color-changing nude man flying toward him. Ari stumbled back from the blow, but managed to grab the chameleon and, using his momentum, flung the man over his shoulders like a rag doll. Marnoy grunted in pain as he crashed through the glass door of a fridge. His skin flickered bright yellow and red as he tumbled to the ground. Ari slowly approached, looking amused.

Marnoy's skin changed back to brown. He groaned and tried to push himself up. The broken glass around him sliced into his hands; blood dribbled out of his palms, causing him to collapse back down in pain. This was it, he briefly thought, his tortured life had finally found itself a suitable end—an excruciatingly painful one.

Marnoy's pessimistic thoughts were directed elsewhere when another deafening gunshot split his hand open in a burst of blood. He looked down at the mangled mess that moments before had been his right hand. He wailed in agony and rolled over onto his back, clenching his destroyed hand in his good one. Jagged squares of glass on the ground dug into his back, leaving red smears on the white tiled floor. His skin began to flare a wide spectrum of colors as he screamed in distress—red, yellow, green, blue. He was boiling with color.

"What the fuck are you?" asked Ari as he aimed his gun at Marnoy's forehead.

Marnoy didn't have a chance to answer before Ari pulled the trigger.

Click.

Ari sighed. The gun was empty. Carefully, he grabbed the barrel of the gun. He looked at the naked man on the floor one more time before slamming the butt of the gun down onto the man's forehead. The skin of Marnoy's face flashed bright white as the handle of the gun crashed against his skull, causing his head to snap back hard against the ground. The chameleon's skin pulsed for several seconds and then slowly faded back to brown.

Ari dropped the gun onto the body and walked back toward Savira. He bent down and scooped the syringe off the floor. Ari uncapped the syringe; the tiny instrument looked awkward in his thick hands. He gently lifted Savira up and laid her down on the top of a bench, carefully sticking the needle into one of her slight shoulders. When he pushed the plunger down, the clear serum slowly disappeared into her.

He set down the needle on the lab bench and stepped back, watching Savira in silence. Linda crawled out from underneath the lab bench and looked around at all of the destruction. Her lab was totaled. Shattered glass littered the floor. Blood seeped out of the lifeless bodies of the two men strewn on the ground. The only audible sounds in the lab were the labored breathing of Savira, the muffled cries of Kim sobbing in her office, and the heavy breathing of the monstrous Ari.

Ari picked up Savira's hand and squeezed it tightly. It looked like he had fallen into a trancelike state as he stared down at her, breathing slowly. His lips were moving, but no sound came out. Ari desperately needed Savira to survive. When he first agreed to his father's plan, he had barely known the woman. But as the months went by, he had become inadvertently attached—willing to do anything for her. His father hadn't understood; nothing that man did was for love. That intangible immeasurable emotion warranted no merit, in his father's opinion: it was always science, science, science.

Fear and love were once foreign emotions for Ari, but now he was caught between both with no idea what to do.

Suddenly Savira started to shake. "What's happening?" Ari howled.

The woman's shaking became a full-out seizure. She convulsed violently and white froth started to bubble out the sides of her mouth. Her eyes rolled up into the back of her head. Ari's face flushed. Tears rolled down his cheeks as he held Savira down to stop her from falling off the lab bench.

"What's happening, Linda?" he yelled again. "Stay with me. Savira, stay with me. Please . . ."

After one final jolt, Savira lay deathly still. Her tongue hung loosely from her slack jaw. Ari whimpered. After a minute, he put a finger to Savira's neck to feel for the fluttering pulse that he knew would not be there. He screamed aloud before burying his face into her stomach and beginning to sob. Ari made a series of unintelligible muted cries until he had exhausted his vocal cords. He lifted himself up and wiped away tears from his red eyes. Snot dripped down his nose as he faced Linda with a crazy violent look in his eyes. "What did you do?"

Linda's face no longer showed any hint of fear, her expression callous and cold. One of her hands snaked behind her to find the suit's zipper. She unzipped herself. The cold lab air rushed in. Ari waited as she shimmied her upper torso out of the suit. She wore an old white tank top underneath. It was against policy to wear it under the suit but she considered the tank lucky and wore it anyway.

She looked him dead in the eye. "How dare you, Ari? Betray your own father. Risk our entire plan because of your own damn selfishness."

Ari blinked in confusion. "What?"

"We all worked far too long and hard on this for you to back out now. Each one of us knew the sacrifices we would have to make. You disgust me," she sneered.

"What did you do?"

Linda laughed. "You idiot. Who do you think made these viruses in the first place?"

Looking down at Savira, Ari realized the truth. He repeated angrily, "What did you do?"

Nodding, Linda laughed to herself. "I told your father over and over again that you and Savira couldn't be trusted."

Rage started to build in Ari like an approaching hurricane. He screamed, "What did you give her? What was in that vial? Tell me!"

Linda stood confidently as Ari approached, bracing for the oncoming assault.

"You wanted a cure—well, the only cure for my viruses is death. That needle was filled with a lethal neurotoxin."

"You bitch!"

He picked up a glass beaker from the lab bench and took a giant step toward her.

Linda lunged forward with a scream, brandishing another syringe full of neurotoxin like a dagger. But Ari was too quick for her. He dodged the needle and smashed the beaker over her head. She crumpled to the ground like a bag of potatoes.

"You killed her! Damn you!" Ari cried. "I'm going to fucking tear you apart."

He picked her up by the back of the neck, his hand easily fitting all the way around her skinny throat, and flung her over the lab bench. Her body crashed sideways through stacks of glass equipment and test tubes. Linda yelped in agony as she landed on the other side, glass raining down around her. Blood trickled down her hands and forearms as she squirmed to get up.

Before she could get her footing, Ari grabbed both her legs in his viselike grip. She made a feeble attempt to kick his hands off, but he was too strong. Using all of his weight, he swung her into another nearby fridge. The glass door exploded as she went straight through it, cutting deep lacerations up and down her back like strips of cloth. Ari didn't let go. Again he swung her at the lab bench, sending her hurtling over it, back to the floor on the other side.

Linda lay bruised and bleeding in the fetal position. She cried softly.

Scanning the lab bench for a good blunt object, Ari picked up another thick glass beaker and slowly approached. He reached in his pant pocket, pulled out something, and threw it down in front of Linda's face.

"Send my regards to my father, you whore!"

She shrieked when she saw the human thumb, lonely, pale, and indeed a long, long way from home.

Ari felt like his chest had been replaced by an angry furnace. He prepared to bring the glass down with blind fury upon Linda's blood-soaked head. He raised his hand for the final blow.

Bang.

Ari's face contorted in pain. He looked behind him to see that a bullet hole had appeared in back of his shoulder. Blood gushed from the wound.

James stood in the open air lock, weapon in hand, doing his best to keep the gun steady, but his hands were trembling almost uncontrollably. When Ari turned around, James' stomach flipped over at the sight of a man possessed. Great veins snaked up and down both sides of Ari's neck and his fierce eyes were blood red.

"James!" Ari snarled as he broke into a sprint. He

was headed straight at James, the blunted weapon of a glass bottle clenched in his right hand.

The fear was paralyzing. James froze. His fingers felt like they each weighed a hundred pounds. The gun trigger felt impossible to squeeze. In a few seconds, the maniac would bludgeon him to death with a piece of goddamn laboratory equipment.

A fitting end for a scientist, he thought.

Then a bloody hole split open in Ari's right thigh. For a moment, James was stunned, his fingers had worked. The bullet didn't slow Ari down though; the man still thundered toward him dragging his wounded leg. James pulled the trigger again and then again.

This time the bullets hit within inches of each other on the left side of Ari's chest. Blood spewed out of holes like Old Faithful. Ari grunted in pain, but the shots didn't stop his momentum. He was only a step away.

James felt like he would have more success shooting down a charging grizzly bear than this mad man who was about to bring down the glass bottle onto his already wounded head. Aiming wildly, James held his breath and squeezed the trigger one more time.

Something hot sprayed his face. Realizing that he had closed his eyes, James opened them to a beautiful sight. The last bullet had caught Ari right between his engorged hate-filled eyes. Ari had been so close that blood was splattered all over James' face. He watched Ari's head jerk back, his body suddenly going limp. Sidestepping, James barely managing to dodge the falling giant, who landed with a splash of blood on the floor. James's hands were still shaking when he dropped the gun.

"Wow!" cried James in relief. Unexpectedly, Ari's big hand clamped over his ankle. Unaware that his vocal cords could reach such heights, James let out a high-pitched scream that would make a thirteen-year-old girl blush. In alarm, he fell backward onto his butt and proceeded to kick Ari in the head repeatedly until the hand released him and became flaccid.

Scrambling up to his feet, James tried to shake off the shock. His whole body quivered. Carefully, he stepped over the collection of dead bodies on the laboratory floor, making sure to stay out of hand's reach, just in case. His wife was still stretched out on the ground, moaning and clutching her various injuries.

He knelt down next to her. "It's okay. Ari is dead. You're safe. I'm so glad you're safe. I was so scared."

She whimpered in pain as James put his arms under her and lifted her up.

"I'm going to get you out of here. We need to get you some help."

Her hand squeezed his arm weakly.

44

Modest found a black leash hanging near the back door. She attached it to Clementine's collar after the dog had eaten her fill of food.

"Let's go for a walk. See if we can find anybody alive around here."

The fluorescent dog trotted alongside her as they exited the house.

On the front porch, Pat had been rocking back and forth in a chair. When he saw the dog he stopped abruptly.

"What the hell is that?"

"A very orange dog."

The animal looked strangely familiar, but Pat couldn't figure out from where. "What are you doing with it?"

"We're taking it for a walk."

"What about this storm? Let's just stay here."

"We have time." Modest walked past him into the fine drizzle. He sighed as he stood up to follow, not wanting to get any wetter than he already was. The dog was already tugging Modest in one direction, as if she knew exactly where she wanted to go.

The dog unexpectedly pulled hard and barked, almost yanking the leash out of Modest's hands. She broke into a jog just to keep up with Clementine, who was furiously scrambling forward.

"Not more running," Pat moaned.

A noise floated toward Modest. At first she thought it was her mind playing tricks on her, but the sound grew louder until she was positive—children's voices. For the first time in her life, her mood actually brightened upon hearing the sound of children. Modest and Clementine rounded the next street corner almost at a sprint. She stopped abruptly, almost colliding with two dark-haired kids who stood there looking terrified. After the initial shock wore off, the kids smiled and approached the orange-furred dog.

"Clementine!" they yelled in unison.

The dog leapt up and put her paws on the chest of the boy, her big tongue lapping at the boy's face. He made a sour expression as he pushed the dog down.

"Clementine, no! Not the face."

The boy began to pet the dog behind the ears. He looked suspiciously at Modest while the girl hugged the dog around the neck. The girl's eyes finally rested on Modest as well. After a few seconds of staring, she said, "You have pretty hair!"

Modest laughed. "Thank you very much."

A wave of relief ran through her upon seeing the children. Her heart was suddenly feeling lighter.

Pat finally caught up. When he rounded the corner, he stopped in surprise. Dumbfounded, he stared at Modest and the children. Seeing the dog and the children together finally sparked his memory. All of a sudden he realized where he had seen the dog.

"I'll be damned."

"Pat, watch your fucking language! Impressionable ears," Modest quickly shot back. "What has gotten into you?" Ignoring Modest's bafflingly direct contradiction, Pat leaned down and offered a hand to the children.

"August and Olive. I am your second cousin Pat—your Great Aunt Rose's son," he said, unable to hide the pain in his voice.

Olivia gasped. Tears welled up in the girl's eyes at the mention of their late aunt.

"So I met you, August, when you were just a baby. I never got a chance to meet you, Miss Olive, but I recognize you from a Christmas card I got a couple years ago from my Uncle James."

It was Modest's turn to be dumbfounded. "You're related to these kids! That's crazy."

The two children looked up at both of them suspiciously. "So you're our cousin?"

"You bet. Now where are your parents?"

"They are in there," said Augustus, pointing toward the pyramid.

"Why are you two wandering around in this storm?"

"We snuck out of school," Olivia giggled.

August shushed his sister. He shot her a dirty look. "You're going to get us in trouble."

"Don't worry. You aren't in trouble, August. So are there more people at school?" asked Pat.

"It's a school. Of course there are people there."

"Touché. So why did you sneak out?"

Augustus shrugged. "We didn't want Clementine to stay out in the storm. We had to. The school told us that none of our parents could leave work today, so if we didn't do it no one would."

"I see."

Olivia looked up at Modest. "What's your name?"

"My name is Modest."

"That's good. Nobody likes a name that shows off." Olivia said with a big smile. Her jet black hair bounced up and down as she skipped next to Clementine.

Modest chuckled.

"That's weird," August said.

"And what are your names again?" Modest asked.

"My name is Olivia and this is my brother, Augustus, but everyone calls us Olive and August."

"It's very nice to meet you."

Pat looked nervously at the pyramid and then at the ugly storm clouds sweeping by above them. He made a quick decision.

"It's not safe for you kids to be out here alone. Modest and I are going to watch you until your parents return. Let's get you two back home."

Turning around, Pat began to lead the group back toward the house.

August walked behind them, looking Modest over. She noticed his eyes on her.

"Are you okay?" Modest asked.

"Why did you make your hair that color?"

"I didn't. This is my real hair color."

"No way."

"Here, look."

Modest showed him the pink hairs that covered her pale arm.

"So you were made that way, like Clementine?"

"Exactly."

Olivia looked at Modest's hair in awe. "Ooo! Neat. My favorite color is pink."

Modest could not say the same.

"I wish I had green hair," August said with his arms crossed.

"With a little hair dye we could make that happen, August. Green is kind of a sick color to put in your—"

The word "sick" stuck on her tongue. An unwelcome thought dawned on Modest. These kids were still alive because they hadn't been exposed to the virus. The thought that they could have just infected these kids cut through her chest. If she had unintentionally exposed them, she would never be able to live with herself. Luckily for her, if she was indeed infected, she would not have to live with that guilt for very long.

Modest didn't know exactly what the best course of action would be. They couldn't leave the kids, especially now, after potentially getting them sick, and especially not while they were all alone out in this storm. She and Pat had no choice but to take care of them until they figured out what to do next.

◎

Linda was finally coming around. James had gingerly laid her down on a table in the nearest break room and proceeded to open the first aid kit that hung on the wall next to the sink. He used antiseptic wipes to clean all of the gashes and cuts she had received from Ari's beating. Her forearms had deep vertical incisions that cut so deeply she looked like a victim of a wild animal attack.

She winced as the antiseptic swab burned the open wounds. "What happened?" Linda whispered painfully.

"Ari was about to kill you, but you're safe now."

"That bitch!" screamed someone behind him.

James whirled around to find Kim standing in the door of the break room. She looked like she had gone mad. Her eyes were swollen and red from crying, her hair wildly out of place. The hood of her biohazard suit hung behind her neck.

"I heard it all. She was the one who made it!"

"Whoa, whoa, whoa! What are you talking about?" James asked. "She made what?"

"She was the one who made the superflu virus!"

James cocked his head in confusion. He looked at Linda and then back to Kim.

"I think there is a misunderstanding. Linda had nothing to do with this."

"No!" shrieked Kim. She took a step forward into the room. "I know what I heard, James. She murdered Savira, too. That's why Ari was trying to kill her. I heard the words come out of her very own mouth. Now step aside."

Her left hand emerged from behind her back holding the gun James had dropped earlier.

His heart skipped a beat when he saw it.

"Fuck me," he said under his breath.

"What is she talking about, James?" Linda cried behind him. "You have to stop her."

Shielding his wife, James said, "You've got the story all wrong. Why don't you put down that gun and let's talk about it. Dr. Weisman was responsible for the virus."

"Move!"

"I will not. Please put the gun down!" He repeated as he held his hands up nonthreateningly in the air.

"James, I have no idea what she is talking about. She's completely lost it. Look at her. She's gone crazy. Please don't let her hurt me."

"Kim, please. Why are you doing this?"

"It's all her fault," Kim sobbed. She took a step forward and gripped the pistol tighter.

"You're not thinking straight."

"That bitch made the virus, James, don't you see? I can't let her live. She's a cold-blooded murderer. If you won't get out of my way, I'll shoot you, too. Now move!" Tears were pouring down Kim's flushed face. The gun shook wildly in her hands.

"No!" he shouted.

Kim squeezed the trigger but nothing happened.

Looking down at the gun, a frustrated Kim tried again, squeezing the trigger as hard as she could, but it wouldn't budge. James remembered that he had put the gun's safety on before he dropped it. The woman couldn't figure out how to release it.

She raised the gun again and squeezed with all her might.

Bang.

James ducked reflexively as a gunshot rang out in the room like a cannon blast, but it was Kim who stumbled forward. She let out a short cry before she fell facedown. A red circle blossomed against the yellow back of her suit. Someone in the hallway had just shot her.

The agent, thought James. "Shit!"

He quickly lifted Linda, set her on the ground, and then overturned the table. Behind it, James crouched down beside his wife. The gun Kim was holding had fallen a few feet away. If he could get to it he would be able to defend himself. As he reached for it, someone stepped into the doorway. He froze.

For a split second James thought Ari had somehow reanimated himself, but to his relief the massive form was none other than Ed. He holstered his gun as he hobbled into the break room on his one good leg. Bloody rags were wrapped around his wounded thigh and shoulder.

"Ed! Damn it! I thought you were one of the agents."

"Nope, they're all dead, I'm afraid. Looks like I was just in time. What got into her?"

Ed looked down at the woman's motionless body. He stepped over her and then lowered himself into a chair near the table. He clenched his teeth from the pain of bending his wounded leg.

"I have no idea. She thought Linda was somehow involved in making the virus. Ed, you need some serious medical attention. You look bad."

"You're telling me. I feel like I need serious medical attention. What happened to Linda? Is she okay? What happened to Ari?"

"Ari is dead. Linda is in better shape than you, but that's not saying much. Now how can I get you two out of here? Neither of you are in any condition to walk very far."

"That won't be a problem. I left the electric cart on the ground floor. We just need to make it to the elevator."

"That'll work."

James helped Ed out of the chair before he picked Linda up in his arms. The two men hobbled out of the room and down the hallway. It was slow going, but when the elevator doors finally shut, James couldn't help but feel hopeful as they ascended back to the surface.

45

Modest and Pat sat at the kitchen table with the kids. The room was silent except for the busy smacking sounds of the children gulping down food. August and Olive ate like starving wolves, rapidly devouring the plate of peanut butter and jelly sandwiches that Modest had made.

After two sandwiches, Modest was finally full. Pat kept on eating, undeterred, seemingly making up for all those missed meals at the retreat.

"Hey kids, do you mind if I turn the TV on?"

Olivia shook her head. "TV on!"

The TV appeared on the wall above them.

"Thanks, Olive. TV channel to CNN," Modest directed at the wall. The TV screen refused to change, full of white static. "CNN," she said again, this time a little bit louder. The sound of static continued on unbroken. Nothing.

"Can we watch cartoons, Modest?" Augustus asked.

"If you can find a channel that works, certainly." Modest sighed.

Augustus faced the wall. "Cartoon Network."

The TV screen still showed nothing.

"Ah, man! The TV is busted!" he cried.

No television. It was an unsettling sign for all of them. If TV was no longer working, then the chaos must truly be real.

"Hey, August, are all the other kids still at your school?" Modest asked.

"Everyone but us."

"Was anybody sick there?"

August shook his head. "Nope."

Awesome, she thought. Now if the kids got sick, she would have no doubt that she and Pat were responsible. She was almost secretly hoping that August would answer yes to help alleviate some of the guilt she was feeling for possibly infecting them. However, she and Pat still showed no signs of infection. Perhaps they had gotten lucky.

She had a strong urge for news of the outside world. Searching the room, her eyes finally landed on a small computer pad in the corner.

"Kids, do you mind if I use your computer real quick?"

August pointed to it, nodding his head. "Sure, it's over there."

She stood up from the table, grabbed the computer, and then sat down with it on the couch. She pulled up NPR's news site. A wave of nausea swept over her.

The site showed images of anarchy, death, burning cars, and riot police lining concrete streets. Rioters clad in bandanas and gas masks were captured in midstride, clenching pipes and bricks with soot-covered hands. She clicked on the headline and began to read:

Chaos erupts as governments and public safety organizations are crippled by the spreading pandemic. In New York City, the National Guard was called in today; however, many of its members have already deserted or fallen ill. Public cries for more vaccinations have been building. A worldwide shortage of the vaccine, which was made available late last night, has left most of the population unvaccinated; However, according to conflicting reports, the vaccine has had little effect on preventing infection. In most major cities, experts estimate the flu has infected up to 80 percent of the population. Many rumors are circulating that the president and most of his staff have fallen ill. So far the White House has refused to comment.

Millions are dead and as of right now there is no end in sight as the superflu continues to spread rapidly.

Modest didn't need to read more. The rest of the article was more of the same. She went back to the home page and noticed that the site had not been updated in six hours. It looked like the news organizations had ceased to function, too. She sighed and set down the computer pad. The wind was picking up outside, its howling getting louder. The storm was almost here.

The electric cart came to a halt at the entrance of the small hospital wing of GeneFirm. James swiped Ed's key card across the touch pad and the doors parted, allowing him to guide the cart down to the emergency center. In the lobby, a group of medical staff were lazily playing a card game. They had been locked in the hospital wing since the quarantine began, so the sight of the electric cart cruising toward them was shocking, especially considering that its passengers looked as if they had come from a battlefield. The group sprang to their feet and rushed the cart as James brought it to a stop.

Dr. Ryan, the only doctor working at the moment, went straight to Ed, who was slumped over in the passenger seat. Ed had been going in and out of consciousness from the amount of blood he had lost.

"Jesus! What happened?" Dr. Ryan shouted.

"It's a long story. Just help them!"

Dr. Ryan swiftly nodded in agreement. One of the nurses wheeled up a stretcher. It took everyone working together to lift Ed's substantial body onto it. A thick puddle of blood lay on the seat where he had been sitting.

"Are these bullet wounds? What is going on, James?" the doctor asked with a worried look on his face. He turned to a nurse, "Get Ed to the shock room and start him on fluids. I'll be there in a second."

As Ed was wheeled off, another stretcher arrived for Linda. The doctor and another nurse carefully lifted her over to it.

"We're going to need you to wait here, James," said Dr. Ryan, "but I'll be back soon. Then you can tell me exactly what happened here."

James nodded. He squeezed Linda's hand as they began to push her away.

"Linda, you're going to be okay, alright?"

She nodded slightly, trying to force a smile as she disappeared down the corridor.

James sat in the waiting room of the hospital, reflecting on the wreckage Dr. Weisman had made of their lives. However his self-pity was interrupted by vibrations in his pocket. He had completely forgotten about his phone and was surprised to see several new voice mails and text messages.

The voice mails and texts were from his kids' school. The blood drained from his face as he read the first message; it explained that his children had gone missing. The second message told him the school had been searched and his children were still missing. The final text made him gag. It was a state weather advisory—a level-red warming storm was about to strike.

Warming storms had several categories. Level green consisted of high winds and rain, level orange could knock down a fence and flood the neighborhood, while a level-red storm meant "call the insurance company, your house is so totally fucked" kind of trouble. At the very least, you could expect hurricane-like winds and tornados. A level red storm was why GeneFirm's storm shield was built in the first place. The message said the storm would hit at 5 P.M. His watch read 4:50.

"Fuckin' fantastic," he said and sighed. Jumping to his feet, he ran at a full sprint from the hospital wing. Using Ed's key card to bypass the quarantine doors, James was able to make his way to the front entryway of GeneFirm, but what greeted him made him yell out a string of obscenities.

In his panic, he had forgotten about the storm shield that stood stubbornly on the other side of the glass doors. He was trapped inside. After a frustrating couple of seconds, he had an idea. He turned and dashed down the hallway, making his way back to the elevator.

James arrived outside Dr. Weisman's office door panting heavily. Feeling light-headed, he paused at the door, preparing himself for the gruesome scene that awaited him. It was dark inside; as he climbed the stairs the only light came from the flickering static of the TV. He made a wide loop around the mutilated figure of Dr. Weisman.

The storm shield had been activated from Weisman's computer, so James figured that was how he could get the shield lowered again. He sat down in front of the computer and touched the screen.

"Bingo!" he said, fist pumping at the sight of storm shield controls.

With a tap of the screen, a deep rumbling filled the room. Above him the tip of the pyramid split open into four descending peaks. Dark green light spilled into the room—the color of a sky about to be torn apart by a tornado. He didn't have much time.

In another minute, the shutters had retracted past the floor of Weisman's office, continuing their descent. In a few more minutes, the metal walls would be gone and he would be able to get out of here and find his kids. The view outside was more spectacular than usual. The surrounding fields and forests shook with wind, caught in an angry green dance. The sky was disgruntled and swirling. Everything was bathed in that eerie greenish gray color. James hoped that if he was not able to find them in time, that his children had enough sense to get somewhere safe before the storm hit. The problem was, even if they were in the safest part of their house, they were still unsafe from a level-red storm. Only the school and the pyramid could protect them from a storm of such ass-kicking proportions.

As he was about to leave the office to run down to the ground floor, he heard a familiar alarm sound that made his heart stop. A female computer voice filled the room.

"This is a severe weather warning. The storm shield is being activated. Please stay away from all exits."

"What?" James shouted at the ceiling. "No! Not now."

He sprinted back to the glass windows and looked down. Sure enough the storm shield was inching its way back up.

"Damn it!" he screamed. He ran over to Weisman's computer and tried to stop the walls. The weather system had overridden the controls. There was no way to stop it. He panicked at the thought of being trapped inside while his kids were out there. This storm could completely level his house, kids and all.

The chair sitting across from Weisman's desk caught his eye. A desperately stupid idea took hold of him. With the chair in hand, he galloped back toward the window. Looking down he could see that he only had a minute before the steel shutters would close above him again. Bracing himself, he swung the chair with all of his strength at the window.

Wham.

The chair reverberated painfully in his hands. The window was barely scratched. He hit it again with the same result. After the fifth blow a crack in the glass appeared. The crack sparked hope. He beat the glass over and over until the splinters in the glass looked like a giant web. The shutters were at the level of his feet. In seconds it would be too high to escape.

"Ahh!" he cried in aggravation. He dropped the chair, took a step back, and ran at the glass, slamming into it with all of his might. The glass crunched but did not give.

"Ugh!" he cried. "You motherfucking glass fortress!"

Grabbing his shoulder in pain, he hobbled backward from the wall. The glass was on the verge of breaking. The metal barricade was almost waist high. There was one last chance. Yelling at the top of his lungs, James charged the glass. When his shoulder made contact with the window, he was surprised to find himself flying through air. The window had shattered, sending him jettisoning out of the building surrounded by an explosion of glass. His thighs caught the edge of the shutter as he flew out, flipping him head over heels. He landed on the flat of his back on the steep slope of the pyramid's wall. His scream continued as he plummeted feet first down the metallic incline. For fifteen stories, he slid. The friction generated by the slide burned through his clothes, making his ass feel like it had burst into flames. The ground was approaching more quickly than he would like. He closed his eyes before impact, hoping for a best-case scenario of only a couple shattered bones.

"Umpf!"

He hit the ground hard. His momentum sent him rolling like a runaway barrel down a mountainside, finally coming to a rest twenty yards away. With his head spinning, he lay there motionless, looking up at the dark sky, in too much pain to move. The air had been completely knocked out of him. After he caught his breath, he began to groan, trying to lift himself up. Miraculously, only one of his ankles had been hurt by the fall. He tested it gingerly. The ankle could only stand a little bit of pressure, but he thought he would be able to limp on it. It was going to hurt like hell. There was no way he would be running anywhere. His backside was on fire. He craned his neck to check himself out. The back of his shirt and pants had been incinerated. Road rash covered his raw exposed skin.

The wind blew hot and humid, the rank breath of the storm, reminding him of the urgency of the situation. In the distance, the redbrick school was barely visible above the rising peaks of the neighborhood's houses.

If they weren't in there, where were they, he wondered?

With the gray clouds churning above, James limped painfully toward the neighborhood. The sky flashed, throwing his bent shadow across the ground. The roar of thunder followed. Grimacing, he picked up speed.

46

Usually, at this time of day, his neighborhood would be swarming with mothers and their playing children, but today this usual scene was replaced with a tense emptiness. James slowly limped along. The trees and bushes lining the street shook in the powerful winds. A few warm raindrops started to slap his skin. After a minute, the few became many. Sheets of rain poured down, drenching anything that lay exposed. The sidewalk, the houses, his clothes, all became a few shades darker with saturation. The rain mixed with his sweat, which he was producing so profusely that it seemed a spigot had been turned on somewhere inside of him. The wind suddenly picked up. It began to scream, blowing hard enough to knock him to the ground.

Out of the corner of his eye, he spotted something

that made him stop. Above the tree line at the edge of the neighborhood, a dark protuberance had begun to snake its way down from the clouds to the ground.

He wouldn't have to worry about Dr. Weisman's immortality experiment much longer if he didn't find cover soon. To pick up his speed, he began hopping forward on his one good leg. He had about three more blocks to his house. With any luck, he would find his kids there. The tornado began to whirl its way toward him. The wind became even more frenetic. It took all of his strength just to fight his way forward. What was left of his shirt and pants flapped violently behind him as he skipped along. Flying sediment and debris stung his eyes.

Finally, he reached the corner of his street. However, his destination was five houses down, directly into the wind, and right in the path of the swirling funnel cloud. James strained his ears. A strange sound approached. It sounded like a very large tin can was being kicked down the road. He cursed when the source of the noise came into view. A very familiar aluminum mailbox bounced by. It looked suspiciously like the one he had installed the previous month. The mailbox clanged its way toward him mockingly.

The short distance to his house was going to be a difficult jaunt. He took refuge behind a fence and braced himself as the winds did their best to thrash him. The fence creaked and buckled under the pressure but it managed to stay together. There was a brilliant flash of light; thunder crashed above. The lightning had struck close. It was now or never.

Without a second thought, he broke the cover of the fence and headed toward a parked car on the other side of the street. Instantly the wind hit him backward. He gritted his teeth and leaned into it, almost crawling on all fours. When he was halfway across the street, a blinding pain struck him in the side of the head. Then an entire barrage began to assault him. Spheres of ice started to accumulate on the ground. It had started to hail. The wind was accelerating the hail to the point where they struck him like major league fastballs. When he was close enough to the car, he dove underneath it, escaping from the icy missiles.

Underneath the safety of the car, he wheezed for air. Exhaustion set in, making him question his ability to make it to the house. From beneath the car, he peered out in search of the tornado.

His view was almost obscured by the thick downpour of precipitation. The tornado wasn't visible, but it was sure as hell audible. It was close, too. The car rocked above him. He had to make a break for it.

Summoning his remaining energy, James slipped out from underneath the car and made a beeline toward his house, straight into the wind. It felt like he was running through molasses with twenty-pound weights tied to his feet. Each step was a battle in itself. He was about ten feet from his front door when he fell to the ground, unable to pull himself up. This was it, he thought. He was a dead man. The tornado would pick him up and rip him to pieces.

Unexpectedly the wind stopped, leaving him in silence. It was now or never.

Desperately, he climed to his feet. Wasting no time, he barreled up the steps toward his front door. Before he reached it, chaos erupted behind him. He felt an overpowering gust of wind as he twisted the doorknob, throwing him through the entryway of his house. As he turned around, the missing funnel cloud appeared, descending into the street. His car began to slide, then lift off the ground, hurtling toward the neighbor's house across the street.

He winced as the sound of screeching metal filled the air. His fine piece of Japanese machinery sliced through the neighbor's garage door as if it were made of wax paper. The car disappeared, leaving a gaping hole behind it. He turned and ran toward the back of the house, praying that his kids were where they should be.

The bathroom closet had been designed to act as a storm shelter. It was a somewhat safe place to ride out a tornado, but less than ideal. The family had used it several times before. It had no windows and thick steel walls, making it a perfect place to hide from high-speed fence posts that pierced through houses like they were cardboard. Rushing into his bathroom, he paused in front of the large door of his closet. He took a deep breath.

"Please," he whispered.

When he threw back the door, a bloodcurdling scream filled the air. He jumped back in fright.

"Olivia!" James shouted.

His daughter sat in the closet looking horrified. August was sitting cross-legged next to his sister. What James hadn't expected to see were the two strangers sitting behind his children. One was a bizarre-looking woman with pink hair, while the other was a fat guy who looked familiar. The pink-haired girl was petting Clementine, who was lying next to her.

"Dad!" Olivia yelled, hopping up and running toward him. She wrapped her little arms around him as he bent down to greet her.

"Oh, watch my ankle, honey," James said through gritted teeth as Olivia bumped into his leg.

"I am so scared," she said. "What happened to you?"

"It's a long story. Are you two okay?" James asked as he looked at the two adults in the corner of his closet. He stood up with Olivia in his arms and took a step backward.

"Who's this?" James eyed them both doubtfully.

The walls shuddered and the house creaked like it was on the verge of collapse. Olivia cried in fear again, burying her face in her father's shoulder. He bent down and sat on the ground with his daughter.

"It's okay. We'll be safe in here."

That is what he hoped anyway. He led his kids back into the closet and shut the door behind them. He took a seat in between his children and the strangers. Leaning over to the man and woman, James whispered, "Who the hell are you and why are you in here with my kids?"

The woman's eyes shined oddly bright in the darkness of the closet. "We came from the health retreat near here. Everyone was sick there, so we left. We found your kids wandering around alone outside. They were the first people we had seen alive in a while. For all I knew, their parents were dead. What would you do?"

James thought about what she said for a second. "If that is true, then thank you," he whispered.

"And I'm your cousin," Pat threw in nonchalantly.

James looked the chubby man over. His brain finally made the mental connection.

"Pat—"

The rest of his words were drowned out by the screams of Olivia and August as the walls of the house bowed under the pressure of the storm. The floor trembled beneath them. His children huddled closer. James could even sense the woman pressing closer toward them. The kids cried out again as they heard the bedroom windows shatter. A flickering green light filtered in beneath the crack under the closet door. The sounds of splintering wood and glass continued. The only thing they could do was sit and wait. No one made a sound as they waited for the great beast outside to move on, as if they were afraid that they might give away their location. James held his children tightly, rocking them back and forth in a soothing motion.

"It will all be over soon. You're safe," James whispered.

Linda awoke startled to find herself alone in a hospital room with no recollection of how she got there. It all came back to her when she looked down at her terribly bruised and lacerated arms. Ari, that damn traitor, would have killed her if it hadn't been for James, her knight with a gun and no armor.

She was elated. Now there was nothing in between her and the future that she had created for them. She and Dr. Weisman had finally done it. And what luck, Dr. Weisman and Ari were dead! Already her mind ran wild with possibilities. She and James would take Weisman's place, leading the survivors of GeneFirm.

Linda swung her feet off the bed and stepped down softly, careful not to bump any of her injuries. She really had to piss. Pulling the IV stand with her, she carefully hobbled to the bathroom, doing her best to hold her hospital gown shut to keep the cold air out. After she returned to her hospital bed and lay back down, she closed her eyes with a smile.

"Explain yourself?"

With a gasp she opened her eyes. The room was empty.

"Who's there?"

"Only God has the right to play with human lives," said the voice.

Linda panicked. The insane thought that God was speaking to her flashed through her mind. Perhaps it was the pain medication?

"Who the fuck is there?"

Suddenly the chair next to her bed flickered with color. The battered nude body of the black chameleon appeared, leaning back comfortably with his legs crossed.

"Shit!" she yelled, nearly jumping out of the bed. Her heart thundered in her chest from the jolt of the man magically appearing out of thin air.

"What are you?" she demanded.

"What does it matter? What I would like to know is, what are you? What kind of monster could be capable of such a thing?"

The question was mere morbid curiosity for Marnoy. Whatever her answer was, he assumed he was still going to kill her. He just wanted to try and grasp what thought process had led a group of so-called doctors to create a viral genocide.

Linda sat up straight in bed, glancing around the room nervously, looking for some way to escape.

"Don't bother," he said. "If you try to call for help you'll be dead before anyone gets here, I promise." As if to prove this were true, he waved the gleaming blade of a scalpel in his hand.

"Now please explain your motives."

The woman's eyes lit up as she began to speak.

"What's there to explain? Look around us! Because of the cancer-proof genes people are living longer and longer. Plus, the recent creation of a new inheritable form of the cancer-proof genes would make every human being from here to eternity cancerless with DNA that is completely unable to evolve. It would mean the certain death of our species."

Marnoy put a hand up. "Whoa, stop. Weren't you and your husband responsible for creating those new genes? If you were so against it, why in hell would you create it?"

"We never meant to actually succeed. We can only blame the brilliance of my husband for that. Dr. Weisman really wanted to develop a viral vector for his own selfish purposes. The project served as a good cover, plus the government gave us grant money to do so. But when James actually managed to create the damn thing, we had to accelerate the planned pandemic before it was too late. This plague will give us the chance to hit the reset button. We will repopulate this world with human perfection. No longer will ignorant politicians, with their rules and ethics, limit my research or stop the progress of science. We will have complete freedom to manipulate the human genome to create a better world."

"So in essence your answer is, to play God?" growled Marnoy.

"Please take your religious fervor elsewhere. I just want to create a world where scientific progress is unhindered."

Marnoy had heard enough. He put up a hand up to silence her. She watched as his hands switched from brown to bright red.

"Unhindered to, say, create freaks like me? I know the end result of scientific progress all too well. Man is capable of doing terrible, terrible things when given complete freedom."

"And wonderful things," Linda cut in.

He shook his head. "I've heard enough. One more thing, though. I've overheard this virus will only kill those with the cancer-proof genes. So what will happen to all the free-births born without those genes? Will they not be susceptible?"

"That is correct."

"I see," nodded Marnoy. He stood up in his chair. Hesitating, he looked at the door and then back at Linda. She watched as the color of his skin started to melt. In front of her eyes Marnoy disappeared, leaving only the crude outline of his body. The scalpel floated in the air, its blade dangerously close.

With a lightning-fast stroke of his hand, Linda's throat split open, showing the fleshy red meat beneath. She didn't have time to cry out. Her hands immediately went up to her neck; blood spilled over them and down her hospital gown like a gory waterfall. She held her red stained hands in front of her face, stunned, as her life bled away around her. Everything she had worked for was now lost, pooling itself on the ground below her. From above, Marnoy recognized the look of unfairness in Linda's eyes. He continued to watch as she writhed in pain. In another minute it was over. The heart rate monitor began to squeal in alarm next to the bed.

Dropping the scalpel on Linda's lifeless form, Marnoy went over to the door and waited. After a second, a couple nurses burst into the room, rushing to Linda's side. He slipped out unnoticed into the hallway. More scrub-clad personnel ran past him toward the room, allowing him to easily creep down the hallway to the exit. Clinched in his one good hand was the dismembered thumb he had brought with him. At the exit, he pressed the lonely digit to the scanner. His job here was done. There would be no promotion, however. Yet he was feeling a sense of satisfaction that had eluded him his whole life. The door whooshed open, hitting him with a blast of damp air. The storm was over. The clouds had broken and the sun was busy roasting the wet earth below. Without any hesitation, Marnoy stepped out into the blinding light. It looked like a perfect day to go fishing.

EPILOGUE

Clouds lumbered across the sky above a small cabin on the edge of a cornfield. An old man sat on the back porch looking across the fields and crops as they swayed in the cool breeze. His ancient senses reignited during storms. As the horizon grew darker, the wrinkled man's eyes and ears became a little sharper. In the thinning light, the world appeared as if it had been dipped in green. The gray clouds blanketed the sky like an oil spill, not a patch left uncovered. The field in front of him had become a concert of shadows dancing between the leaves and the cornstalks. He closed his eyes and took in the sound of a million leaves rubbing softly together. The hushed sounds of the world came to him on winds that smelled like rain—the damp smell of a brooding sky. Past the field, tree branches creaked and leaves rustled. The clammy air transported him back to a time long ago, almost entirely forgotten.

He rocked back and forth in the chair that one of his grandchildren built him, pale hands clinging feebly to the armrests. The shirt he wore hung down loosely over his bony shoulders and arms like a blanket. A year ago it had been a perfect fit. In the past months, he had been shedding weight. Lately, when he looked in the mirror he was reminded of a picked-clean turkey carcass, his limbs nothing more than naked bones sucked clean by the hungry mouth of some clandestine disease.

Behind him a screen door creaked open. A button-nosed girl, no older than nine, poked her head outside and shouted at the man.

"Great-great-grandpa! Mom says you should come inside soon. The storm is getting close."

He ratcheted his head around; pain shot through his neck with the effort. A big smile crossed his face at the sight of the grinning girl. Her big smile was interrupted by two missing front teeth. She looked just like her great-great-grandmother did, with long flowing dark hair, dark skin, and piercingly dark eyes.

"I will be fine, sweetie. Tell your mother this old man would like to stay out in the rain for once."

"Okay!" said the girl merrily.

The screen door banged shut. A muffled shout of a woman inside the house floated out to him, but he ignored it. He was lost in the growing peace of the powerful winds. Leaves from nearby trees began to smack into the side of the house, some landing in his lap. He picked one up and examined it. Now that this leaf had separated from its tree, they had something in common. Inevitably, they would both dry up with nothing left to do but decompose and merge with the dirt below.

The old man awoke to the cold splash of rain on his forehead. Somewhat surprised, he looked around, momentarily forgetting where he was. He had fallen asleep in the rocking chair.

The screen door once again swung open. A tiny hand beckoned him in.

With a grunt, he managed to push himself out of the chair. By the time he had inched his way to the door, his clothes were wet and heavy. Shivering violently, he entered the cabin. Waiting at the door was his bright-eyed great-granddaughter and her mother, a woman who towered on long legs. The mother had long pink hair that reached all the way down her back. She gave him a pitiful glare.

"James! Look at you! You're freezing and soaking wet. You're going to catch pneumonia. What did I tell you—you need to be watching yourself in your condition!"

He tried to smile through the pain, but he was feeling fatigued. Getting himself out of the chair had taken too much out of him.

The old man winced. "I'm sorry, dear. Can you help me sit me down, please? I am not feeling well."

Her eyes flashed with worry. She quickly wrapped a slender arm around him, helping him cross the room toward a faded brown couch.

"Thank you, dear," he said as she carefully leaned him back onto the soft cushions. When he was safely sitting down, he let out a well-practiced sigh.

The rain grew louder. A steady roar filled the room as the roof was pounded from above by the liquid fury. He felt the presence of someone next to him. The couch cushion shifted with the weight of a small guest.

He turned to find his tiny descendant snuggling up next to him.

"I'm scared," said the girl.

"Why's that?"

"The storm!"

"Oh, a little bad weather is nothing to be afraid of," said James, wondering if what he said was true or not.

The crack of thunder exploded outside. The little girl screamed, jumping at his side. James wrapped one of his arms around her, doing his best to give her a comforting hug. The act was temporarily interrupted by a hacking cough. He coughed loudly into his sleeve, which left him wheezing for air and his chest burning with pins and needles.

The thunder outside, the tiny girl clinging onto him: it all brought back distant memories of a dark closet, a stormy night, and blood—more blood than he had ever seen. The older he got, the more he found himself caught in the act of remembering.

The girl's mother came in and draped the man and the girl with a thick blanket. He leaned back and closed his eyes, letting the sounds of the storm carry him off to sleep.

It was a sun-baked Sunday afternoon. The towns-people were flocking down the road toward the great pyramid rising out of the amber fields of wheat.

James was slumped over in a wheelchair being pushed by the tall pink-haired woman. She had a sour look on her face. Despite her pleas, James had demanded that she take him to the gathering. She was unsuccessful in convincing him that he was much too weak and sick to leave home.

"Are you sure you're okay, James? This heat isn't good for you."

James scoffed, "I'll be fine. Just keep pushing."

He was lying of course. The effort that it took to climb into the wheelchair had greatly fatigued him. Deep down, he knew he didn't have long, which is why he was so insistent about today's journey.

James and the woman joined the throngs of people heading toward the pyramid. As they neared the entryway, the shadow of the building consumed them. When he looked up, the sharp tip blotted out the sun while its rays of light formed a harsh halo around the apex.

Soon the gaping mouth of the building's entryway swallowed them into its cool interior.

The town hall consisted of a large space crammed with old tables and wooden benches. It looked drastically different than the commons that James once knew. No longer was it white, shiny, and sterile. Now the floors and walls were brown with dirt and age, the air hazy with dust. Slices of the outer metal wall had been removed to provide the room with air and natural light.

The gathering place buzzed with busy conversations as people mingled. When James was pushed

into the room in the creaking wheelchair, a noticeable hush quickly fell over the room. He could feel
hundreds of eyes upon him.

"Take me to the front," said James.

Behind him, the woman breathed a sigh of frustration. "You shouldn't even be here, James. Let's
stay in the back."

"The front, please," said James, sternly resolute.

As she pushed him forward, a path opened up immediately. People whispered and pointed as James
was wheeled by. She stopped at the very front row,
putting the wheelchair at the end of a row of benches.
A man immediately offered his spot on the end of
the bench to the woman. She sat down next to him
and clasped her hands tightly together. Her eyes
searched James for any sign of trouble.

At the front of the room, next to the stage, a man
emerged followed by a small group. They were all
dressed in well-worn business suits. The man in the
lead was average-looking with brown hair. He sur-
veyed the crowd packed into the dingy room.

One of the men at the bottom of the stage stepped
and up and shouted, "Silence! Silence! Mayor Edward Logan has the floor."

Edward stepped forward, raising his hands for silence.

James watched with pride as his thirdborn looked
over the crowd. Edward's eyes came to a halt when
they saw the collapsed figure of his father in the
wheelchair; his brow furrowed in surprise.

"Good morning, people of Gene Farm. I see we
have a special guest today. Despite his sickness, we

are honored by the appearance of my dear father, James Logan."

The room broke out into applause as people cheered for their oldest and most famous resident.

Edward looked down at his father and said, "I'm happy to see you here, Dad."

Looking back at his audience, he continued, "I'd like everyone to join me and congratulate Dr. Logan on his hundred and forty-fifth birthday last month."

Edward paused for a moment. On the inside, he was not nearly as composed. The sight of his dying father was incredibly hard to deal with. His dad had been there for him for the past sixty years and, up until a year ago, James had still looked relatively young, vibrant, and healthy for his very old age. It seemed he would live forever. But now here he was, sick and near the end.

James did his best to nod his head at his son, but he could only manage a slight dip of the chin.

Feeling his eyes starting to water, Ed wiped them quickly. "Today marks an important anniversary in our town's history. So let's take a moment to give thanks to the woman who saved us. Without her wonderful work, without her vaccine, none of us would be here today. Today marks the hundred and fifteenth anniversary of the tragic death of our savior, Linda Nguyen."

At the podium, Edward waved his hands again to silence the various shouts that were coming from the crowd. He turned and faced the large mural behind him. A painting of Linda stretched up the wall. A mane of black hair flowed around her shoulders.

Her eyes stared out at the room with a look of un-yielding strength. After a few seconds, he solemnly faced back toward the audience.

"Linda Nguyen—without her, humanity's achievements would have been lost to time. Let us all take a moment of silence to remember the woman who created the vaccine that saved us all from the great plague so long ago."

Hundreds of heads lowered in unison and the room went silent. Only James sat there with his head up, looking at his wife's image with painful longing. It had been so long ago that he watched her get wheeled away on the medical stretcher. How could he have known it would be the last time he would see her alive? Not a day went by since her murder that he didn't ache for her. However, Linda was no longer his to cherish. She belonged to the people now—a piece of mythology.

"Let's go," whispered James.

"What? Now?" asked his great-granddaughter.

When she saw James, she didn't have to ask again. Tears were beading down his reddened face. She slowly got to her feet, hunching over to push James down the aisle. Everyone watched in complete silence as they moved toward the exit. On stage, Edward held back tears as his father left.

The hot glare of the sun awaited them outside. The warmth beat down on James and he was glad for it. The woman pushed him down the road through the fields of corn and wheat. The rough and cracked concrete beneath gently bounced James around in his seat. He thanked her for taking care of him. Her hair glowed bright in the sun like a pink flame above him. He thought about all of his children, his grand-children, his great-grandchildren, and his many great-great-grandchildren. His blood practically flowed through the fields around him. The genes inside his cells were now part of the town's genetic foundation. With four generations of his DNA coursing through the town of Gene Farm, it was impossible to tell how many of his descendants shared his special genes.

Dr. Weisman's last experiment could undermine everything the man had worked for. James' descendants were spreading like a forest fire, with the potential to live longer, pollute more, and proliferate faster than ever. Progress was inevitable.

James knew Dr. Weisman had been wrong about mankind. There was no saving humanity because it needed no saving. Overpopulation, disease, and even the weather were no match for their resilience. The growing bands of survivors roaming the globe would rebound and, in a hairbreadth of time, the world would be crawling with civilization once again. He took comfort knowing that his children would restore the world he once knew, and maybe, just maybe, this time around they would choose a better path. In a moment of clarity, he looked back on his long life. All the people he had watched come and go in his many years flashed before him like the thick corn plants in the fields around him—familiar faces stretching on forever. The heat of the sun began to cook his skin, but he wasn't uncomfortable. He closed his eyes. The sounds of the fields were lulling him to sleep. All the discomfort that had plagued him for weeks started to fade, his mind going peacefully blank. Death and its microscopic scythe had finally found him after all these years, seeding his body with a long-forgotten cancer. All he could do was crack a smile in the cheerful sunlight and ask himself, "Why the long wait?"